The assassin stood naked, head thrown back, arms stretched high . . .

A table before him had been covered with a sheet to serve as a makeshift altar.

"O Zeus," he intoned, "even as you rule on Olympus, there is in this city a false ruler—a woman of infinite treachery. I have suffered the faltering hand. O Zeus, I swear to you that I shall strike her down without mercy." He brought his right fist down on the altar with a mighty blow.

The assassin then came to the bed and sat down next to the young woman. He caressed her shoulder. "Zeus," he said slowly, "I will do your bidding with Aphrodite. I will make love to her. But you know, mighty ruler, that it is not love that is in my heart tonight. It is vengeance."

Books by Ben Mochan
from Jove

BRASS KNUCKLES
THE ASSASSIN CODE

BEN MOCHAN

THE ASSASSIN CODE

A JOVE BOOK

THE ASSASSIN CODE

A Jove Book / published by arrangement with
the author

PRINTING HISTORY
Jove edition / October 1985

ISBN: 0-515-08361-5

PRINTED IN THE UNITED STATES OF AMERICA

Preface

Let me begin by making the usual disavowal: Any resemblance between the characters of this book and actual persons, living or dead, is coincidental.

With that out of the way, I now tell you that no research effort was spared to make the events and places described herein 100 percent accurate. There is a "Sound and Sight Show" in Athens; the interior of Buckingham Palace is as pictured; the Barbary apes do roam on Gibraltar's upper rock.

All this research had but one purpose: to put you in the story. I wanted you to see what happened, and where, through the eyes of the characters. Above all, I wanted you to ask yourself if, given similar circumstances, you would have acted as they did—or differently.

As you will see, this is a weighty question. It will perhaps become especially self-revealing when you consider the actions of the person who dominates this story. When you have finished it, you will know who I mean.

—B.N.M.

THE
ASSASSIN
CODE

PART ONE

Chapter 1

THE HORSEWOMAN RODE exuberantly, with superb skill. Wheeling the great stallion into a tight circle, she pressed inward with her left calf and moved her right foot backward along his body. The roan answered the signal by moving smoothly into a full canter.

She felt the familiar exhilaration as the September wind, cold and numbing, buffeted her face. The trail ran along the moor, halfway down from the towering top hidden in mist; far below she could see the dirt road that led across a stone bridge to the village beyond. At this distance, the wisps of smoke rising from the thatched roofs etched black, lacy tendrils against the gray sky.

Half a mile into the canter, she reached the point where the trail began to descend, and brought the stallion to a gradual stop. As he shook his head, exhaling geysers of steam, she sat erect, looking at the panorama of Scottish Highlands stretching far to the north.

It was her favorite moment of the day, a time for renewing her commitment to the countryside where she had spent most of her forty-seven years. The ride back to her manor would be made at a leisurely pace, giving her time to relax, planning her day.

Five hundred yards away, the assassin waited. Unhurried, dispassionate, he adjusted the center wheel of his binoculars and watched the horsewoman move into sharp focus. He noted with amusement her impeccable riding habit and her visored cap fixed at precisely the right angle. He smiled wryly: It would never do for the gentry to appear in other than proper uniform.

Moving the binoculars in a slow traverse of the moor, he assured himself that no one else was there. He was not surprised to find it so; for the past three mornings he had studied the same scene from his vantage point behind an outcropping ledge. He looked behind him, down to the road. His MG, pulled over behind a clump of trees, was completely hidden.

No, there would not be any hitch. He reached over and picked up his rifle. Lying prone, he shifted himself into a comfortable position and sighted along the barrel to a point just before the bridge. There the dirt road made a sharp turn. And there it would be, in a few moments, that his target would ride into his sights.

The horsewoman had resumed her progress. The stallion, attuned to the wishes of his mistress, trotted steadily past the clumps of heather that grew along the descending trail. The wind was higher now, testimony to the deteriorating weather. A fine mist of rain began to drift down from the low-hanging clouds.

The assassin reckoned the horsewoman to be an eighth of a mile from the bridge. He held his binoculars on her face for a moment, impersonally studying the firm chin; the lean, aristocratic nose; and the expression, which, even at this distance, seemed cold and imperious. Casually, with automatic deftness, he pushed the bolt of his rifle forward to place a bullet in firing position.

The shot would be difficult, he knew. He estimated that it would be made at a distance of ninety-five yards. With the drifting rain and the darkening sky, the chances for failure were increased, a fact that concerned him not at all. With total confidence, he waited.

Now little more than a hundred and fifty yards away, the horsewoman was thinking ahead to the warm fire and breakfast that awaited her. Her first appointment of the day would be at ten. That obsequious banker of hers would be making his semiannual report. She smiled thinly, relishing the thought that her own calculations had already told her the estate's investments were doing well. It wouldn't hurt, she supposed, to offer him some praise. Not enough to turn his head, but enough to spur him on.

The assassin calmly raised his rifle and trained it on the bend in the road. With his peripheral vision, he monitored the steady trot of the stallion, nearer and nearer to the selected spot. He waited ten seconds, and then inhaled deeply, holding his breath. His finger began to squeeze slowly, relentlessly.

The horsewoman was twenty yards from the bend, then ten, then five. At the precise moment when she reached the turn, the assassin's finger completed its squeeze. The shot crashed into the stillness with appalling force. Instantly the stallion reared high in the air, forelegs pawing in fear. The horsewoman, jolted back in her saddle by the impact of the bullet, threw up a hand in a grotesque farewell to life. Her body, dead from the instant the bullet had penetrated her skull, tumbled heavily to the ground.

The assassin heard the echo of the shot rolling back from the surrounding moor. With unhurried movements, he stood up, collected his gear, and began the walk down the slope to his car. As he reached the road he passed close to the body lying in the dust. A quick glance verified that no life remained. He continued on to the car, disassembled the rifle with swift, skillful motions, and placed it in its case. He returned the case to its secure hiding place under a blanket.

With the binoculars trained on the distant village, he noticed that a small knot of people had gathered. They appeared to be uncertain, trying to decide on the direction from which the sound of the shot had come. Well, they'll find out soon enough, he told himself sardonically.

He turned the key in the ignition and started the engine. Putting the car into gear, he was careful to keep undergrowth between him and the villagers' line of sight until he had rounded a corner. Then, leaning back in his seat with a contented sigh, he lit a cigarette and settled down for the long drive south.

Seated at his large mahogany desk, Sir Benjamin Wembley, GCB, GCVO, OBE, Private Secretary to the Queen, frowned with annoyance. The lilting strains of an American show tune carried to his ears from the quadrangle of Buckingham Palace. With spritely enthusiasm, the Regimental Band of the Coldstream Guards was beginning its daily concert for the benefit of the tourists. Thronged along the tall wrought-iron fence surrounding the palace, clicking their cameras, they gaped in wonderment at the scarlet-clad troops before them.

Sir Benjamin's frown deepened as the band swung into "Oklahoma." As a former colonel, it had always seemed to him incongruous to hear a military band descend to show tunes. To do so at the very seat of Majesty seemed to him an intolerable affront.

Sighing, he took a sip of his coffee. Through the open door of his office he gazed absently at the Privy Purse Corridor. Along its length, on the ground floor of the palace, were located the most important elements of the palace hierarchy: the Keeper of the Privy Purse, the Press Secretary, and various other departments. At its far end, the corridor terminated in a semicircular area containing the Queen's entrance from the side court and, across the corridor, the Queen's lift.

Sir Benjamin gave up his idle contemplation and returned to the task at hand. It was the part of his daily routine that he liked least—sifting through the piles of nonpersonal mail to the Queen and routing them to the proper staff members for handling. Already this morning he had plowed through an invitation from a village of no historical importance to attend the five hundredth anniversary of its founding. The bloody cheek, he had thought irascibly, to presume that the Monarch could possibly appear.

Now he picked up a letter that poured forth a gush of spontaneous love for the Queen. In an aloof way, he approved of such letters, for they indicated an attitude toward the Crown that seemed to him entirely proper, reflecting his own feelings. He marked the letter for reply by one of the ladies-in-waiting and placed it on a pile beside him. The next letter held his attention instantly. He stared with foreboding at the words, obviously cut from a newspaper. They had been painstakingly pasted to the paper to form the message.

His eyes scanned the words swiftly, and then looked at the attached envelope. Its address had also been formed with newspaper type. Sir Benjamin pushed a button, and waited impatiently until a subordinate appeared.

"You've seen this one?" he demanded, holding up the letter.

"Yes, sir," the subordinate replied. "When I was slitting open the envelopes, it was hard to miss it."

"You read it, I suppose?"

"Yes, sir."

"And what do you make of it?" Wembley rubbed his chin absently.

"Just another one from a crank, sir, as far as I can see. God knows we get enough of them from time to time."

"I suppose you're right," Sir Benjamin agreed doubtfully. "There wasn't anything else that came along with it, was there?"

"No, sir, just the letter."

"I see. Still, it does make quite an extraordinary statement, doesn't it? It's worth a bit of a check, don't you think? Please ask the Press Secretary to step in for a moment."

The subordinate inclined his head in assent and left the room. Wembley took up the letter and read it slowly, his face creased in worried concentration.

YOUR MAJESTY—
WHEN YOU READ THIS, I WILL ALREADY HAVE KILLED ONE OF YOUR RELATIVES.

I DEMAND £100,000. PLACE AN UNSIGNED AD IN THE PERSONAL COLUMNS OF THE LONDON *TIMES* SAYING YOU WILL COMPLY. THEN AWAIT MY FURTHER INSTRUCTIONS.

IF YOU DO NOT DO THIS WITHIN TEN DAYS, SOMEONE CLOSER TO YOU WILL DIE. IF YOU STILL DO NOT OBEY, YOU WILL DIE SOON AFTER THAT.

REMEMBER, THE COCK CROWED THRICE TO TELL OF TREACHERY. YOU WILL BE THE THIRD VICTIM OF MY TREACHERY, UNLESS YOU DO AS I ORDER. THE THIRD STRIKE WILL BE AGAINST YOU, AND YOU WILL BE OUT—OUT OF POWER, OUT OF LIFE.

I DO NOT ASK. I COMMAND, AS MY DUE. FOR I MUST BEAR THE FALTERING HAND—YOU HAVE SO MUCH, AND I SO LITTLE.

ACHILLES

There was a light knock on the open door. Wembley looked up and motioned the Press Secretary into the room. "Have a seat, Alec. I have something I'd like to ask you. Probably a waste of your time, but no harm done."

"Sir?" The Press Secretary folded his long frame into a leather chair and waited expectantly.

Wembley passed across the letter. "Look this over. You'll know what my question is."

The Press Secretary's newspaperman's instincts were alerted with his first look. He adjusted his horn-rimmed glasses and read swiftly. Finished, he shook his head. "Typical for a loony letter. A shade more lucid than most, but still loony. You want to know, of course, if we've had any report that one of Her Majesty's relatives has been murdered?"

"I do."

"Reassuringly, thank God, the answer is no. There was a report over the wire earlier that a Lady Lawton was shot yesterday. Somewhere in the Highlands—the name escapes me for the moment. But she's not related. The police are still mucking about, trying to sort out what happened. I suppose—" The Press Secretary stopped short, his face suddenly apprehensive.

"What's the matter, Alec?" Sir Benjamin demanded.

"Do you have a copy of *Burke's Peerage*?" the Press Secretary asked quietly.

Wembley scanned the titles of the books on a shelf behind his chair. He felt the swift building of dread as he selected a leather-bound volume and held it out.

The Press Secretary leafed through the pages almost frantically. "Lady Lawton. Lady Dorothy Lawton, if I remember the wire story. Didn't jog any memory at the time but now that I've seen that letter I wonder. It seems to me I remember from somewhere— Wait, here it is." His finger stopped midway down the page. He read as if transfixed. "I'm afraid your letter is a live bomb, sir," he said, trying to keep his voice even. "Lady Lawton is an obscure relative. Obscure, but still a relative. Fifth cousin."

Sir Benjamin nodded. "I see." He picked up his telephone. "Please connect me with CID, Scotland Yard," he calmly instructed the operator. "I'll speak to Assistant Commissioner Adams."

Chapter 2

THE ASSASSIN RETURNED the rented MG to the Avis agency, paid his bill, and sauntered the two blocks to Piccadilly Circus, snarled with its usual traffic.

He was relishing the walk after the long confinement in the small car. Pausing for a moment, he debated whether he should stop for lunch at one of the fast-food restaurants that dotted London's central area. Reluctantly, he decided against it. It would be wiser to return straight home; after all, the suitcase he carried still contained the rifle. Better to stow everything away neatly in his flat.

He came to the entrance of the underground tube and paid the fare to Chancery Lane. During the long descent of the escalator to the level of the tracks, far underground, he idly examined the advertisements lining the walls. At the bottom, he picked up his suitcase and walked along the narrow tunnel that led to the northbound platform.

At one point, he paused to listen to a harmonica player entertaining the passing crowds. He fumbled in his pocket for a coin, tossed it into the cap placed at the player's feet, and resumed his progress.

His wait on the train platform was short. The Blue

Line train braked to a stop. The doors to the cars slid open; he entered and sat down gratefully, placing the suitcase firmly between his feet. The train accelerated smoothly. At Tottenham Court Road he disembarked and changed to the Red Line. Five minutes later he got off at Chancery Lane and walked the short distance to his flat.

It was good to be home, he thought contentedly. He removed his coat and shoes, fixed himself a snack and a drink, and sat down at the telephone. He placed a call through the international operator and waited, totally relaxed, savoring the sharp taste of the whiskey. The phone jangled; it was the operator, reporting that his call was ready.

"Thank you," he said, and then switched to a heavily accented Greek. "You are there, Paul?"

Thirteen hundred miles away, in a sixth floor room of an Athens hotel, a swarthy man with thick black hair answered quickly. "I am here. So it is you. I thought as much when the operator said London was calling."

"You are making progress?"

"Very much so. All will be arranged soon."

"Good." The assassin took a long pull at his drink. "I thought I might fly there tomorrow. Just for a quick visit. I want to make sure we have no areas of misunderstanding."

"That will be fine," the swarthy man replied. "Ring me when you get in. Oh, by the way—"

"Yes?"

"Your Greek is improving. Quite markedly."

The assassin placed the telephone in its cradle and got up to fix a second drink. Stretching out on a divan, he fell into a pleasant reverie, savoring the way events were progressing.

New Scotland Yard is a drab pile of stone set firmly on London's Embankment. What it lacks in architectural beauty is more than made up for by the quality of its tenants: the Criminal Investigation Department of the

Metropolitan Police. Inheritors of the zeal of Sir Robert Peel, who founded the Metropolitan Police in 1829, the CID tempers dedication with fairness, imagination with common sense.

Sir Henry Adams, Assistant Commissioner in charge of the CID, was presiding, with customary efficiency, over a meeting in a second-floor conference room. A powerfully built man with large features and a firm jaw, he still projected the vigor of the championship boxer he had been at Cambridge. Born in India, the son of a prominent barrister, he had come to the Yard after a distinguished career as a solicitor.

Without question, the asset that had served him best, after his brain, was his eyes. Dark, unblinking, direct, they invariably riveted the attention of anyone to whom he spoke. This commanding effect was heightened by his dark tortoiseshell glasses and the black suit he invariably wore.

At the moment he was listening impassively as a young inspector made his report. "I see," he said, when the inspector had finished. He drummed his fingers reflectively on the oak table. "You seem to have covered matters well enough. You're sure of the men who looked over the moor up there?"

"I am, Sir Henry. Plenty of experience, both of them. They arrived very promptly at the point where Lady Lawton's body was found, and immediately went over the area with exceptional care. Nothing to go on, really. It was misting, but not enough to leave tire tracks. And all their grubbing around on hands and knees didn't turn up anything we could send to the laboratory. No cigarette stubs, food wrappers, or anything like that. Nothing."

"Even at the spot where the killer was holed up waiting for her?"

"I'm afraid not, sir. As I mentioned, there's a rock ledge—it's the only cover around. It had to be where he was, so my people gave it a special go. Nothing."

Sir Henry nodded. "So you didn't have much to send to the laboratory."

"No," the inspector agreed. "They'll give us their report on the bullet a bit later on. And of course there's always the letter they sent over from Buckingham Palace. Maybe the lab can come up with something solid after they've checked that through."

"I have a question about the letter," a thin officer put in. "You say the words were taken in their entirety from newspapers and pasted on a sheet of paper. It must have taken a great deal of time to get the message together. Days, maybe weeks, I should judge."

"You judge incorrectly," the inspector replied earnestly. "I thought the same thing myself, until I got together some newspapers and tried it. It's rather remarkable how quickly you can find the words you want."

Sir Henry grimaced. "Especially when it's not a labor of love, but of hate," he commented. "All right. There's nothing more we can do until we hear from the laboratory, so I suggest we break. Before we do, I'd like to make a short statement." The group around the table waited attentively. "I don't have to tell you where we stand," the Assistant Commissioner went on. "Our job is twofold. First, of course, we've got to find this man. He's killed once, and in his letter he says he'll kill again within ten days unless the Queen pays his demand. So we've got precious little time. We'll be meeting again as soon as the laboratory report is ready. I suggest between now and then you bear down hard on developing any ideas you might have." His dark eyes regarded each man in turn. "Hard."

He paused for a moment and then resumed crisply. "There's a second part of our job. We've got to clear this up without alarming anyone. Especially the Queen. At this point I don't propose to tell her anything about this; she's got enough on her plate as it is. And I don't want anyone else—*anyone*—to know what's going on. That goes for the press, of course; I think we all know what they'd do. But it also goes for the rest of the force, and for your wives. Be sure you bear that well in mind." He stood up quickly. "That's it, then."

•   •   •

The laboratory report was ready in the late afternoon and was surprising. The technician who presented it to the group read carefully, pronouncing each syllable with a pedantic, emotionless monotone. He held up a large tag that was attached to a bullet by a thin wire. "Here, gentlemen, is the missile which caused death. It was unquestionably fired from an American carbine, a small rifle used by the American forces for specialized purposes during World War II. The striations are unmistakable. The carbine had an effective range of one hundred yards; up to that distance it did the job, but beyond that it was, to all practical purposes, useless. Any questions?"

Sir Henry signaled with a hand. "You say the Americans used the carbine for specialized purposes. What specialized purposes?"

"Some noncoms carried them. They're remarkably short, light, easy to clean. Service troops used them, too. They had nothing like the range or stopping power of an M1, of course, but they did provide a bit of security, you might say."

"How about ammunition?" Adams asked. "Can it be readily procured today?"

"Yes. It fires special .30-caliber bullets, but they're not hard to get. No need to buy at special shops or anything like that, if that's what you mean."

"How about the carbine itself? Is it easy to pick one up in a gun shop?"

"No sir, it is not, and I should say impossible in England. Our chaps never used the carbine."

"All right," the Assistant Commissioner said. "So much for the rifle. What did you get from the letter?"

"Not much there. The words were obviously clipped from the London papers—they match the type styles. The sheet on which the words were pasted is pretty ordinary; so was the paste, and the outer envelope. No fingerprints of any significance. The postmark, as you know, was central London—several million people could have mailed it. Pretty much of a blank, all in all, except possibly for one thing."

"And that is?" Adams asked.

The technician hesitated. "Well, sir, as you know, one of the phrases in the letter said 'the third strike will be against you, and you will be out—out of power, out of life.' "

"Right. What do you find significant about that?"

"The reference to a third strike and out." The technician was apologetic, no longer the complete professional. "It's not the function of my department to deal in speculation, sir—only in facts. But one of my people is a bit of an encyclopedia on all sports. He tells me 'three strikes and you're out' is an American baseball expression." The technician shrugged. "What with the carbine being an American connection, too, so to speak, he thought I should mention it."

"Quite right," the Assistant Commissioner replied tersely.

The meeting continued for an hour after the technician had left. Each member of the team outlined the investigative steps he would suggest taking; together they added up to an effort of enormous proportions. But there was no general feeling any one approach would provide a quick solution; the digging promised to be hard and painstaking.

Sir Henry brought the meeting to a close with an additional thought of his own. "We've agreed on what's to be done and it's to be devoutly hoped we make fast progress. But meanwhile we simply can't neglect any avenue. Some of you know Tom Haynes of the American CIA office here. He's been of help to us before when we've had something with an American angle."

He permitted himself a wry smile. "We seem to have one now, what with a bullet from an American carbine and an American baseball expression. I'll get Haynes over here as soon as I can reach him."

Chapter 3

THE PILOT OF the incoming TWA jet throttled back, then studied his instrument panel for an instant. His approach to Heathrow Airport was going the way he liked it: routinely. Casually he glanced from his cockpit window; fifteen thousand feet below, the English countryside moved beneath the port wing.

Suddenly he focused on a small aircraft far to his left and several thousand feet lower. Eyes straining, he stared at it intently, then nudged his copilot and pointed. "What the hell is it?" he asked. "Looks like something put together in a garage."

The copilot leaned over and looked at the aircraft, then shook his head wonderingly. "Jesus, I've never seen one of those except on a screen. What's the matter? You never saw any old war movies?"

With fresh interest, the pilot noted the way the aircraft banked smartly and headed toward the north. "Look at that, will you? The thing handles pretty well all right."

"Ought to. If I remember right, it was the best Allied fighter plane in World War I. Good speed for then, plus the wings stayed on in a dive."

"That could be important." The pilot chuckled. "What do you suppose it's doing here?" His radio crackled, and Heathrow Tower came on the frequency; instantly his attention turned to receiving landing instructions.

Ten miles away, the small plane swept in low over power lines and touched down in a pasture. With a staccato burst of its small engine, it turned and taxied toward a shedlike structure at one end of the field. When it was twenty yards away, the engine was cut and the wooden propeller windmilled to a stop.

Flying glasses shoved up on top of his thick black hair, a tall man struggled to hoist his way out of the cramped cockpit. Succeeding, he jumped to the ground and stretched luxuriously.

A mechanic garbed in a loose coverall came from the shed and watched him with amusement. "You know, Tom, for a guy your size you have the craziest hobby. Flying a Spad, for Pete's sake. Better a Flying Fortress; you'd fit it better."

"Now don't go insulting my pal here," the tall man said, patting the fabric-covered fuselage fondly. Ever since he had bought the plane from a defunct air museum, he had tended it carefully. "You sure don't know any great-grandmas as spry as this one."

"I'll take care of rolling grandma in," the mechanic offered. "You spent a little more time up there than you usually do."

"Great." The tall man waved his thanks and headed for his car. Driving down the motorway to the west side of London, he kept to a steady speed of seventy, maneuvering through traffic with relaxed skill, listening to the soaring strains of Tchaikovsky's Sixth pouring from the tape deck. Pulling up in front of his flat, he sat in the car, savoring the final movement.

Jill Blake watched him through the curtained windows of the living room. In the late-afternoon light, his strong, aquiline profile seemed to her handsomer than ever. But then, she reminded herself, she could hardly qualify as a competent critic. From the moment he had come to the American embassy two years before, to look up a friend, he had filled her life.

She could remember every detail of their meeting. She had looked up from her typewriter to find him standing there, a towering, astonishingly good-looking man in his early thirties, smiling with an easy confidence. Was her boss in? he had asked pleasantly, identifying himself as a friend from the States. No, she had answered automatically, Mr. Clayton was out of town and wouldn't be back for a week.

In that case, he had said, he would like to leave a note. Would she be kind enough to supply paper and a pencil? She would, and long before the note was completed they had talked at length. He learned that she was a Vassar graduate, an Ohio native, in her second year as an embassy secretary, a ski enthusiast, and a collector of waffle glass. She learned that he would be with the CIA in London in an unspecified assignment for an unspecified time, that he had never been married, came from Connecticut, hated fishing, and was named Thomas Edison Haynes, with the middle name stemming from his engineer father's reverence for an inventor.

They both learned that they liked steak, small restaurants with dark-paneled walls, and each other. On their second date she had taken him back to her tiny room and they made love with passion and enormous pleasure. Three weeks later, after a fun-filled search for a flat, they had come upon airy rooms with plenty of light for her beloved plants, and had promptly signed a three-year lease.

In the months that followed, it seemed to her that her love for him deepened with each day. Since he was away frequently and oftentimes for an extended period, she treasured each moment they spent together as a great gift. They visited the theater frequently, did the museums, ate adventurously in small ethnic restaurants, and returned with anticipation to their comfortable bed.

Only one thing disturbed her, and she struggled constantly to keep it from her mind. From the beginning she had longed for the day when he would ask her to marry him. But he had never touched even remotely on the subject. From time to time, she had wondered if his work could be the reason; he was away so much and mentioned little about his trips. On more than one occasion, she had come close to raising the question of marriage directly, but lectured herself sternly on the foolishness of pushy women.

Now she waited impatiently, knowing his predeliction for listening to the ending of music he particularly liked. She took one final glance at a mirror, thinking despairingly that her tousled blond curls and eager face made her look like an insipid teenager.

He was out of the car now, striding up the walk briskly, taking the three steps up to the door with a jaunty bound. She hugged him vigorously and drew him into the kitchen; a delicious aroma filled the air.

"*Voilà*," she announced proudly, drawing him over to the glass-paneled oven door. "Look within and see the Cornish pasties all a-bubble. You've arrived in time's nick."

"If they taste as good as they look, you've done it again." He grinned, knowing how much pride she took in her cooking. "By the way, what's a Cornish pasty?"

She sighed mockingly. "Ignorant men! If you cared about the finer things of life, dear sir, instead of smelly airplanes, you'd know what a Cornish pasty is. In Cornwall the men went down into the lead mines, twelve thousand feet deep. They needed stick-to-the-ribs food, and Cornwall is a poor area. So guess what the women of Cornwall did?"

"What? Open up a McDonald's?"

"Not at all," she answered haughtily. "With the brilliance of women everywhere, they invented the pasty. It looks like an apple turnover, as you can see, but inside there's meat, and potatoes, and onions, and turnips, and all sorts of good things. Good hot, good cold." She peered into the oven and pulled the door open. "Make us a drink, will you, while I get this stuff on the table. Oh by the way, there's a message for you. A Henry Adams called. Wondered if you could stop by first thing in the morning."

He was measuring the Scotch into the glasses and

looked up inquiringly. "Oh? I don't suppose he said anything more, did he?"

"No, just left a number to call if you'll be able to make it. It's on the telephone table." She was setting the table with swift, deft motions. "Henry Adams. Sounds like a proper Bostonian, that. Is he?"

"Not exactly. He's with Scotland Yard."

"I see." She placed the plate of pasties on the table and turned to face him, her expression suddenly anxious. "Does this mean you'll be going away again, Tom?"

He looked at her evenly. "I haven't the slightest idea what it means, Jill. Suppose we wait and find out."

She thought she detected a faint irritation in his tone. "Right," she said dully, trying to hide her hurt. "Sit down, we're all set."

The clock in the conference room read ten minutes to eight. The Assistant Commissioner leaned forward in his chair and returned some papers to an aide. "Doesn't look like there's much in the morning reports, does there?" he commented. "Just as well. With this thing on our minds, a bit of a let-up in the general crime rates is more than welcome."

"Let's hope it keeps up, Sir Henry," the aide said.

Adams rapped the table for attention. The group of men who had been chatting quietly were instantly silent. "All right," he said, "we have a few moments before Haynes gets here. For the benefit of those who don't know anything about him, I'll fill you in with a few facts." He smiled wryly. "Some of you aren't too fond of Yanks, I daresay. Maybe we can change your mind.

"To begin with," he went on, "he's hardly the kind of man who can get lost in a crowd. Six feet three or so, and I should judge fourteen stone. Which tells you he's got the kind of build crew and tennis coaches favor. As a matter of fact, I'm told he could have made it very large indeed in pro tennis, if he'd wanted to go that route. His brains aren't exactly underdeveloped, either

—Harvard summa cum laude and all that. He joined the Yanks' CIA station here maybe two and a half years ago.'' He turned to a bulky man seated close to him. "Suppose you tell them how we got on to him, Evans.''

"Glad to.'' There was a reminder of his Welsh upbringing in the bulky man's accent. "We were looking into a particularly nasty dope business. A more unsavory cast of characters I've never seen, including an American who seemed to be instrumental in bringing the stuff in. So we asked the CIA if they could give us a hand in running down the American connections and so on, and they nominated Haynes for the job.''

"I take it he did all right,'' a scholarly-looking inspector asked.

The bulky man smiled. "That's a mild way of putting it. We finally got down to a push-and-shove contest with them. They were holed up in a Soho loft, threatening all sorts of hell with a bloody arsenal. The Yank just picked up a slab of wood, smashed through the door, and began laying about him like an avenging angel. Three of them wound up in hospital.''

"He's lucky he wasn't shot,'' the inspector commented acidly.

"Ordinarily I would agree with you, but he's still very much alive, isn't he? I think Sir Henry will agree he's got a bit of a derring-do record.''

The Assistant Commissioner nodded emphatically. "So my friends over at CIA tell me. They're pretty close-mouthed, of course, but I've gathered enough to know he's either the luckiest man in the world, or he knows precisely what he's doing. He's made a couple of trips behind the Iron Curtain, for example, on some sticky assignments. Plus some sleight-of-hand maneuvering in Berlin that was just plain brilliant.''

The scholarly-looking inspector shook his head dourly. "Doesn't this American paragon have any faults? Surely there's no such thing as the perfect man, is there?''

"I'm afraid you're right,'' the Assistant Commissioner replied. "He's helped us on one or two occasions other than the Soho business. Not as spectacular, but just as important. And I must admit he's much more inclined to take matters into his own hands than I like to see in our people. But on the other hand, it's still true you can't quarrel with success." A telephone next to his elbow rang quietly; Adams picked up the receiver and listened. "Very well," he said, "ask him to step in."

Haynes strode into the room with easy confidence, showing no surprise at the size of the group. He shook hands with the Assistant Commissioner, nodded to Evans and two other men he recognized, then plopped into a vacant chair.

"We appreciate your joining us, Tom," Adams began. "If you don't mind, I'll dispense with formal introductions around the table and get right on with it." He adjusted his tortoiseshell glasses and picked up the laboratory report. "A Lady Dorothy Lawton was shot yesterday morning in Scotland. We were brought into the matter by a call from Sir Benjamin Wembley; you may know he's the Queen's Private Secretary." Swiftly, he described events up to the moment, dwelling in detail on the laboratory report.

Haynes listened carefully, without interruption. The Assistant Commissioner concluded his comments with a question: "Do you think we're right in assuming there might be an American angle to this?"

"Of course," Haynes answered. "Your assassin used an American carbine and a baseball expression; he knows Times Square isn't in Iceland. Tell me, this place Glen Walk, where Lady Lawton was killed. Just exactly where is it?"

"It's a little village about eighty kilometers northwest of Glasgow."

"How long will it take me to get there?"

The Assistant Commissioner was surprised. "You're sure you want to go? It's a pretty long haul, and as you've seen from the report of our men up there, they've been pretty thorough. You'd be wasting your time, I'm afraid."

"Probably you're right," Haynes agreed. "But I'd

still like to take a firsthand look."

Adams smiled with resignation. "As you wish. I was telling the group just before you came in, Tom, that you like to do things your own way. You've proved me right. I also told them you always give us some really solid help. I hope you'll prove me right there, too."

"Amen to that," Haynes said, rising and stretching his arms. "We'll see what we will see."

An hour after his arrival in Glen Walk, Haynes stood at the thick oak door of the home where Lady Lawton had lived. Inside the house, in answer to his use of the heavy knocker, there was a sound of footsteps; then the great door was slowly opened, and a diminutive maid bowed a welcome.

"Come in, sir," she beckoned, the rich Scottish burr rolling the *r*. "Lady Marston is expecting you."

Haynes stepped across the threshold and was escorted into a drawing room furnished with massive oak pieces and dark tweed drapes. The maid withdrew, promising that her mistress would appear shortly.

Haynes occupied himself with reviewing in his mind the interview he had just concluded. The two CID men who had been handling the investigation had answered his questions politely, with professional detachment, but he had sensed their resentment. He couldn't blame them—his appearance inevitably must have seemed a check on their competence, and in a sense, he supposed, it was.

His reverie was interrupted by a soft, melodious voice. "Mr. Haynes?"

He swung around and stared in amazement. The woman who was standing a few feet away was extraordinarily beautiful. Black hair, falling in waves to her shoulder, glowed in the late-afternoon sunlight; her features were delicate, in contrast to the sensuous mouth and challenging eyes.

"Mr. Haynes?" she repeated as he continued to stare. "You seem preoccupied."

"Guilty as charged, I'm afraid. Forgive me."

"Of course. I daydream myself now and then."

"That's not quite it. As a matter of fact, some lines from a poem came into my head."

"Oh?" She was interested. "Would you share them with me?"

"You might like them," Haynes said quietly. He raised a hand in salute and recited:

> She walks in beauty, like the night
> Of cloudless climes and starry skies;
> And all that's best of dark and bright
> Meet in her aspect and her eyes.

The girl laughed delightedly. "An American who knows Byron. You're a surprise, Mr. Haynes."

"Not one-tenth the surprise you are, Lady Marston."

She regarded him with amusement. "At the risk of seeming to be returning a posy, I'll answer your quotation with another . 'His figure is handsome, all girls he can please.' Do you please all girls, Mr. Haynes?"

"At the moment I'm only trying to please one."

"And doing a very good job of it too." She studied him challengingly. "Does it shock you to hear me say that?"

He met her look steadily. "I'm unshockable, Lady Marston. Quite unshockable. Under any and all circumstances."

"Indeed?" she answered coolly, moving gracefully to a chair. "Frankly, when the officers rang me up to say you'd be stopping by, I was puzzled. You must know they already interviewed me at some length."

"Yes. But I thought perhaps there might be something you overlooked telling them."

"Such as?"

"Well, suppose you start by telling me why you disliked your aunt?"

She straightened in her chair angrily. "That's an impertinent thing to say."

"True. But accurate, isn't it? Let's put it this way. I

understand they called you in Glasgow when they found
your aunt, and you came right over. That was two days
ago.'' He grinned disarmingly. ''You hardly appear to
be in deep mourning.''

There was a long pause, and then unexpectedly she
chuckled. ''You are the most direct man, aren't you?
Well, you're right. My aunt was a self-centered, nig-
gardly witch. I doubt if you'll find anyone in the Highlands who liked her. But I'm equally certain you'd never
find anyone who would harm her. We just don't have
that kind of violence here.''

He looked at her thoughtfully. ''They haven't given
you any idea of why your aunt was killed?''

''No.'' She seemed puzzled. ''Why? Do you know?''

''I wouldn't think so,'' he answered evasively, getting
to his feet. ''Look, Lady Marston, you've been most
kind to see me. I do have one last question, however.
Will you have dinner with me tomorrow night?''

Her reply was direct. ''There's nothing I would like
better. But the nearest decent restaurant is fifty kilometers away.''

''I know. So we'll enjoy the drive there. This is scenic
Scotland, isn't it? Suppose I pick you up around five?''

She looked at him for an instant, her brown eyes
appraising. ''That will be fine. Five it is.''

Driving back to the room he had rented, he reflected
on the day. Sir Henry had been right; he had learned
nothing new. But he had made the trip with no fixed
purpose except one. He had always made it a rule, in
any investigation, to see the scene and talk to the people
there. Somehow, in his later thinking, that had always
seemed to help.

His thoughts swung to Lady Marston. Instantly a picture of her came into sharp focus: the total beauty of
her face and figure, the disturbing mixture of daring
and reserve. He felt a sudden excitement, knowing that
he would be seeing her again soon.

•   •   •

The morning mist was still drifting across the valley when he came to the spot where the dirt road turned sharply. A few feet away the stone bridge spanned the rushing brook, and beyond it the great moor loomed, a massive bulk shrouded at its summit by drifting gray vapor.

He stared for a long moment at the dirt where Lady Lawton had fallen. Finally he glanced around and easily located the rock outcropping from behind which the shot had been fired. It was almost a hundred yards away, he judged; whoever pulled the trigger had been a hell of a shot to stop a moving target so neatly.

Walking to the rock ledge, he gazed back at the road, trying to put himself in the assassin's place, imagining the scene as the horsewoman had drawn nearer and nearer still.

As the sun struggled to clear the mist, he spent three hours painstakingly walking over the ground for two hundred yards in each direction. He was under no illusion that the CID men had been less than exhaustive in their search, but reasoned that they probably hadn't combed the area beyond a radius of seventy-five yards. Even so, his widened search yielded nothing until he was almost ready to quit. Then his attention was caught by a torn piece of a newspaper page, trapped in the gnarled branches of a heather bush. He examined it curiously, wondering if it might have any significance. There was no date, and the only type legible on the six-inch-by-ten-inch scrap, discolored by the rain, was an account of a Liverpool football match.

He raised his head and estimated the distance to the ledge where the assassin had hidden to be almost a full two hundred yards. Disappointed, he shook his head; it was baying at the moon to think that the paper had any significance. Still, he reminded himself hopefully, there is often wind on the moors, and its vagaries could blow a scrap of paper a good distance. Debating with himself, glad the tedious search was over, he trudged slowly back to his car.

Chapter 4

THE WINDOWS OF the Flying Grouse provided a spectacular panorama of star-filled sky. Haynes studied it appreciatively, savoring the moment, content to watch the moon riding the scudding clouds. Across from him Lady Marston, magnificent in a black dress relieved only by her diamond pendant, leisurely sipped an after-dinner liqueur. "You like our Scotland, don't you?" she asked.

"Yes, very much." He turned to face her, his eyes intense. "I suppose it may seem a bit odd, but it has an almost mystical quality for me. It doesn't take much imagination for me to picture the Highland clans marching south to the battle of Culloden, or Mary, Queen of Scots, riding to the arms of Lord Bothwell." With a quick grin, he shrugged. "Who knows? Maybe it's because my maternal grandfather came from Scotland. Not too far from here, actually, Ardrossan."

"Well, well. A fellow Scot." She leaned forward, cupping her chin in her hands. "There's a great deal more I'd like to know about you. But much more up-to-date than your grandfather."

"For instance?"

"How about the women in your life? Is there someone special?"

He looked at her seriously. "Special? That depends
on how you define the word, doesn't it?"

"A nice evasive answer." She laughed. "Come on,
tell me."

"Now wait a minute." He held up a hand. "Before I
get into the story of my life, how about a little cooperation from you? About all I got out of you on the drive
up here was that your first name is Hope. Outside
of that, I got the standard travelogue lecture on the
scenery."

"Fair enough," she acknowledged. "I suppose it is
get-acquainted time. All right—I suppose the first question you'll want to know is whether I'm married. It
always is."

"Not too surprising, is it? Well, are you?"

"No, and the answer to your probable second question—Have I ever been married?—is yes. Once, to an
architect, for four years. We've been divorced for two."

"I suppose I should say I'm sorry, but I'm not."

"No reason why you should be." She twirled her
glass idly. "More than fifty percent of marriages today
end in divorce, right? Well, it's a private theory of mine
that eighty percent of the marriages that do survive
shouldn't survive; the people in them are staying
together for all the wrong reasons. Only about one in
ten marriages should have happened in the first place.
Mine wasn't one of them."

He nodded. "How about since then?"

"Since my divorce?" She shook her head. "Now
that's really none of your business, is it? As long as I'm
not deeply involved with someone at the moment, it
doesn't really matter who there was or wasn't in the
past, does it?"

"I guess it doesn't," he said, knowing that in her case
it mattered very much to him.

"It's your turn," she prompted. "A moment ago you
slid very neatly off my question about whether there's
someone special. Now that I've told you what you

wanted to know, don't you think a bit of reciprocity would be nice?"

He hesitated. 'I'm living with a girl," he said finally. "Whether or not she's special in the sense you mean, I just don't know. Sometimes I think yes, sometimes no."

"That's an honest answer," she replied. "You're not as footloose and fancy-free as I would hope, but then it could be a lot worse, couldn't it?"

The waitress approached their table, trying to look discreet yet giving an unmistakable reminder that they were the last in the dining room. Reluctantly, he signaled her and settled the bill, then waited until she had retreated with profuse thanks for his tip.

He felt his heart thudding now that the moment of decision had arrived. "Look," he said, his voice tight, "we could stay the night here. I won't say it's a long drive back or use any other phony argument. The plain truth is that I want you more than I think I've ever wanted a woman."

She tilted her head and looked at him directly, as if weighing his fate, enjoying his suspense. Then she smiled with amusement. "It is time we got to bed, isn't it? Why do you think I suggested an inn, rather than a restaurant?"

They came together as they closed the door of their room behind them, exchanging a long, passionate kiss. Finally she pulled away lightly and began to disrobe. He watched with surging excitement as she took off her dress and hose. The soft curves of her figure in her panties and bra were exquisite, and then she was naked, her hair tumbling about her face as she bent to draw back the bed covers.

He finished undressing and came to her, drawing her close, his organ distended and throbbing as he sought her lips. Her tongue met his, building his desire to an incredible height. With relief he saw that her urgency was as great as his; she drew him on top of her, uttering a low moan as he entered and began the first slow, lingering thrusts.

•   •   •

There was sex in room 370 of the Athens Chandris Hotel, too.

The assassin had landed in Greece four hours earlier, in the last moments of the fading day. The approach to the airport had for many miles been at low altitude, the DC-1011 winging over small islands separated by narrow straits. It had seemed incredible, as the aircraft made its final descent, that a city of three million could lie so close to an almost uninhabited area.

Passing through the efficient Greek customs quickly, the assassin had been successful in securing a cab with his first hail. Settling back, completely relaxed, he'd given himself over to enjoying the sights of the city he loved so much. Nestled in a semicircle of mountains, Athens faced the Aegean Sea, with modern office buildings dominated by the lofty plateau of the Acropolis, and in the far background the looming presence of Lycabettus Hill.

The Chandris, as ever, was a welcome oasis. He had asked for a room overlooking the Fuliro Racetrack, and treated himself to a long hot shower. Toweling, he'd glanced at the room's main illumination, bulbs encased in a huge square of sculptured glass; it never failed to please his aesthetic sense.

With a quick phone call, he had confirmed his appointment for the next afternoon, and descended to dinner in the Chandris's restaurant. Its floor-to-ceiling centerpeice of frosted glass, constructed to look like cakes of ice, contrasted with blue tile sidewalls to form a setting at once stark and exotic. At that hour, well before the normal Athens 9:30 P.M. dinner hour, only three tables were occupied.

The assassin had eaten a leisurely dinner of small cheese pie appetizers, followed by a very good moussaka, and then returned to his room. He had called a familiar number, then stretched out on the bed to await the girl.

Her knock had been brisk and businesslike. When

he'd opened the door, he had beckoned her in brusquely, noting with approval her small thin figure and typically Grecian good looks, even to the delicate but unmistakably curved nose.

She had gone about her purpose with dispatch, disrobing with impersonal efficiency and stretching out on the bed. "What do you like?" she asked. "It is fifty thousand drachmas, of course, but for French it is ten thousand more. Also there are special prices for other things. What is your wish?"

He answered slowly in Greek, searching for the right words. "I wish to place my big toe in your vagina. It will stimulate me, and maybe you too. How much for that?"

For an instant, her professional unflappability was tested, but was quickly regained. "It is an unusual request," she answered. "That is all you want?"

"Yes, except I will, of course, when I am fully stimulated, fuck you in the usual manner."

She considered carefully. "I see. Then it will be twenty-five thousand drachmas extra for what you want. Is that satisfactory?"

"It is."

She nodded and lay back, awaiting his ministrations.

Up early, the assassin took a cab to the port of Piraeus. He queued up at the line in front of the Flying Dolphin Hydrofoil ticket office and paid 650 drachmas for the round trip to Aegina.

The great yellow and black hydrofoil made the passage to the island in thirty-five minutes, churning the water behind it into a foamy streak that stretched half a mile. Disembarking, the assassin walked through the town to a beach, where he changed into his bathing suit and spent a relaxing morning swimming in the clear blue water.

He was back in his room at the Chandris by noon. Selecting a light tan summer suit, he dressed carefully for his appointment. He arrived at the foot of Lycabettus

Hill in good time, and took the cable car to the summit. Glancing at the restaurant there, he saw that Paul had not yet arrived. For the next several minutes, he enjoyed the unmatched overview of the city, amusing himself by training the large coin-operated binoculars on the Olympic Stadium, the temple of Zeus, and an American aircraft carrier anchored in the harbor.

When he made his second check of the restaurant, Paul was there, drumming on the table with characteristic impatience. He was drinking strong black coffee, and shoved across a second cup, already poured. "Here. It's probably cold. I thought you'd be on time."

The assassin dispensed with any explanations and launched brusquely into their business. "So where do we stand?"

The Greek scrutinized him intently. "Everything is set. What happens now, of course, is up to you."

"I am prepared to go ahead," the assassin said firmly. "Provided, naturally, the price is right."

"If you are prepared to accept the contract, the initial payment will be ten thousand drachmas. When the job is done, forty thousand drachmas more. How does that strike you?"

The assassin answered coldly. "It is not as good as I had hoped."

"These things are always difficult," Paul commented smoothly. "No one can compel you to accept, of course, but I am certain it is the best deal you will get." He switched from Greek to English. "What is your expression? Take it or leave it."

Sipping his coffee, the assassin concentrated heavily. "All right," he said finally, "I will accept. You will, of course, notify me precisely when you expect completion. I will have to be ready."

"Understood." Paul glanced at his watch. "Unless you have anything further, I take it we've covered everything."

"Except for one thing. The manner of payment. I'll get back to you later on that."

"Good." Paul got to his feet and extended his hand.

"Have a nice trip back. You're taking the evening flight out?"

"Not tonight, tomorrow," the assassin replied. "There are certain things I must still do here." His expression was thoughtful. "They are important."

Hope Marston stepped out of Haynes's car and turned back to face him, her hand lightly caressing his cheek. In the harsh morning sunlight, her skin was flawless, her eyes a brilliant brown. "Thank you for bringing me back," she said quietly. She studied him for an instant. "What will it be, Tom? Is this it, or will there be more?"

Haynes drew her toward him. "That's a question that doesn't need an answer. I'll call you; we'll work out a way to get together. How often do you get down to London?"

"Not as often as I'd like," she replied. "But as it happens, I've got to be there next week. My sister and her husband will be passing through. He's in the Foreign Office, and he's coming in for a conference."

"How long will they be there?" he asked.

"Probably not more than two days or so. But it will give me a good chance to visit with my sister."

He smiled wickedly. "It will also give you a good chance to visit with me. Why don't you plan on staying for a week or two after they leave?"

"And what about your lady friend?" she asked teasingly. "Would she like that?"

"Suppose you let me worry about that," he answered with a faint irritation. "How about it?"

"All right," she agreed. "I'll plan at least a week extra."

"Make it two." He kissed her firmly. "I'll be talking with you before then," he said, reluctantly putting the car in gear. "Lots."

He took a final look in the rearview mirror as he approached a corner. She was still standing where he had left her, motionless, her hand half-raised in farewell. He turned right at the corner, and she was no longer there. Not at all to his surprise, he found that he missed her already.

The Athens night was cool. The assassin sat on a folding metal chair on Filopapou Hill, in the third row of the audience that had assembled for the nightly "Sound and Sight Show." Across a broad valley the Acropolis was in darkness, the ruins atop its summit silhouetted against the sky.

Engrossed in his musings, the assassin waited patiently, oblivious to the conversations of the tourists who surrounded him. As the hour drew close to eight, the loudspeakers placed near the rows of spectators suddenly came alive with the sound of heralding trumpets. A recorded voice bade a welcome and announced that the show was a salute by France to the glory of ancient Greece. Simultaneously the Acropolis, half a mile away, was flooded with a soft yellow light.

The recorded voices of other actors were heard, playing the roles of Grecian leaders in the centuries before Christ. They were expressing their anguish at the advance of the Persians against Athens; as they spoke, the lights illuminating the Acropolis changed in color, adding a high drama to the recital. Then a climactic moment was reached, a description of the battle that had surged across the Acropolis. The lights changed to a fiery red, simulating the flames that had engulfed the Parthenon.

At that precise instant, without warning, a streak of lightning flashed across the sky. Before the thunderclap faded away, sheets of rain swept across the hill, drenching the audience, turning the dusty ground into mud.

The assassin, torn from his deep concentration on the show, was completely disgusted. He watched the tourists hold handbags, packages, and newspapers over their heads in an effort to find some protection against the driving wetness. Finally, as the heavy downpour continued, they began to run back down the hill in the direction of the buses that had brought them.

The assassin was one of the last to leave, walking defiantly, in a black mood, the rain coursing through his hair and down his cheeks.

By mid-morning the next day the temperature had already reached ninety-seven degrees, but the air was dry and comfortable, the sun bright in the cloudless sky. The assassin's temper had improved with the improvement in the weather. He was looking ahead with eagerness to his visit to the National Archaeological Museum. It was always one of his favorite Athens attractions, but today his visit would have a special purpose. The business that awaited him on his return to London, he knew, would need every last iota of careful attention; the morning's arrangements would—in his planning—play a key part.

He dismissed his taxi and entered the cool, spacious rooms of the museum. Despite his preoccupation with his purpose, he could not resist spending a relaxing hour in the square, white-painted series of chambers that housed his favorite Mycenaean artifacts. Finally, refreshed in spirit, he tore himself away and made his way to the collection of vases that the ancient Greeks had called amphorae. Formed in pottery, they were decorated in colorful, individualistic ways, most depicting mythological scenes. The assassin proceeded slowly, studying each amphora, searching for the one that would best match his needs. Two of the amphorae came close to his specifications, but after pondering abstractedly he decided against them and continued his search.

It was approaching noon before he found exactly what he was seeking. He stood before it, elated that his patience had at last paid dividends. Then, raising his Polaroid camera, he snapped a picture and waited for it to develop. Satisfied that the picture was sharp, clearly delineating the scenes of the amphora, he placed it carefully in the pocket of his jacket and left the museum.

Twenty minutes later he emerged from the Metro underground into the bustling madhouse of Monastiraki
Square. A large sign on the side of a building pro-
claimed that this was the Athens flea market. Shops
bordered the square and extended up into side streets,
their narrow windows and the sidewalk space before
them crammed with an astonishing array of merchan-
dise. There were copper buckets and wool sweaters,
blouses and Greek boatsmen's caps, candies, fruits and
jewelry, flowers and toys, liquors and leathers.

The assassin made his way into this kaleidoscope of
wares, savoring the bustle as tourists trooped from shop
to shop, stopping to pick up and handle articles that
caught their fancy. There was no difficulty in finding
shops that sold amphorae; they were a standard fixture
all over the city. Stopping before the largest, the assassin drew the Polaroid picture from his pocket and began
scanning the vases, looking for a match.

Almost instantly the proprietor was at his elbow, a
slightly built man with rimless glasses and an earnest,
sympathetic air. "You are looking for something special," he announced with the profound assurance of a
Delphic oracle. "You have come to the right place."

"We will see," the assassin countered, enjoying the
bargaining game. He held out the Polaroid picture. "Do
you have an amphora that will exactly match this?"

The proprietor took the snapshot and eyed it closely.
"You are asking a great deal," he complained in heavily
accented English. "I would guess this is one of the
museum pieces."

"It is."

"You must realize all of the pieces there have not
been copied. I have never seen this particular one."

"Then I shall have to look elsewhere." The assassin
made as if to leave.

The proprietor was galvanized into action. "Wait,"
he said commandingly, "do not be so hasty. I am sure I

can find something very close to this. Very close indeed."

The assassin, who had not expected to find an exact match, pretended to consider. "I don't know," he said doubtfully. "How much would something such as you describe cost me? Bearing in mind that it is really not what I want?"

With an offended expression, the proprietor shrugged. "I can see you are a hard man in a transaction. So be it. I recognize that to sell you I must make you a special price. It will be only eight hundred drachmas."

"Six hundred will be more like it, or I will not waste my time."

"Very well." The proprietor threw up his hands in mock dismay. "Come with me." He led the way through the shop, down a stairway, and into a corner room of the basement. Without hesitation he reached into a display of amphorae and withdrew one deftly.

The assassin took it and examined it at length. "It will do," he announced grudgingly. "Six hundred drachmas. I wish you to package it securely, so it will not break as I travel."

"If you wish that kind of packaging," the proprietor declared, "then I must charge you an additional one hundred drachmas."

"Twenty-five."

"No, I cannot do it."

"Fifty, then."

The proprietor acceded with a grave nod, satisfied that this latest exchange had at least restored some of his bargaining skill. He took the vase and retreated into a small back room, reappearing in a few minutes.

"You will have no worries," he commented, handing over the package. "It is well protected."

The assassin paid the bill and left, absently acknowledging the proprietor's affable invitation to return soon. Back at the Chandris, he took a short nap before he checked out and took a cab to the airport.

An hour and a half later his flight 822 to London lifted smoothly from the strip and headed up the long climb to cruising altitude. The assassin was in a window seat, cradling the packaged amphora in his lap. He sat quietly, absorbed in his thoughts, until the stewardess arrived with his dinner tray.

Chapter 5

ASSISTANT COMMISSIONER SIR Henry Adams felt uncomfortable. It wasn't the impressive surroundings of 10 Downing Street that bothered him; he was accustomed to interviews with the nation's leaders, in government or in business.

What was causing him to shift restlessly, feeling like an awkward schoolboy, was the necessity for admitting that his proud CID was floundering. Trying not to appear defensive, he kept his face impassive. "That's where we stand, Madame Prime Minister," he explained. "As you can see, the investigation is in an early stage."

The Prime Minister adjusted her glasses, idly tapping a pen against the polished surface of her desk. "I believe I would rephrase your last statement, Henry," she said flatly. "Wouldn't it be more accurate to say you are at a dead end?"

The Assistant Commissioner bowed his head stoically. "If that is the terminology you prefer." It is not for nothing, he was thinking, that this lady has been called the Iron Leader. "Personally I do not subscribe to it."

Taking notice of his pique, the Prime Minister smiled thinly. "Come now, Henry, sulking does not go with your character. I am glad that you alerted me on the matter. And I approve of your decision not to alarm the Queen. At least at this stage."

"We are hopeful it will not be necessary to do so." Adams could not resist adding a further comment. "This is not the first time, Prime Minister, that we have dealt with threats against the Crown. And we have always managed to cope."

"As I am sure you will this time. But I think you will admit there is a most disturbing aspect to this situation. We are not dealing with an idle boaster. Whoever this person is, he or she has already murdered, and threatened to murder again within ten days if the hundred thousand pounds is not paid. You have no intention of recommending payment, and I agree with your viewpoint wholeheartedly. But time is becoming critical—you have six days left. I believe the threat is real. Very real."

"As do I, Prime Minister."

"Then I would feel much better if you could be more definitive in the actions you propose to take."

The Assistant Commissioner maintained an outward calm. "We have called upon every informant who might possibly be of help," he began patiently. "Our people who work on extortions are reviewing their files, looking for any possible parallel situations. We're also winnowing through a list of people who recently left the employ of the Queen—servants and so on. The grudge angle can't be ignored, of course."

"Needle-in-the-haystack procedures," the Prime Minister interrupted. "Routine. But I know they can't be overlooked." She stood up, signifying that the interview was over. "I want you to keep me fully posted. You can phone me a report around five each day—that will be quite sufficient. Unless, of course, something special arises, in which case I shall expect to be notified immediately."

"As you wish." Adams prepared to leave.

"Henry," the Prime Minister said, "we've known each other for a long time. I think you know I have the greatest respect for you and your organization. But where the well-being of the Crown is concerned, I will not have much patience. I want this matter resolved, and fast. Do you understand?"

The Assistant Commissioner regarded her gravely. "I believe my concern for the Crown is quite as deep as any of Her Majesty's subjects. Even yours, Prime Minister."

"Doubtless," the Prime Minister agreed dryly. "Good afternoon, then."

On his way through the anterooms, Adams noted the strained, almost apprehensive look of several who waited. It is as if they are awaiting their turn to enter the lion's den, he told himself sardonically. Well, they're not very far off at that.

"How did it go?" Adams's aide asked solicitously.

The Assistant Commissioner sank gratefully into his leather chair. "About as I expected. But she's right, and she had to know. Anything new here?"

"I'm afraid there is," the aide answered reluctantly. "This certainly is not your day, sir. There's been another letter."

"Oh?" Adams came out of his lethargy sharply. "Let's have it."

"I've sent the original over to the laboratory. I thought you might want them to have their go at it as quickly as possible." The aide passed over a folder. "Here's your Fax copy."

Adams took the folder. "When did it come in?"

"They sent it over from Buckingham about forty minutes ago. It was in their morning post."

The Assistant Commissioner nodded and opened the folder. He stared down at the letter, noticing that the same technique of using words cut from a newspaper had been employed. As he read, the muscles of his firm jaw tightened visibly.

Your Majesty—

Thus far you have seen fit to ignore my demand. Only a few days remain before I will kill again.

5 will become 3 unless you act. Signify your surrender by placing an unsigned ad in the personal columns of the London *Times*. Then await my further instructions.

Do not misjudge my resolve. I have sworn a mighty oath before the Temple of Athena. In the wind and the rain, with the glory of her home towering high above us, bathed in noble light, I vowed to let nothing deter me from my course.

Through the long night that followed, as I stared at the deserted oval, I pledged anew to persevere until I receive or exact justice. If that justice ultimately will demand your life, so be it.

The choice is yours: comply or die.

Remember, I must bear the faltering hand. It is your moral duty to ease my anguish.

Achilles

Adams tossed the letter aside angrily. "It tears me apart to think of this madman dictating terms. Have you sent a copy to the other members of the group?"

"No, sir," the aide replied. "I thought you should see it first."

"Well, I've seen it, more's the pity. Have some copies run off and get them around." Adams glanced at the wall clock. "Give them a chance to digest it before we get together. Set the meeting for eleven-thirty."

"Eleven-thirty it is, sir. Oh, by the way, Mr. Thomas Haynes is waiting downstairs; I told him you were expected back shortly. Would it be convenient to have him come up now, sir?"

"It will." Adams occupied himself with a morose inspection of the letter until Haynes was ushered into the office. "I hope you bring some good news," he said then. "It seems to be in short supply today."

Haynes shook his head. "I won't be of any help." Swiftly he went over his visit to Scotland, careful to avoid any reference to Lady Marston beyond a simple statement that he had talked with her.

The Assistant Commissioner listened glumly. "Well, we're no further forward, are we? I'll send this bit of newspaper you've picked up along to the laboratory, but from what you tell me you don't expect much from it."

"Not really." Haynes clasped his arms around his knees. "What's been happening isn't good, obviously."

"Hardly." The Assistant Commissioner gestured toward the folder on his desk. "There's been another letter. I've called my people together for eleven-thirty, and I'd like you to sit in. Get a copy before the meeting, will you? See what you can make of it."

"Right."

Adams sighed and picked up his telephone. "You'll have to excuse me. The Prime Minister wants to know about any new developments." He frowned heavily. "Frankly, I'm not looking forward to this call."

Jill Blake looked up from transcribing a dictation belt and gave a soft cry of pleasure. "Tom, you're back."

He crossed to her desk and gave her a quick kiss. "I am indeed." He pretended to look carefully around the room. "As an American citizen I'm pleased to see you've got everything under control. That's the way an American embassy should look: shipshape, efficient, alert." He picked up a paper bag in mock dismay. "Here, what's this?"

Jill laughed. "That's my lunch, a cheese sandwich and milk. Which I'll be eating in about ten minutes—want to join me?"

He shook his head. "Nope. I've got a meeting in half an hour. In the neighborhood, so I thought I'd stop by here first."

Her eyes were warm with pleasure. "I've been wondering what the occasion is. You hardly ever come here."

"With you looking so beautiful, I should make it a habit."

"Why don't you?" She smiled. "Tell me, how was the trip?"

He hesitated slightly. "Fine. Scotland never looked better—there's nothing quite like the heather on those hills."

She looked at him curiously. "I wasn't thinking of the scenery especially. Did you get anything accomplished?"

"Not really," he answered, doing his best to sound offhand.

"How about the Scotsmen?" she asked teasingly. "Are they as dour as they're supposed to be? And the Highland lassies? Did you meet Lorna Doone or someone like her?"

"Oh for God's sake, be serious," he snapped, walking to the door. "I'm late. See you at home tonight."

Outside, in the bustle of Grosvenor Square, he lashed at himself angrily. What stupid sense of guilt had made him go to her office in the first place? And why couldn't he at least have kept his cool once he was there? He stepped up his pace, trying to work off his annoyance.

Jill Blake was trying hard to get back to her work. But a specter of doubt had risen within her; it sat triumphantly on her mind, grimacing at her, bringing a chill to her heart.

From the outset the gathering was spirited, spurred by a new sense of urgency. The Assistant Commissioner brought his fist down on the table. "Quiet. We're sounding like the Tower of Babel. All right—we'll start by taking a quick look at what's been done."

He called in quick succession for a series of reports. All were negative: no sale of an American carbine had been reported recently in London; no informant seemed able to help; the new letter was as clean of fingerprints as the first; no former Crown employee disgruntled enough to murder had as yet been uncovered.

"So much for our progress," Adams commented worriedly. "There just isn't any, unless of course you count as progress eliminating possibilities that were remote in the first place. Let's get on with it and see what fresh ideas we have." He turned to a senior inspector. "Bill?"

A lean official responded by pulling some notes from his pocket. "I think this latest letter is encouraging—at least it gives us something to go on. All this raving about temples and pledges in the rain and what not, along with that Achilles signature, makes me certain that we're confronted with a psychotic. I think we should check the mental hospitals all over the UK. There's always a chance one of them has recently released a patient with an obsession about Grecian history. It wouldn't be a bad idea to check the psychiatric outpatient clinics of the London-area hospitals too."

Adams nodded wearily. He was remembering the Prime Minister's caustic reference to "needles-in-the-haystack procedures." "All right; it's worth a try. How about the reference in this new letter to 'five will become three, unless you act.' And the reference in both letters to 'the faltering hand.' Do you have any theories there?"

"No, I'm afraid not," the inspector admitted.

Haynes signaled for attention. "I'd like to offer something on that 'five will become three' business," he said. "Lady Lawton, the first victim, was a fifth cousin of the Queen. In the first letter, Achilles stated that the next victim would be someone closer. Now I submit this: A third cousin is closer. Perhaps that's exactly what Achilles means—his next target will be chosen from the Queen's third cousins. As he puts it, five will become three."

Several officials agreed instantly. "If that's the case," a red-haired officer suggested, "it seems to me we'd better warn the Queen's third cousins to take special precautions. Oh, I don't mean to get their wind up by giving them the full details. That would mean a leak to the press for sure. But I'm certain we can find a way to handle a warning discreetly. Remember, we've only got five days before the next killing is supposed to take place.''

"That seems to me to make good sense," the Assistant Commissioner observed. "And I imagine it's entirely practical. The Royal family is large, of course, but there can't be all that many third cousins." He indicated the red-haired inspector. "I'll leave you to set that up and carry it through.''

The inspector nodded. "Will do. Do you think we should perhaps go a step further and actually provide protection?''

Adams reacted explosively. "Absolutely not. If you want to have the regular uniformed patrols keep a special eye on their places of residence, fine. But nothing beyond that. Providing personal protection to that many people would really put the press in full gallop.'' He directed his attention back to the group. "Now let's move on. Does anyone have a suggestion on that phrase 'the faltering hand'?''

"A number of us were turning that over," a young inspector answered. "It seems to be an obsession with this man." He qualified his statement with an expressive shrug. "At least I'm assuming it's a man. Well, I'm sure we'll all agree that this faltering-hand fixation is at the root of the bitterness—the reason for demanding retribution.'' There was a general murmur of concurrence. "Then the question becomes," the inspector continued, "how the disability occurred. If it's a birth injury, and our man holds it against society in general and the Queen in particular, we're out of luck. There's no way of tracing anything like that. On the other hand, if one of Her Majesty's employees, recently separated for one reason or another, suffered a hand injury in her employ, that would be extremely interesting. Injury in the armed forces is another possibility, of course, but I'm afraid we'll have to put that in the birth-injury category—there's just too much ground to cover."

Adams appeared disappointed. "If you've finished, and I gather you have, all you're really saying is that we should bear down even more on finding any disgruntled ex-employees of the Crown. Which, of course, we were planning to do in any event." He swept the group inquiringly. "Anybody else like to say anything before we get into an approach I'd like to suggest?"

There was a silence until Haynes cleared his throat. "There's one point I'd like to make," he observed. "I don't think we should assume automatically, as has been suggested, that Achilles is a raving madman obsessed with Greek history. I'm not implying, of course, that anybody who takes the course he is taking is necessarily sane. But on the other hand, he could be deliberately attempting to confuse us, to throw us off the track, by all these Grecian references. Or he could certainly be interested in Greek history without being completely zany."

"What are you getting at?" Adams asked.

"I'm not quite sure," Haynes admitted frankly. "Somewhere I think I may have the beginning of an idea, but I can't quite flush it out. What I would like to propose, however, is that someone get with an expert on Grecian history to look into these Grecian references. As a matter of fact, if there's no objection, I'll nominate myself."

"I suppose you're right," the Assistant Commissioner conceded. "If you'll see me after we've broken up, I'll suggest a couple of chaps over at the British Museum who will fill the bill." He directed his attention to the group. "Now about that approach I mentioned a moment ago. I think we've got to put an ad in the personal columns of the *Times*, exactly as Achilles demands." Apparently he was expecting the shocked reaction he got. "Just a minute," he went on, holding up a hand. "I'm not proposing that we pay one hundred thousand pounds or one farthing of it. But we're running right out of time. We've agreed to alert the Queen's third cousins, and if Haynes's guess about 'five will become three' is correct, that could conceivably help. At least in preventing a second killing. Yet that won't flush our man out. The newspaper ad will. I believe we should run it and wait for his instructions. Then we plan our next step, looking toward taking him.''

"This man is smart," a senior inspector protested. "I'm not at all sure we can bring off what you're suggesting. And if he finds out what we're up to, I wouldn't want to be responsible for the action he might take."

"I'm aware of the risks," Adams countered. He paused a moment. "One of the reasons I was put into this job was to make exactly the kind of decision I'm faced with now. I do not propose to debate the matter further. We will place the ad in tomorrow's *Times*."

Haynes applauded mentally. It was refreshing to hear a leader acting like a leader.

The assassin walked briskly to the kiosk at the corner. Even at this early hour, there was a knot of homeward-bound customers waiting to buy cigarettes and their evening papers. He stood in line patiently. "London *Times*," he said, as the proprietor finally glanced in his direction. Tucking the paper under his arm, he retraced his steps, entered his flat, and busied himself with preparing his tea and mutton chops.

Only after he had eaten a leisurely supper did he permit himself to pick up the paper. Even then he forced himself to read the front page and the sports pages thoroughly. At last, half-hoping, half-prepared for disappointment, he turned to the personal columns and began to read deliberately. He was almost at the bottom of the first column before he found what he was seeking. The message consisted of four words, sandwiched between an appeal for a missing husband to return and a plea urging someone named Aaron to telephone.

Taking in the words avidly, the assassin read them again and again:

ACHILLES. I WILL COMPLY.

Involuntarily his hands had tightened on the newspaper. A great exultation rose within him. Caught up in his elation, he absently brewed another cup of tea and sat down again, sipping the hot liquid, reveling in staring at the four words.

ACHILLES. I WILL COMPLY.

Half an hour later, calmer now, he methodically washed the dishes and placed them on their shelves. Moving into his small living room, he settled himself and began to block out in his mind his next action.

Twice, as if to reassure himself, he returned to the kitchen and reread the fateful four words. They were still there, set off by the white space around them, telling him that he had won.

Chapter 6

THE BRITISH MUSEUM rises in grandeur on London's Great Russell Street. Its spacious halls are a mecca for scholars worldwide, for throughout its illustrious history the museum has accumulated an incredible treasury of antiquities.

Haynes speedily discovered that this vast depository of human achievement, at first bewildering in its scope, is in reality carefully organized into three main departments. The largest by far encompasses the antiquities of Greece, Rome, Eygpt, the Western Asiatic, the Orient, Britain, and the Middle Ages.

Like a great amoeba, the Antiquities Department subdivides into its various specialized areas. Working his way through a labyrinth of directories, Haynes came at last to a tiny office tucked at the very end of a long corridor.

The young man who rose to greet him was far from the stereotyped conception of a curator. Broad-shouldered and slender, he fairly glowed with an exuberance of good health and restless energy. "Come in, come in," he boomed after Haynes introduced himself. Brushing his wavy blond hair away from his forehead, he transferred a pile of books from a chair to the floor. "It's a bit crowded in here, but I think you can shoe-horn yourself in."

Haynes sat down and regarded his host with interest. "You didn't get that tan poring over dusty tomes, did you?"

The young man laughed. "Hardly. If you'll forgive an atrocious pun, I got it poring over dusty tombs. Out in the field—on some digs in Crete."

Haynes chuckled. "Professor Harte, I'd suggest you stick to archaeology. Writing comedy would not be your forte."

"Oh, I don't know." Harte grinned. "You're obviously not familiar with some of our more popular shows." He dug a pipe from his pocket. "We're not called upon by Scotland Yard very frequently, and I'll admit I'm curious. Just how may I help you?"

"You might start by telling me about Achilles."

Harte raised an eyebrow quizzically. "If you say so. He was the son of Thetis, a sea nymph. You might say he began life with a built-in insurance policy: His mother dropped him in the river Styx, making all of him invulnerable except the heel by which she held him."

"That sounds like most insurance policies," Haynes observed sardonically. "Always a loophole—in his case the unprotected heel."

"Exactly. Well, when Achilles had grown up to be a chieftain, a bad apple appeared on the Greek scene. His name was Paris, and he was a son of the King of Troy. The first thing he did was to talk Helen, the beautiful wife of a Greek king, into running off with him."

"Which started the Trojan War, if I remember my ancient history."

"You do. The Greeks were pretty pissed, so they charged off to Troy to get her back. Nine years later they were still trying. During those years, Achilles was the Greeks' mightiest warrior. At least until he sat out part of the war."

"How come?" Haynes asked.

"Well, it seems there was a little misunderstanding

about a woman that Achilles had captured. The Greek leader made him give her up, and Achilles was miffed. I'm sure you've heard the phrase 'Achilles sulked in his tent.' "

"I have."

"They finally got him out of his funk, and he got around to slaying Hector, the bravest of the Trojans. Even that didn't end the war, but Achilles finally got a look at Polyxena and that did it."

"Polyxena?"

"Daughter of the Trojan King. A real looker. Achilles started negotiations with the Trojans, looking toward marriage. Things were going well, until one of the Trojans who was a sore loser shot Achilles in the heel with a poisoned arrow. That, naturally, did him in. Guess who the sore loser was?"

"I haven't got the faintest idea."

"Paris. Who else? The same rascal who started it all by making out with Helen."

Haynes was amused. "Do you always conduct your seminars in such a breezy way?"

"Not exactly. The trustees wouldn't be too thrilled." Harte tamped tobacco into his pipe and touched a match to it. "Can you tell me why you're so interested in Achilles?"

"I wish I could. But it's just not possible."

The young man was unperturbed. "I thought that would be the case. Is there any other ancient Greek you're interested in?"

"Yes. One. The goddess Athena."

"What do you want to know about her?"

"First of all, are there many temples to her in Greece?"

Harte spread his hands expressively. "You'd better believe it. Don't forget—she was the goddess of wisdom and of the arts and sciences. Athens was named for her; after all, she had given man his most useful boon, the olive tree. She was the city's protector, too. And she was up to it—she's the one who sprang full-armored from the head of Zeus."

"I suppose some of her temples are more prominent than others."

"Of course. The Parthenon, of course, would have to be Number One. The temple at Delphi is pretty famous, too."

Haynes studied him seriously. "Professor, a moment ago I told you I could not explain my interest in Achilles. I do, however, have clearance from Scotland Yard to read you something. If you can give us a clue as to what it means, that would be very helpful to us. But I cannot answer any questions about it. Do you understand?"

Harte took his pipe from his mouth. "I do."

"All right, listen." Haynes drew a sheet of paper from his pocket and read slowly: "I have sworn a mighty oath before the temple of Athena. In the wind and the rain, with the glory of her home towering high above us, bathed in noble light, I vowed to let nothing deter me from my course." Hopefully, he looked at Harte. "Does that mean anything to you?"

The young man was clearly excited. "It most certainly does. Whoever wrote that had to be in Athens, and I think I can pinpoint where. That phrase 'her home towering high above us, bathed in noble light'—that's the tipoff. Every night, on Filopapou Hill in Athens, they put on the 'Sound and Sight Show.' I've seen it a dozen times. You sit there and look up at the Acropolis, and they illuminate it completely. The building that stands out above all is the Parthenon. That was where the great forty-foot statue of Athena was placed; that was her home."

Haynes felt a rising excitement. "You're sure that description couldn't fit any other place in Greece?"

"Absolutely," Harte answered emphatically. "There simply isn't any other temple of Athena that description would match."

"Good. Now there's another phrase I'd like to read you. It is this: 'Through the long night that followed, as I stared at the deserted oval, I pledged anew to per-

severe.' " He glanced up from the sheet of paper.
"Well?"

"No luck on that one. 'The deserted oval'—it just
doesn't ring a bell."

"Maybe later?"

"No, I'm afraid not," Harte admitted ruefully. "I
just haven't got a glimmer."

"All right. Let's get back to that 'Sound and Sight
Show' you mentioned. It's on every night, you said.
Who goes to it—tourists?"

"Hundreds. Every performance."

Haynes wrinkled his forehead. "That doesn't make
matters any easier." He stood up and shook hands.
"Professor, I'm deeply indebted to you. But quite hon-
estly, at this point, I'm not sure how I can make any use
of what you've told me."

"Anyway, hang in there," the young man replied.
"Listen, if you get to a point where you can tell me
what's going on, keep me in mind, will you?"

"You'll be the first to know."

Haynes left the museum and strolled toward Russell
Square. For many years, when faced with a problem, he
had found that walking helped.

It was twenty minutes later, as he was waiting for a
light to change, that an idea came to him. Standing on
the curb, he considered it from many angles, then set off
purposefully for a public telephone.

The clerk at London's Weather Bureau thought he had
heard everything, from callers who vilified him for an
inaccurate weather report to others who demanded to
know what the temperature would be a week from
today; he had suffered them all. Now, however, he was
listening incredulously. "What's the weather like in
Athens? What is this, some kind of joke? Why in
bloody hell don't you go there and find out?"

"No, no, I'm serious," Haynes said, quickly con-
cocting a story. "I'm thinking maybe I'll spend my holi-

day there. But you know how it is, mate, I work too hard all year to want to go there and run into rain and what-all. I could ask a travel agency, of course, but all I'll get out of them is a song and dance. They're out to sell tickets."

"I won't argue with you there," the clerk said, remembering what a disaster his last holiday in Spain had been. "All right, what is it you want to know? Temperature and that sort of thing? If you can ring back in ten minutes, I'll look up our back overseas reports—"

"Wait a minute," Haynes cut in. "I don't mind the temperature so much. Can you tell me how often it rains there this time of year?"

"Oh, if that's it, I can tell you right off. Not very often at all."

"When was the last time it rained?"

The clerk hesitated, then decided to be accommodating. "You are the one for details, aren't you? You must be a bloody engineer or the like. All right, call me back and I'll see what I can do."

Fifteen minutes later, Haynes had his answer. "It rained in Athens two nights ago," the clerk informed him jovially. "Pretty heavily, too. Before that, dry for two weeks. Have a good holiday, chum."

Haynes had a gut feeling that he should go to Athens. For the first time, he felt a link with his quarry. He knew something about him; he knew where he had been as recently as forty-eight hours ago.

"I pledged in the wind and the rain," the assassin had written, and it had rained only once in the last fortnight. All right, Haynes cautioned himself, let's not go off the deep end. So we know that he was one of hundreds of people attending a show—so what? How will that fact help you to isolate him, to say this was the one person among the hundreds?

Logically, he had to admit, going to Athens could be as fruitless as his trip to the Highlands. But the gut feeling was there, urging him to go, reminding him that the assassin had also written "As I stared at the deserted oval, I pledged anew." Find the meaning of the deserted oval, the gut feeling insisted, and you will find your answer.

In the end, it came down to one thing—he would go because he would not rest until he did.

Lord Ernest Travers, eighth earl of Woolton, stared through a leaded window of his country home. A panorama of rich green lawn, planted with magnificent oaks, stretched a full five kilometers to a range of hills. Close to the great house, a meticulously trimmed English garden made a formal, elegant pattern.

It was a view that never failed to bring Lord Travers a sense of security. Three hundred years ago, when the first earl had come here, the land would have presented the same fresh, inviolate look. Travers could recite its history since then, citing the year the garden had been started, knowing when many of the trees had been planted, and by whom.

This sense of continuity with his ancestors always reminded him of his family's distinction through the centuries. Wealth, power, unassailable position—these had always been the Traverses' due. That is why he was finding the subject of the present interview an outrage, almost impossible to comprehend.

Turning from the window, he regarded his visitor with a cold gaze. "Am I to take it, Constable, that you are seriously suggesting that someone may attempt to harm me?"

The CID man was adamant. "Yes, sir. That is precisely our feeling."

"And yet you refuse to tell me who or why."

The constable managed to maintain an untroubled appearance. He had been assigned, along with several other CID officials, to warn the Queen's third cousins of possible trouble. He had also been given a plausible story to use if necessary, and he decided to employ it now.

"Refuse is not the word, sir," he said, adopting a confidential manner. "Actually, sir, you are not the only one we're speaking to. I happen to know that quite a few other prominent people are being alerted too. If I were to guess, sir, I'd say that we're dealing with one of those loony anarchists who pop up once in a while. You know how they are—always ranting and raving against people with more than they've got. We simply want to warn you about possible trouble, sir, in order that you may take proper precautions. There's never any telling what one of these crazies might try."

The earl, somewhat placated, persisted in a milder tone. "But you can't tell me who this person is?"

"Not at this point, no sir. I understand that we got word something might be afoot through an informant. In cases like that, it always takes a while to get more specific information." The constable smiled reassuringly. "But we will, sir. We invariably do."

"Let us devoutly hope so," the earl snapped. "Very well. I will, as you put it, take precautions. Just what would you suggest?"

"Try not to go out without someone else along, sir. Actually, I would recommend that you cut down as much as possible on leaving home at all. Just until we've worked this out, sir."

"If you're so concerned, don't you think you should supply protection for me?"

"We would, of course—for you and the others—if we had more definitive word. But at this point, sir, we've only got pretty sketchy information. Still, we thought it best to warn you."

The earl selected a cigar without offering the humidor to his visitor. "Thank you, Constable," he remarked stiffly. "You may consider that I have been properly alerted. And now, if there's nothing further, I have some matters that need attention."

The constable picked up his hat. "Nothing further, sir. I appreciate the time you've given me. And do take care."

• • •

Lady Hope Marston finished dialing and waited impatiently for her London call to go through. After several rings, a male voice answered. "Yes?"

"Mr. Haynes, please."

"Sorry, he's not here."

"This is where he works, isn't it? This is the number he gave me."

"Yes, but he's out of town."

She carefully concealed her disappointment. "I see. Can you tell me when he'll be back?"

"I'm afraid not," the voice replied noncommittally. "Would you care to leave a message?"

"Thank you, yes." She paused for a moment. "Just tell him that Hope Marston called. I plan to be in London on the eighteenth and am hoping to see him. I'll be at the Connaught."

"I'll tell him."

She placed the telephone back in its cradle and returned to polishing her nails. Just exactly what do I feel about this man? she was asking herself—it's not at all what I felt for the others.

Her memory drifted back over the years since her divorce. There had been two affairs: a short encounter, soon after her divorce, with an Edinburgh physician; and then, more notably, a two-year liaison with a German executive. He had provided companionship when she needed it, sex when she needed it, and that was all. A month before, having for a long time recognized the sterile nature of their relationship, she had terminated it.

Then suddenly there was Haynes. What did he really mean to her? she wondered. In the one night they had spent together, she had experienced the greatest sexual satisfaction she had ever known. But it was much more than that: the sense of happiness in just being with him, her delight in watching him covertly as he drove, the warm conviction that they belonged together.

I'm like a fifteen-year-old schoolgirl, she mocked herself. But the excitement was there, clear, unmistakable. She glanced at a calendar. The eighteenth—two endless days away. But it would come. It would come.

Haynes spent his first afternoon in Athens reading the guidebook he had purchased in the lobby of the Hilton. Sprawled on the bed, he read swiftly, taking careful note of the illustrations. At no point did he come across anything that might give him an insight into the meaning of the phrase "I stared at the deserted oval."

In mid-afternoon he took a break, went down to the lobby, and approached the travel desk.

An attractive girl looked up as he approached. "Can I help you, sir?" she asked in an accent with French overtones.

"Yes. I understand there's a nightly 'Sound and Sight Show.' Can you tell me where I can buy a ticket?"

"Right here, sir. We handle all the tour tickets. How many would you like?"

"Just the one."

"Oh." She eyed him with new interest. "You're traveling alone, sir?"

"That's right."

"You'll like the show," she said. "As a matter of fact, it's been a while since I've seen it; I've been thinking I might go again one of these nights."

Haynes smiled politely, ignoring the obvious invitation. "How much will that be?"

The girl continued to study him challengingly. "Nine hundred drachmas. Not bad, huh?"

"Not bad," he agreed with a smile, aware that she didn't mean the price of the show. "Tell me, do all the travel desks in the hotels sell tour tickets?"

"Uh-huh."

"Anybody else sell them?"

"Not really. Tourists are about the only ones that go." She held his eyes steadily. "Except, of course, people like me."

He picked up the ticket and counted out the money.
"How do I get there? By taxi?"

"No, by tour bus. They'll stop by the lobby about
seven-fifteen."

"Fine." He was a few steps from the desk when he
heard her call.

"Sir."

Haynes turned around. "If you change your mind,
sir," she smiled, "let me know."

He raised a hand in genial acknowledgment and went
on to the elevator.

The tour bus driver was prompt, and by seven forty-five
had guided his vehicle to a position reasonably near the
site of the show. A line of similar buses was also discharging passengers, who strolled along a pathway bordered with flowers, following signs that directed them
toward the top of the hill.

Haynes emerged into a clearing and felt an instant
reaction. There before him, across a valley on the lofty
Acropolis, was the Parthenon, the home of Athena—
exactly as the assassin had described it. He found a seat
among the folding chairs, and almost immediately, with
the recorded sound of trumpets, the program began.

Throughout its course, as colored lights illuminated
various sections of the Acropolis to match the narrative,
Haynes was acutely conscious that the assassin had been
here just three nights before. What thoughts had run
through his mind, what plans, what emotions, what
dreams?

The music soared to a climax as the program ended.
Walking back to the bus, and through the evening,
Haynes sensed the presence of the assassin all around
him. It was as if he had left an invisible aura, filled with
evil, behind which his identity was hidden.

The mood continued the next morning. Haynes tried to
project himself into what had been the assassin's

thoughts and actions. If he had decided to go on the "Sound and Sight Tour," then the odds were over-whelming that he had purchased his ticket at the travel desk of a hotel. Haynes recalled that the girl who had sold him his ticket had said that almost all the tickets were sold through hotels.

All right, he reasoned, fine—but which hotel? There were scores in Athens, from the deluxe Hilton to the pensions renting a room for a few hundred drachmas a night. No, trying to pick the hotel was impossible.

But was it? he debated. The assassin had written "Later, as I stared at the deserted oval." The "Sound and Sight Show" ended at ten, and the tour driver would have dropped off his passengers at their various hotels. Wasn't it logical to assume that the assassin had returned to his hotel? If that were the case, then his hotel must have commanded a view of "the deserted oval." Even if he had taken a walk, the chances were high that the oval would have been nearby.

Excited by the thought, Haynes quickly finished his breakfast and bought a pamphlet with a city map and a listing and photographs of the principal attractions. Sitting in a corner of the lobby, he studied the photographs, looking for any that might have an oval shape.

He ran through the listings of attractions: the Academy, the Acropolis, the Agii Asomati, and down through the *A*'s and on to the *B*'s. He had worked his way into the *O*'s before he stopped short, his finger resting on a paragraph that was headed "Olympic Stadium." There was no accompanying photograph, but a stadium must have a track, and the shape of a track is oval. With a sudden elation, he snapped the pamphlet shut and went out to hail a cab.

The cab driver maneuvered his way through the heavy Athens traffic with a mixture of foolhardiness and skill. On Vassileos Konstandinou Street, in the heart of the city, Haynes paid his fare and found himself standing in front of the open end of the stadium.

He reread the paragraph in the pamphlet:

Olympic Stadium: Tucked into a natural ravine of
Ardettus Hill, the Panathenic Olympic Stadium
seats 70,000. It was designed by Lycurgus in the 4th
century B.C., covered with white marble 500 years
later, and entirely restored for the first modern
Olympic Games in 1866.

Walking to the chain barring entrance to the stadium
enclosure, Haynes stared beyond it to the tiers of seats
and the immaculate field. Unmistakably the track was
oval. With an unconscious sigh of satisfaction, he
turned and looked about, hoping to see a hotel rising
close at hand.

There was none clearly visible. Undiscouraged, he set
out to search the streets bordering the stadium. The first
two streets yielded nothing; shops displaying a bewildering assortment of material were interspersed with office
buildings and professional offices. On the third street,
however, there were two possibilities. Both were modest
pensions, but rising higher than their neighboring buildings. He studied each in turn, his initial reaction dwin-
dling to disappointment. Neither was high enough to
present an overview of the stadium track.

By the end of his second hour of patrolling, when he
had worked his way back six streets from the stadium,
he had to conclude that he had drawn a blank. Trying
to beat down his disappointment, he left the area and
stopped at a sidewalk cafe for coffee. Leafing through
the pamphlet idly, he picked up reading the list of attractions where he had left off at "Olympic Stadium."

This time he had little enthusiasm, but plowed his way
resolutely through the list until he came to the S's. Suddenly he felt a fresh wave of hope, for there was a
heading "Racetrack: the Faliro Horse Race Course." A
track is oval, he said to himself, whether it's a stadium
track or a racetrack.

Nevertheless, reluctant to face a second disappointment, he tarried over his coffee, taking care to complete
his reading of the list of attractions. There were no other

possibilities; it would be the Faliro Race Course or nothing.

It was almost anticlimactic. His cab was a mile away from the race course when the driver turned around. "You sure you said the race course?" he asked curiously, in accented English. "Not open now. Tonight."

"The race course," Haynes answered firmly.

"Okay. I thought maybe you meant the hotel across from the race course. My English is not so good."

Haynes was suddenly sitting upright. "There's a hotel across from the racetrack? You're sure?"

The driver looked at him scornfully. "I drive cab in Athens for six years. I'm sure."

Haynes beamed at him excitedly. "What's its name?"

"Chandris. Like there." The driver pointed ahead. Now only two blocks down the road, a huge vertical sign, with large blue block letters on a white background, read HOTEL CHANDRIS.

"Take me there," Haynes ordered jubilantly.

The driver shrugged and in a moment pulled off from the traffic on Singrou Avenue into a side road. After a few twistings and turnings he rounded a corner and drove into the hotel's circular driveway.

Haynes got out and stared up with joy at the hotel's seven floors. Across the divided highway he could make out part of the racetrack's grandstands.

The driver grew tired of waiting. "Two drachmas," he said impatiently.

"Make it three," Haynes replied expansively, handing over the bills. The driver looked at the bills, shrugged, and grinned. "Thank you." With a last curious look, he put the car in gear.

Haynes entered the lobby and approached the reception desk. "Tell me," he asked the clerk, "do you have rooms that overlook the racetrack?"

"We have lots of them, sir," the clerk responded politely. "But I'm afraid they're booked at the moment. Would you like another room?"

"No, thank you." Haynes noticed the travel desk near the elevator and walked over to it.

A plump young man was engrossed in stacking travel folders. Haynes waited until he had finished. "Oh, I'm sorry, sir," the clerk said apologetically. "I didn't realize anyone was waiting. What would you like?"

"It rained last Tuesday night, during the 'Sound and Sight Show.' I wonder if you could tell me how many people you had booked for it?"

The young man was instantly suspicious. "That's an odd request, sir. Would you mind telling me why you'd like to know?"

Haynes had determined that a frank approach would be best. "I'm looking for information—a description, actually—of a person who was staying here and attended the show. In all probability the show ticket was purchased from you."

"That sounds like a police matter. Is it?"

"It is an official matter, yes."

"Then may I see your credentials?"

"I'm sorry, but that will not be possible. Quite obviously I am not with the Athens police. But I am not at liberty to tell you whom I represent."

The young man hesitated. Quite obviously an American, he was thinking. Maybe from the embassy. Or even one of the armed services—the American navy, he had observed, liked to keep a low profile in the city. In any event, he concluded pragmatically, it's never wise to antagonize officials, no matter what their nationality.

"Very well," he said. "What you're asking doesn't seem too confidential. Just give me a moment." He riffled through some papers. "Yes, here we have it. Last Tuesday night we booked nine people here at the Chandris for the 'Sound and Sight Tour.' "

Haynes was pleased. "With that small a number, it's possible you might remember them."

The clerk shook his head. "Not a chance. After a while, in this job, everybody looks the same."

"I see. You say you sold nine tickets. Can you tell me how they were sold? Let's say, for example, to four couples and one person."

"That's easy." The clerk consulted his records. "Yes,

two tickets were sold during the day on four occasions. I presume that would be couples. One ticket was sold separately.''

"That one ticket," Haynes urged. "Think. Can you recall the person?''

The young man concentrated for a long moment. "I'm sorry. I just don't remember.''

"Can you perhaps recall if it was a man or a woman?''

"Not definitely, no. It was probably a man. Women alone buying a ticket are not too common, and I think I might have noticed that.''

Haynes decided on one more try. "All right. Do you recall them coming back from the show? In all likelihood they were soaked: the storm came up pretty fast, and they must have been caught up on the hill.''

"I wasn't here. We close the travel desk at eight. Maybe someone at the reception desk noticed them coming in.''

"Perhaps.'' Haynes thanked him and inquired at the reception desk for the clerk who had been on duty Tuesday night. He was informed that his name was George Papalos, and he would be coming on duty at seven.

The hours before then dragged interminably. Haynes tried to take a nap, but gave it up as a bad job. He was reduced finally to soaking himself in a long bath.

Promptly at five minutes to seven he entered the Chandris lobby, and was relieved to see shortly that George Papalos was on time. A curly-haired man of middle age, wearing wire-framed glasses, took over the reception duties.

He was barely at his post before Haynes approached him. Once again persuasion was necessary before cooperation was obtained, but the discreet offer of two ten-thousand-drachma notes proved the winning argument.

"All right,'' Papalos said at last. "You wish to know if I remember when the 'Sound and Sight' tourists came in from the show Tuesday night. Yes, I do remember—very clearly.''

Haynes looked at him carefully. "You're sure?"

"Very. In the first place, when I saw the tour bus pull up, it was almost half an hour earlier than usual. Due to the rain, of course. In the second place, they were very, very wet. Now what specifically do you wish to know?"

"Did you happen to look at them closely or just glance?"

Papalos reflected for a moment. "That is a hard question to answer. Let me put it this way. It was somewhere around ten o'clock, and at that time the lobby is pretty empty. So when the group came in, they were talking and laughing, and I called out something about bad luck with the rain. One or two of the couples just waved and went on into the bar. The other people went over to the elevators."

"Could you describe any of the individuals in the group, do you think?"

"Not really. One of the men was wearing a white jacket. I've been thinking of getting one something like it, so I noticed." Suddenly Papalos grinned. "One of the women was blond, with a particularly good figure. I noticed that, of course."

"No doubt," Haynes agreed dryly. "You spoke of couples. Everybody who came in seemed to be paired off with someone else?"

"Yes, except for the man who came in a few seconds later." Papalos shook his head eloquently. "He was by himself. And him I remember."

Haynes suppressed his excitement, keeping his voice level. "Why? What was unusual about him?"

"He was strange," Papalos replied. "I said something to him, too, about bad luck with the rain. But he stopped, and said something to me like 'You're right.' Then he cursed. I have never seen such anger in anyone's face."

"Can you tell me what he looked like?"

"Yes. He was very tall and on the slender side. His hair was soaked, and I remember it as being rather dark. And he was British—no doubt about that."

"How do you know?"

"A lot of English come to Athens on holiday. You get to know their accent."

"I see." Haynes went on deliberately. "Can you be a little more specific about him? What were his features like, for example?"

"I'm afraid I can't help you there." Papalos adjusted his wire-frame glasses. "You must understand that I'm not much good at describing people. I do remember his eyes—they were very unpleasant."

"Unpleasant?" Haynes asked, surprised at the description. "How do you mean that?"

"There was so much anger in him, spilling over. It was not a nice thing to see."

"His age?"

"Forty or so. No more than forty-five at the very outside."

"The color of the eyes?"

"I don't know."

"Was there anything special about his hands? Were they crippled?"

"Not that I noticed."

"Well, then, can you tell me how you would judge his social status? Did he seem educated, for instance?"

Papalos adjusted his glasses again. "To me an Englishman is an Englishman. One is like the other."

"You've been very patient," Haynes said, noticing that Papalos was getting weary of the questions. "One last thing—and the most important. You have the room records there. Is there any way you can find out his name?"

"It is impossible. We have almost four hundred rooms here, and always more than seven hundred guests. Even if he were by himself, there's no way of telling. We have many, many men traveling alone—businessmen, tourists, and so on."

"From something he wrote, I have reason to believe his room overlooked the racetrack. Would that help?"

"No. Almost all the rooms on the front of the

building and the sides have at least some view of the track.''

Haynes hesitated, tried again. "Perhaps you can suggest someone else who might be of help."

"Believe me," Papalos said fervently, "that is a question I have been turning over in my mind for several minutes. Unfortunately, there is no one."

The conversation had reached the point of no return.

Haynes was in a quandary. He had come to Athens with two great questions in his mind: Who? and Why?

On the one hand, he felt he had made some headway in finding the answer to "Who?" Sketchy information, yes—but information where before there was none. At least, he said to himself sardonically, I now know the assassin is male and British. That narrows the list of possible candidates from billions of male adults in the world to several million British males.

But on the other hand, the question of "Why?" loomed large, completely unexplored. Why had the assassin come to Athens? Surely he had not traveled from London simply to attend the "Sound and Sight Show." Then why? Whom had he seen, what had they discussed, what decisions had been made?

Haynes wrestled with the question of "Why?" For hours, unceasingly, he probed his imagination, seeking actions he might take that would yield an answer. Finally he reached the disturbing conclusion: There was nothing further he could do here. He would return to London.

Chapter 7

THE ASSASSIN PUT down his pencil. He was seated at a table in his kitchen, composing the note that would detail how and where £100,000 would be paid to him.

He was worried. His spirits had continued to soar after he had read the advertisement in the personal columns of the *Times*. Until a few moments ago. Then a sense of wariness, of something wrong, had intruded into his consciousness.

He did not try to brush it away. This was not the first time he had experienced the feeling, and he had learned to take it seriously. On three prior occasions it had saved his life.

What the feeling was telling him was that he should make absolutely sure that the advertisement was all that it seemed. Perhaps, just perhaps, the feeling whispered, the ad had been placed to set a trap, with him as the prey.

It would do no harm to check, the assassin reasoned. He considered various possibilities and decided to visit the neighborhood pub. At this hour, six o'clock, there was every reason to believe Timothy Kelley would be there. And Kelley, if he remembered correctly, worked

73

in the offices of the London *Times*.

The assassin rose and put on his coat. Ten minutes later he walked into the Golden Bow. There was a lively game of darts in progress, punctuated by loud exclamations of triumph or despair. At one end of the long room, grouped around the bar, a crowd of men sipped their pints and chatted. The assassin was pleased to note that one of the group was Kelley.

Waiting until he had been served, the assassin edged his way toward the burly Irishman. At an appropriate moment, he smiled a greeting. "Well, well, Timothy Kelley. Nice to see you."

"So it's you, is it?" Kelley responded. He was an imposing figure of a man, fully six and a half feet tall, with a freckled face and the watery eyes of a heavy drinker.

"It's me." The assassin eyed Kelley's glass. "Your ale seems a bit low there. Can I order you another?"

"Very kind of you, I'm sure," Kelley said, hurriedly draining his glass.

The assassin ordered the refill and then lit a cigarette. "How's the job going?" he inquired conversationally. "You're with the London *Times*, as I remember."

"Right you are. Same bloody old rat race, day in, day out. I'm with the circulation department, and they're always hounding us to get more readers, more readers. Christ, there's no end to it."

The assassin nodded sympathetically. "Must be a real pressure cooker." He paused as if a sudden thought had come to him. "Say, you might be able to help me settle a discussion."

"How's that?"

"Well, I was having lunch with a couple of friends today. One of them mentioned an ad in this morning's *Times*. We got to guessing who might have placed it, and we came up with all kinds of ideas—some of them pretty wild. It would be really interesting to know the answer."

The Irishman was curious. "What did the ad say?"

"That's the thing. Not much. It was in the personal columns and all it said was 'Achilles. I will comply.' "

"No signature?"

"No signature."

"I see what you mean," Kelley remarked. "It does set you to wondering, doesn't it? What do you want me to do?"

"Well, if it isn't too much trouble, I thought you might be able to find out who placed it. My guess is that it's some kind of business code." The assassin signaled the barman. "You'll have another with me, won't you?"

"Don't mind if I do," Kelley answered appreciatively. "Yes, I think I can find out for you. I know a chap in the advertising department and I'm sure he'll look it up. Suppose you drop by here tomorrow night."

"Fine. I'll do that. You're sure it isn't too much trouble?"

"Not at all, not at all."

The assassin was in the Golden Bow promptly at five forty-five the following night. Kelley arrived within a few minutes and greeted him eagerly. "I saw my friend in the advertising department today. Guess what? It appears your ad was probably placed by the police."

The assassin took an instant to answer. "The police? What makes you think that?"

"Well, it seems that everybody who places an ad in the classified columns has got to give a name. It's a rule of the paper. But all the records showed on this ad was a post office box number for billing purposes."

"That hardly proves it was the police, does it?"

"No, but my friend says he's seen that box number used before, maybe once a year or so. He says no one in his department knows for sure who the box number is, and his boss won't say. But there's always been a feeling that it's the police."

The assassin managed to keep his sudden rage in check. "I see," he said quietly. "Well, I must say none of us guessed that. Thanks for looking into it."

Lady Marston disembarked from the *Flying Scotsman*

and took a cab from the station to the Hotel Connaught. She set about unpacking, and was almost through when her phone rang.

"Welcome to London," Haynes greeted her. "I got the message you'd called, and I'm delighted. I have two questions: Are you still as beautiful as ever, and can we have dinner tonight?"

"You haven't changed, have you?" She laughed. "Still as direct as always. How have you been, Tom? I understand you were away."

"Right. To Athens. Just got back this morning, as a matter of fact. Well? I can't stand the suspense."

"Well what?"

"How about dinner tonight?"

"I can't make it," she answered regretfully. "You remember I told you my sister and her husband are coming in. I simply have to spend the evening with them; it's been three whole years since I've seen them."

"I was afraid you might say that," he replied mournfully. "But you also said they won't be here long." His voice became urgent. "Hope, when can I see you? I just can't get you out of my mind."

It seemed to her that she had never known such happiness. "I know how you feel," she said, almost inaudibly. "Somehow we'll make it tomorrow night—call me around five."

Sir Henry Adams seemed haggard, an impression that was not helped by the dark suit and tie he habitually wore. "I don't wish to seem negative, Haynes," he was saying, "but you'll agree the information you've brought back doesn't put us that much forward."

"No, it doesn't," Haynes agreed. "But at least we've filled in some of the empty spaces. We know we're looking for a man who is British, tall, on the slender side, and probably has dark hair. We know he's got some sort of a handicap; at least he keeps referring to 'the faltering hand.' And he can shoot—handicap or not. That shot that brought down Lady Lawton proved that.

We know he used an American carbine. We know, too, he's been in Athens recently. So we're not totally in the dark."

The Assistant Commissioner looked disturbed. "Granted. Ordinarily I'd say we're making progress. But we've only got three days left." He resumed his restless pacing. "Why hasn't he gotten in touch with us? We put the ad he wanted in yesterday morning's *Times*. What's he waiting for?"

"I don't know. Maybe he was out of London yesterday. You know, Sir Henry, I keep coming back to why he went to Athens. If you'll accept a suggestion, I think it might be well to ask Interpol if they've got anything on a man fitting his description, sparse as it is."

The Assistant Commissioner stopped his pacing. "Just exactly what are you getting at?"

Haynes spoke earnestly. "We don't know why he went to Athens—there's no saying otherwise. Perhaps there's an international aspect we just haven't gotten onto. God knows what's in the minds of some of these terrorist groups today."

Adams shook his head lugubriously. "Yes, I suppose there is a possibility of something like that. All right, I'll have someone get in touch with Interpol directly." He crossed to his intercom. "You know, Haynes, that's what makes this whole matter so alarming. It just doesn't follow any cut-and-dried pattern."

Hope Marston was radiant in a white evening dress with a mandarin collar and artfully molded lines. Throughout the performance of *Evita,* Haynes kept his eyes on her more than on the stage. Her black hair, falling in lustrous waves, was accented by her diamond earrings and pendant. There was a faint flush in her cheeks, as if the evening held a special magic.

As they walked through the theater lobby after the final curtain, he was aware of the admiring looks from the men and the appraising looks from the women. "You're quite the show stopper," he said, "and that's as it should be. Goddesses don't appear on earth too frequently, now do they?"

She smiled at him happily. "You do say the nicest things. If I'm all that wonderful, don't you think you might offer me an after-theater supper? Would it sound too un-goddesslike if I say I'm starved?"

But as they were finishing their supper she turned to him, suddenly serious. "Tom, this girl you told me you're living with. Where does she think you are tonight?"

He looked at her steadily. "I wish you hadn't asked that. Quite frankly, I'm not too proud of myself. I just said I wouldn't be home; no explanation."

She nodded. "I see. She knows, of course."

"How could she?"

"Oh, I don't mean she knows who I am. But believe me, she knows something's wrong. It goes with being a woman."

"You're probably right," he conceded, reluctantly recalling the expression on Jill's face earlier. "Look, can't we get onto a more cheerful subject?"

Her hand on his arm was light. "Forgive me. It was stupid of me to ask. All right, suppose you tell me the story of your life. Did you have mumps? Were you in love with the little girl next door? How many brothers and sisters?"

"There's not much to tell, I'm afraid. Actually, I was an only child and that's a marvelous thing to be. You learn to be completely selfish from the very first day. You grow up with a big self-esteem and the conviction that the world revolves around you—only you."

"Sounds delightful."

"It's wonderful. Outside of that I guess the only other important thing was my parents. They're super. My father's an engineer, and a very good one. My mother's a doctor, and a very good one. And they love each other very much and me very much. End of story."

"Short and sweet." She laughed. "I can see where you got your self-confidence."

They huddled together, talking easily for a long while, and it seemed to both of them natural that they were holding hands. Finally, by some unspoken agreement, they stood up and left. As they entered the lobby of the Connaught, it never occurred to either of them that he would not be going up with her. They lay down on the great bed, holding each other tenderly for an instant, and then their passion rose with wild urgency.

Later, as the first faint light of the new day entered the room, she cradled him as he slept. "All's fair in love and war, Thomas Edison Haynes," she whispered fiercely. "All's fair."

In a quiet section of the CID laboratory, a middle-aged man named Charles Harrison worked happily. From the time he had first learned to read, Harrison had been fascinated by crime and the men who work to solve it. He had pored over book after book detailing the machinations of criminals from Charles Peace to Lord Haw-Haw; gradually, his admiration focused on the men whose anti-crime post was the laboratory. There in his opinion were the real heroes, objective, dispassionate, impossible to deceive.

It was inevitable that with this passion, backed by a considerable scientific ability, Harrison would enter police work—in the laboratory, of course. His total dedication and obsession with accuracy matched even the CID's tough standards, and in short order he emerged as a key employee, called upon for the most difficult assignments.

Perhaps the only flaw in Harrison's approach to his work was his inability to accept even the slightest suggestion, let alone criticism. In his view he lived in a world unto itself of test tubes and chemicals; it was unthinkable, intolerable, for anyone who wasn't part of that world to venture an opinion.

He was pleasantly immersed in his test tubes and reagents when Haynes put in an appearance. Instantly

Harrison's mood changed; he had not been looking forward to this interview.

"Well now," he said with a civility he was far from feeling, "you've come about that bit of newspaper you picked up in Scotland."

"That's right."

"Very frankly, I was surprised when the Assistant Commissioner rang up to say you'd be stopping by. You've read the report I sent him, I daresay."

"I have."

"Then you know precisely what our findings were," Harrison said reproachfully. "Look, as I understand it, you picked up this scrap of newspaper fully two hundred yards from the spot where Lady Lawton's body was found. That's right, isn't it?"

"Yes," Haynes agreed.

"Then you probably assumed that it had no connection with the case. Am I correct?"

"You are."

Harrison stared at him coldly. "You are aware we established that your scrap of newsprint came from the Sports Pages of the London *Evening Times* for September sixth—one day before the shooting. That would strongly indicate a probability that your assassin bought the paper the evening of September sixth and took it with him when he drove up to Scotland. That is information, Mr. Haynes—where you expected none. But as I understand it, far from being grateful, you are still not satisfied."

"Mr. Harrison," Haynes said patiently, "the man we're looking for could have bought that paper at any one of hundreds of places in London. Knowing he bought it doesn't help us, does it?"

"We do not manufacture evidence here," Harrison snapped. "There were no fingerprints, no stains, no writing on that newsprint. What, precisely, do you feel we can do further?"

"I was hoping there might be additional tests you might apply."

Harrison reacted angrily. "Are you suggesting that

we do shoddy work here? I assure you we utilize every possible test—always."

"Mr. Harrison," Haynes answered calmly, "I am suggesting no such thing. As I told the Assistant Commissioner, there is something about the report that troubles me. I can't pinpoint it, but I am sure it is there."

"Indeed?" Harrison remarked icily. "Fortunately, it is not a laboratory function to deal with vague 'somethings.' There is nothing further we can do."

"I'm sorry to have taken your time, and I admit it was illogical of me to come." Haynes couldn't resist a wry smile. "The Assistant Commissioner warned me you might be a bit resentful."

"The Assistant Commissioner is a very knowing man," Harrison responded sharply.

The assassin drank steadily, unaware of the late hour. He could not credit the treachery of the police. What madness, what arrogance, could have led them to act so rashly? How could they possibly assume that he would walk blindly into their ambush?

His rage feeding upon itself, he got up frequently to replenish his glass. Deep within him, in every fiber of his body, he suffered the shattering knowledge that the prize he had thought so near had never been near. From the very beginning, he told himself bitterly, they must have planned to lead him on like some country idiot.

Well, they would learn that he could retaliate. He had warned them and they had not listened. The deadline he had set would soon be at hand—the blood for a second death would be on their conscience.

He went to a closet and brought out the package he had carried from Greece. Unwrapping it carefully, he saw that the merchant from whom he had bought it had done his packing well. The vase had survived the air trip without damage; its smooth glazed surface was unmarred.

The assassin placed the amphora in the center of

the table with almost ceremonial deliberateness. He examined it with intense concentration, marveling at the graceful curve of the handles, gently tracing the outline of the delicate figures.

The central figure riveted his attention. The strength and agility of the warrior were evident in the firmness of his stance and the sinews of his outthrust arm, holding a lance. His head was protected by a helmet that reached to the back of his neck, and his left arm held a round shield, on guard against attack.

After many minutes, the assassin was satisfied. He sat down to finish his drink, reveling in the knowledge that he had chosen well. The vase fit perfectly into the plan that he had formulated, and that he had never believed he would have to use.

Again the rage returned, stronger than ever, flooding him with the galling certainty that the Crown and the police had conspired against him. So be it. A line learned long ago burst upon his mind: "Even so my bloody thoughts, with violent pace, shall ne'er look back."

Chapter 8

THE SECOND-RANKING official of the American embassy looked at his secretary with concern. A kindly man, it distressed him to see her obvious unhappiness. "What is it, Jill?" he asked. "Any way I can help?"

Jill Blake shook her head. "No, sir, I'm afraid not. I'm sorry, I wasn't aware it showed so much."

Andrew Clark, still in his thirties, had gone through a trying divorce six months earlier and was sure he recognized the symptoms. "Trouble with your boyfriend?" he asked solicitously.

"Sort of. At least I think so," Jill answered. She paused, deep in her misery. "That doesn't make much sense, does it?"

"It makes perfect sense. Besides, if it's making you feel bad, that's what counts. Is there anything I can do? Time off, anything like that?"

"No, I'm afraid not. But thanks."

Clark nodded. "Just remember, if there's anything, let me know."

Jill was near tears as he walked away. His concern had triggered a wave of emotion she was unable to get under control for several moments. There is nothing you can put your finger on, she tried to reassure herself. So he's away from home for a night. Is that anything to get panicky about? Probably he's off on an overnight trip and he'll be waiting for you when you get home tonight. But she remembered with sudden despair his evasiveness when he returned from Scotland. Something was wrong, awfully wrong.

Haynes was astonished to get a call from Charles Harrison. "Do you suppose you might come over to the laboratory?" Harrison said quietly. "I think I might have something for you."

"Of course." Haynes was in his office at the CIA station, catching up on some work, but left immediately and took a taxi to Scotland Yard.

This time, Harrison greeted him with a conciliatory smile. "You know, I'm very grateful to you. After you left yesterday, I must admit I sat here stewing. I was thinking how damned cheeky it was of you to imply I might have overlooked something; at least that's the way I took it. Then—right in the midst of my mental grousing—it struck me like a bolt: There was a point I had overlooked." Haynes waited expectantly. "It is difficult for me to admit this," Harrison continued hesitantly, "but my error was quite unforgivable. I failed to take into account the fact that newspapers generally publish more than one edition. Actually, I find, the London *Times* publishes three editions. The first edition comes off the press early and is sent by train to the north of England and Scotland. The other two editions are sold principally in the London area. Do you follow me?"

"Yes, I do."

"All right, then. Originally, I simply assumed that your scrap of newsprint was from a paper purchased in London. But after you left yesterday, when I checked and found there are three *Times* editions, I looked to see from which edition the newsprint had come."

"And?"

"Well, as you probably know, newspapers frequently vary the length of a story from edition to edition. For example, in the first edition, a particular story might be shorter than in a later edition, when more details are available. Sometimes, too, the story might be on a different page than in other editions."

"I understand." Haynes was very much on edge. "When you checked the three *Times* editions, what did you find?"

Harrison wagged his head somberly. "This has been a very humbling experience for me. I found that the piece of newsprint was not from one of the London editions, as I had assumed, but from the first edition. The piece contained an account of a Liverpool soccer match. It was a much shorter story than in the later editions."

"The first edition," Haynes cut in urgently. "You said a moment ago it is sent by train to the north of England and Scotland?"

"Exactly. It travels during the night and is put on sale the morning of the next day."

"Aren't any copies of the first edition sold in London?"

"None. The minute it comes off the press, it's packed off to the train for shipment."

Haynes leaned forward intently. "Then you're saying the scrap of paper I picked up, from the evening September sixth issue, must have been from a copy bought in Scotland on the seventh—the day of the shooting."

"Either bought in the north of England or Scotland," Harrison amended. "I must caution you, however, that we cannot say flatly that it was the assassin who bought the paper. It could have been someone else."

Haynes grinned. "I propose to find out. Until I do, I prefer to be an optimist." He shook hands warmly. "Thank you very much."

"No need to thank me for making a stupid error." Harrison regarded him curiously. "Tell me, Mr. Haynes, just what was there about my report that bothered you? What made you think there might be more?"

"To tell you the truth, I just don't know," Haynes said. "It was just something. You know, right after I got out of college, I worked for a paper for about a year. Maybe subconsciously I missed in your report any mention of a particular edition. I just don't know."

Harrison nodded. "I see. Well, in any event, good luck."

"Amen to that," Haynes responded seriously, crossing his fingers.

Haynes decided to fly his Spad up to Scotland. His maps showed there was a landing strip about ten miles from Glen Walk, and a phone call confirmed that ground transportation would be no problem.

The Spad flew due north, its Hispano-Suiza engine beating a steady rhythm. A thousand feet below, the traffic on the motorway was almost matching its speed. Haynes was under no illusion that he would save much time. But he sensed that he needed a chance to sort out his thinking, and the solitary, remote experience of flying was very welcome.

The day was clear, with an early crispness that was invigorating. His thoughts switched back and forth from the purpose of his trip to Hope Marston and Jill. He was not the first man to be living with one girl and sleeping with another, he told himself reassuringly. Yet he could not shake the feeling that what he was doing was far from admirable. Maybe it was a heritage from his Scottish forebears, or maybe it was a sense of fairness, but he knew he would have to choose, and soon. The picture of Hope, the memory of her passion, would come to him, and then Jill's bright, trusting face would intrude.

He had been glad, in a way, that Hope had stayed on in London. Her brother-in-law's conferences at the Foreign Office had been extended by two days, and she had felt she should spend the time with them. If I am away from her, he had reasoned, I will know clearly how I feel. So far, he admitted, his confusion was still as great as ever.

The Spad passed over Harrogate, the antique capital of England, and then Carlisle at the border. The afternoon sun was still high when, buffeted by the Highland crosscurrents, he located the strip and began his descent.

As promised, the airport's self-styled manager put away his mechanic's tools and drove him to Glen Walk in a battered truck. Haynes patiently answered his questions about the Spad, enjoying the panorama of heather and hill that bordered the route.

In the center of town, he climbed down from the truck and headed for the general store where the mechanic had told him a paper could be obtained. "Good afternoon," he said, entering the crowded interior.

The proprietor interrupted his rearrangement of bolts of woolens and regarded him with friendly interest. "And the same to you," he responded in a rich burr.

"Would you have a copy of the London *Times?*"

"Aye. It's possible. Gie me a minute." The proprietor crossed to another counter and rummaged underneath it, reappearing after an instant with a loosely folded paper. "Ye're in luck. But it's nae today's, of course. Yesterday's."

"Of course." Haynes paid for the paper and lingered on.

"Ye're a stranger, then," the proprietor prompted.

"Yes and no. I was here a few days back, looking into Lady Lawton's murder."

"Ah, so that's it? A bad business, that." The proprietor eyed him with a heightened interest. "Ye're wi' the police, is it? If you dinna mind my saying so, ye're nae typical. An American, if I dinna miss my guess."

"You're right. And I work with your police only occasionally—a matter of American cooperation, you might say."

"I see." The proprietor nodded sagely, pretending to understand. "Ye've talked wi' Henderson and McLeod, then," he said, naming the two area CID constables.

"Yes, last week when I was here. They're good men."

"Aye."

Haynes took the plunge. "Tell me, do you sell many copies of the *Times?*"

"Not the noo. It's nae the tourist time. Three a day, sometimes four or five."

"Do you remember the day Lady Lawton was shot?" Haynes asked. "That was last Thursday, the seventh. Did you sell copies that day?"

"I did," the proprietor answered without hesitation. "The usual three, of course. They've been coming in for years. And then there was one other—a stranger."

"How can you be sure it was the seventh, not the sixth or eighth?"

The proprietor snorted. "People around here will nae forget what they were doing on the seventh. Lady Lawton's murder was the biggest thing to happen in a hundred years."

Haynes bored in, preparing himself for disappointment. "Do you remember what the stranger looked like?"

"That I do. They're nae sae common in Scotland, usually the lone fisherman on holiday or summat like that. But this man was nae fisherman."

"Suppose you describe him for me." Haynes covered his suspense by lightly rubbing his cheek.

"Well, he was a big fellow, very tall. Maybe around forty. Not bad-looking, when you come down to it. Not heavy—on the thin side, if anything." The proprietor paused, searching his memory.

"Was he British?"

"Oh aye, nae a question about that."

"Color of his hair?"

"Dark, I think."

"Can you be more detailed? How was he dressed, would you say he was a working man or not, any scars, color of his eyes—that sort of thing."

The proprietor pondered dutifully. "Nothing special.

I dinna think he was a farmhand or a factory worker, if that's what ye mean."

Haynes felt the familiar disappointment welling up inside him. So it was going to be the same old generalities. "How about his hands?" he asked. "Was he crippled—anything unusual about them?"

"Not that I noticed." The proprietor shrugged, absently moving an order pad on the counter. "Look, that's not why I remember him. It was the matter of the headline."

"The headline?"

"Yes. It was something about a bombing by the IRA in Ireland. This chap read it and started in swearing. He dinna like the Irish, that I can tell you. Called them filthy cowards and some other things a lot worse."

"Why?"

"Why?" the proprietor echoed. "You mean did he say why he hated them?"

"That's right."

"Aye, as a matter of fact he did. To tell you the truth, I'm nae fond of them mysel'. I said that, and he yelled that I couldn't possibly know what complete bastards they are. He hollered something like, 'Fight them like I did, lose your men to their filthy tricks—then you'll find out.' He was proper wild, believe me. Especially when he got onto his wound."

Haynes interrupted sharply. "What kind of a wound was it?"

"He dinna say exactly. But I remember seeing the veins on his temple, he was so crazy. 'The sons of bitches wounded me, they wrecked my life forever'—he was yelling stuff like that." The proprietor bent forward confidentially. "I would ha' asked him about the wound, but it occurred to me, what with his screaming his life was wrecked forever, that he might have been hurt in his private parts. And that's no mon's business, is it?"

"You're sure he didn't mean his hands?" Haynes countered.

"I've already told you I did na' notice them especially."

"So you did. All right. Go on—what did he do then?"

"Well, he calmed down finally, and I think he felt a bit funny about the way he'd been acting. He picked up his paper, sort of mumbled a good-bye, and left."

"Did you notice where he went?"

"Aye," the proprietor answered earnestly. "Not far, to be sure. He just went out and got in his car. I watched him through the window—he was there quite a while. It looked like he was going through the back part of the paper—you know, where the ads are." After a second's pause, the proprietor smiled apologetically. "Of course, I canna' help you there. I have no idea what he might have been looking for."

"I do," Haynes said. "What kind of a car was he driving?"

"Ach." The proprietor tossed up his hands. "One car's the same as another as far as I'm concerned."

Five minutes later, Haynes thanked the proprietor profusely and left. In the interim, nothing further had been learned. But he was content. He was carrying with him a precious nugget of information. The assassin had fought in Ireland and had been wounded there.

And that may prove to be the wedge we need, he thought hopefully.

At five forty-five, Sir Henry Adams entered the gymnasium of New Scotland Yard, feeling a great need for his morning workout. His muscles were taut and aching; the strain of a sleepless night had left him edgy and irritable.

"Good morning, sir." Sergeant Whitcombe, the department's physical instructor, stood up respectfully. "What'll it be this morning, Sir Henry? A bit of work with the weights or the rowing machine?"

"Neither," the Assistant Commissioner answered

crisply. "There are a few extra kinks this morning, so
we'll have a go with the gloves."

"As you wish, sir," the sergeant replied, inwardly
wincing. Even at forty-seven, the Assistant Commissioner's lean frame could put jolting power into his
punches.

They sparred for three spirited rounds before Adams
held up a gloved hand. "That's enough. I'll take my
shower now."

The sergeant nodded. "I'd hate to have faced you in
your Cambridge days, sir. No wonder at all you were
the school champion."

Adams ignored the compliment and left with a preoccupied wave. Upstairs in his office, only slightly refreshed by his workout, he breakfasted on tea and a
biscuit. Outside his windows, the day was in full swing;
he could hear the noises of traffic moving toward London's teeming businesses. The city was awake and stirring.

He walked to the window and gazed dispiritedly at the
jumble of buildings stretching to the horizon. Somewhere, in one of thousands of buildings, a man was
probably up and about, his mind focused on his dark
plans.

The Assistant Commissioner brought his hand down
sharply on the windowsill. His frustration boiled within
him—frustration and fear. The assassin's deadline was
now one day away. One day, Adams repeated urgently
to himself, and still he has not acknowledged the ad.

Why, in God's name, why? "Achilles. I will
comply." The words in the paper had been stark, impossible to overlook. Why had the expected response
not come? Why?

Adams sensed, deep within him, the gnawing dread
that the assassin had learned the ad was a deceit. He
had rejected the thought a dozen times, asking himself
coldly how that could be possible. But it persisted in
returning, terrifying, assaulting.

One day more, and if he knows, he will strike. God

grant that the Queen's relatives, forewarned, will stand on their guard. Swiftly Adams reviewed in his mind the many avenues of the investigation. They were thorough, but so pitifully slow. Inevitably, he was sure, they would prevail—but would they prevail in time? There was one day left before the inexorable deadline. And beyond that, the awesome threat to the Crown itself would remain.

The sound of the telephone pulled him from his brooding. "Good morning, Sir Henry." Haynes's voice was vibrant with a controlled excitement. "It's a wet Scottish morning here, and I didn't get much sleep, but I definitely feel encouraged. This time lying awake doing mental homework might just pay off."

They talked intensively for a long time, considering various courses of action, invariably coming back to one central idea. Finally they were of one mind, and hung up immediately.

The Assistant Commissioner instantly summoned his task force. His earlier despondency swept away, he outlined tersely his talk with Haynes; the group reacted swiftly and positively.

Three minutes later, the head of New Scotland Yard's computer section was urgently called from his whirring machines to the Assistant Commissioner's office.

Adams was alone, impatiently sucking on his pipe. "I've got a crash assignment for you, Peter," he announced without preliminary. "Let me tell you what I have in mind, and then you tell me if it's possible."

Peter Wycoff listened intently. A small man with close-cropped gray hair and a neatly trimmed beard, he projected an image of impersonal, confident ability. "I'm sure it can be done," he said flatly, when Adams had finished. "I'll not take up your time with the details, but yes, it can be done."

"How long?" Adams demanded.

Wycoff pondered carefully. He had long ago learned that the Assistant Commissioner's direct gaze reflected a realism that tolerated only facts, unpleasant or otherwise. "My estimate is at least seventy-two hours. Possibly more. I'll be able to tell better after I've gotten into it."

"There are no ways to cut that time?"

"I have already considered them. Seventy-two hours would, I think, be the minimum."

Adams nodded in dismissal. "Then I suggest you get on with it. I'll call General Leonard and set it up."

The International Criminal Police Organization, Interpol for short, is headquartered in Paris. A giant clearinghouse, Interpol serves the police of over ninety countries, exchanging information on individuals or groups who are or may be engaged in international crime. It has no agents, no patrol cars, no riot squads. Its weapons are an extensive radio network and circulars, but it uses them superlatively well.

On the second floor of the Interpol building, on a blustery September afternoon, an official painstakingly examined the report on his desk. He satisfied himself that it contained all the pertinent information the files could yield, and finally punched a buzzer for his secretary. "This is the report Scotland Yard wants," he said as she entered the room. "It seems to be in order, and they appear to be in a great rush for it. See that it gets off at once."

"*Oui, monsieur,*" the secretary responded. "*Immédiatement.*"

Chapter 9

LORD ERNEST TRAVERS managed to make his way to his car without undue difficulty. But it required several attempts, complicated by fumbling, before he fitted his key into the Bentley's ignition lock and started the engine.

He sat motionless, prudently trying to clear his head before he put the car into gear. The night had been eminently successful, he congratulated himself, trying to estimate the extent of the winnings that now jammed his pockets. The effort proved fruitless, and he soon gave it up.

Switching on his headlights, he negotiated the driveway that bordered the gambling house and reached the highway. Driving with the exaggerated care of the drunk, he guided his car through the deserted Birmingham streets; without incident he soon gained the motorway and headed north.

In an effort to fight off the drowsiness that was beginning to steal up on him, he rolled down the windows and switched on the radio. Ahead of him lay a drive of thirty kilometers before he could turn into the gates of his country home. It was a drive he had made many times under similar conditions, and he had no doubt of his ability to make it again.

Listening to a recording of the *Brandenburg* Concertos, he found his mind drifting over a variety of subjects. As he did frequently, he mulled over possible additions that could be made to his formal garden, a favorite pastime. But tonight his musing gave way to a recollection of his interview with the CID constable.

Travers was still smoldering over the warning he had been given: Never leave your estate unaccompanied; never leave at all unless it is absolutely necessary; there is a crazy who might wish to harm you. It was intolerable that some raving anarchist—at least that's what the constable had implied—could go around plotting mischief against his betters. Why didn't the Yard nail the bugger right off? With all their publicity, you'd think they'd collar him in jig time.

Preoccupied with his anger, he almost missed the exit ramp for the side road that led to his estate. A scant fifty yards away he jammed on the brake and decelerated enough to make the turn. The Bentley shot onto the side road, wobbled for an instant, and then straightened away.

At that precise moment Lord Travers felt a small, hard object pressing firmly against the back of his skull. "Don't turn around," a quiet voice said. "That pressure you're feeling is the muzzle of an American carbine. A very efficient instrument. Very."

Travers emerged from his daydreaming abruptly. "Who are you?" he roared. "What do you want?"

"There's a grove two hundred yards down the road," the assassin answered easily. "Turn in there."

The thought sped through Travers's mind that he was carrying a great deal of money. He was about to be robbed, that was obvious—and at the worst possible time. "Don't be a bloody fool," he blustered. "You'll spend years in Dartmoor. You're not picking on some grocer's clerk—I'll see to it they hunt you down."

"I know who you are," the quiet voice answered. "Ernest Charles Travers, sixth earl of Woolton."

Suddenly a great, numbing fear came to Travers. "What do you want?" he said weakly, remembering the constable's warning.

The muzzle of the gun increased its pressure. "Turn off now," the assassin commanded. "Park behind that clump of trees and turn off the motor." Travers did as he was ordered. "All right," the quiet voice said, "walk straight ahead, over behind that large tree. And don't turn around."

Centuries of family arrogance had not conditioned Travers to accept orders well. Starting to comply, the rage erupted in him and he spun around sharply. "You damned miserable bastard," he yelled, lunging out wildly.

The assassin easily evaded him, stepping back lightly, rifle at the ready. In the strong moonlight, he was silhouetted against the line of trees, a beam of light falling across his features. "I must compliment you, milord," he said mockingly. "Your courage does credit to your lineage."

Travers was staring at him fixedly. "I've seen you somewhere," he said. "In London."

"Indeed? Very possible, I suppose. But completely irrelevant, since this is the last time you will see me."

"You intend to shoot me?" Travers asked with resigned dignity.

"I do."

"Then shoot and be damned."

"I will be, I assure you," the assassin answered sardonically, raising the rifle.

Travers catapulted forward in a final, hopeless fighting gesture. The bullet took him in midair, ripping through his heart.

For an instant the assassin stood somberly, then walked back to the Bentley. Reaching down to the floor of the back seat, he picked up the vase he had selected with so much care in Athens. He returned to the body and set the vase against it, in an upright position. Well satisfied, without a backward look, he set off through the forest to the spot where he had left his car.

•   •   •

The hue and cry arose almost from the moment a small boy, out for an early morning walk in the woods with his dog, spotted the black Bentley. Curious, he drew nearer, and then was running wildly, eyes wide with fright, legs pumping hard to carry him away from his gruesome find.

The news was headlined in every large metropolitan paper. Lord Travers had served many years in the House of Lords, and was well known for his blustery, harsh baiting of the Labor and Socialist parties.

"EARL OF WOOLTON DIES IN SAVAGE MURDER" the Manchester *Guardian* trumpeted, using a sensational tone that was reflected elsewhere. But it remained for a sharp-eyed reporter on a London tabloid to spot a link between two murders and launch a fierce attack.

"Where is Scotland Yard while the Queen's relatives are being butchered?" his article demanded in its opening sentence. He went on with his tirade:

> Just a short ten days ago, Lady Dorothy Lawton, a relative of the Queen, was gunned down while on a peaceful early morning horseback ride. Now the body of Ernest Charles Travers, sixth Earl of Woolton, a third cousin to the Queen, has been found in an isolated grove near his Yorkshire estate.
>
> Local rumor has it that Lord Travers was returning from a night of successful gambling, and that he was followed and murdered as a result. Police refuse to confirm or deny the rumor, and are keeping their own counsel. We submit that their silence may perhaps stem from a paucity of ideas. Indeed, no theory has as yet been advanced for the murder of Lady Lawton.
>
> When members of the noble families of the land are not immune from violence, is it not reasonable to ask how any of us can feel secure? We call upon Scotland Yard to brush away its mental cobwebs

and live up to its past glory. If it is unable to do so, then one must seriously question whether the time for a change in its leadership is not at hand.

Sir Henry Adams read the article, and was relieved to see that it had not occurred to the reporter that the two murders might be directly connected. It was not the first time the Yard had been under fire, nor would it be the last, and he had always made it a policy to ignore criticism until events proved it wrong.

This time, however, the storm was far more severe than usual. He was not surprised, therefore, to receive a summons from the Prime Minister.

The Iron Leader, as usual, wasted no time. "Henry," she fairly snapped, "you are of course aware that a substantial segment of the press, albeit the yellow segment, is calling for your head."

"Madame Prime Minister," the Assistant Commissioner replied, "it is of course your prerogative to give them what they wish, if you so decide."

"Don't talk idiotic twaddle. You've been faithful in keeping me up-to-date, and I know you're doing everything possible. And I have strong hopes that calling in the computer people on the basis the American outlined will get the job done." The Prime Minister set a loose wisp of hair firmly back in place. "But we must face it, we're still twenty-four hours away from getting that computer report."

"Twenty-three hours, to be exact."

"Twenty-three hours, then." The Prime Minister waved a hand impatiently. "The point is, what further can we do today? Now."

"Unless I misheard, Madame," Adams countered, "you said earlier you are confident we are doing everything possible."

The Prime Minister sighed. "Henry, at times you're a very stubborn, difficult man. You know very well what I mean. I hate to admit it, but there are politics involved in everything, even in this instance. Can you give out a positive statement, perhaps, that would say you are making important progress, but are not now at liberty, etc. etc. You know the sort of thing I mean.''

"I do indeed, Madame, but what you suggest is impossible. The Yard is simply not in the business of public relations.''

There was a glint of irritation in the Prime Minister's eyes. "Spoken like a man who does not have to face questions in Parliament every week. You know I could order you to issue that statement.''

"You could indeed," the Assistant Commissioner responded calmly. "You could then accept my resignation.''

Unexpectedly, after a pause, the Prime Minister chuckled. "You can't fault me, Henry, for trying. The government has enough sticky wickets at the moment. Standing up to the bombardment of Parliament's questions is not the most pleasant part of this job; I'd just as soon head off any new ones.''

"I quite understand. Please do not feel I am unaware of the burdens you carry so well, Madame. I regret I am unable to help.''

"You help constantly by the excellent job you do," the Prime Minister answered seriously. "I am sure you will prevail.'' She hitched her straight chair closer to her desk. "There is one thing I should like to say to you.''

"And that is?''

The Iron Leader spoke quietly. "I should have thought the less of you, Henry, if you had accepted my suggestion.''

Sergeant Alan Clarke had been the first officer to arrive at the Yorkshire grove. Even before he had spotted Travers's crumpled figure, he knew who the victim was; the license plate of the Bentley was as familiar as his own.

A seven-year veteran of police work, Clarke was inured to viewing the aftermath of violent crime. He set about his business with meticulous efficiency, searching the car and the nearby area thoroughly, going through the victim's pockets to see if he had been robbed.

His eyes kept straying to the vase that was propped against the body. He had first noticed it with astonishment, wondering what it was doing there. It was unlike any vase he had ever seen—the delicate figures on its face seemed alien, and therefore forbidding. Try as he might, he could not think of any possible explanation for the vase's presence; yet he was certain that it must have great significance.

Clarke's feelings were reflected exactly in a conference room at New Scotland Yard. Four men were studying the vase intently: the Assistant Commissioner, Haynes, Professor Harte from the British Museum, and the chief of the Department of Psychiatry at London Hospital.

"The central figure is Achilles," Harte said. "The defeated warrior at his feet is Hector, the son of Priam, King of Troy. You'll note Achilles has his spear raised; he's about to administer the fatal thrust. Mercilessly, I might add. The vase is a copy, obviously an inexpensive copy, of the original in the Archaeological Museum in Athens. It's the sort of cheap copy you can pick up in almost any souvenir shop in Greece."

"Thank you very much, Professor," Haynes said. "We appreciate your coming by so promptly."

"Not at all." Harte absently rubbed his blond hair. "You know, Mr. Haynes," he said, grinning, "when you came to see me at the museum, I asked you why you were so interested in Achilles. As I recall, you said you weren't free to tell me then, but when you could I'd be the first to know. I take it the time is not just yet?"

"I'm afraid not," Haynes replied. "But my promise still stands."

"I'll hold you to it," the professor said, with a farewell flip of a hand.

The group resumed its contemplation of the vase. "You say there was nothing else at the crime scene," the psychiatrist said after a moment. "Just this vase."

"That's right," the Assistant Commissioner answered.

"And the two letters you spoke of were both signed Achilles?"

"Yes."

"Well, of course there's no question," the psychiatrist said, tapping the table for emphasis. "Whoever this man is, he has identified with Achilles. You say he has killed twice, and I'm sure in his mind he is acting exactly as he believes Achilles would have acted. The vase placed next to the body? I can't be one hundred percent sure, of course, but I venture that your man put it there as a sort of signature. He was rubbing your nose in it, so to speak. It was his way of gloating 'Look, I told you I would do this, and I've brought it off, haven't I?' "

"That's pretty much the way we see it," Adams commented, "but we wanted to get your slant. There's one other point we'd like your opinion on, too."

"Which is?"

"In both these murders, the assassin used a rifle. Admittedly they didn't take place in Piccadilly Circus, but even in remote areas the sound of a rifle shot carries a long way. Then why not use a knife? Or a piece of pipe or whatever? Why run the risk of firing a rifle?"

"I don't see anything odd about that at all," the psychiatrist replied. "Bear in mind that Achilles is a god. Now gods don't go skulking around, hiding in the shadows, waiting for their chance to use a knife. No, they act boldly, defiantly, confidently, on the grand scale."

"I see what you mean," the Assistant Commissioner said. "Well, it appears we have a god to contend with, and an angry god at that."

The psychiatrist was grim. "No doubt about it. That phrase you say he uses—'the faltering hand.' Do you have any idea of how much venom it packs? Clearly, there's an obsession with a handicap at work here, and in that type of case it's not at all unusual to blame someone else for your misfortune. The result is hate, the deepest, most gnawing kind of hate, fueled by a constant, burning rage."

Haynes cut in. "Is there anything further you might

tell us, Doctor, about this man's profile? Anything that might suggest an additional line of investigation, for example? We can use all the help we can get."

"I'm aware of that," the psychiatrist answered testily, "but I've given you all I can." He shot a baleful glance at the Assistant Commissioner. "After all, I haven't even been shown the two letters. You've given me a general idea of their contents, to be sure, but that's not the same as seeing them, is it? Under the circumstances, it's extremely difficult to be of much help."

"Doctor," Adams responded patiently, "I believe I made it clear that there is information in those letters that we cannot at the moment divulge to anyone who is not directly involved in the investigation. All I can do is ask for your understanding."

"Very well," the psychiatrist replied curtly. "If you are holding to that position, you cannot fault me for any future developments."

The report from Interpol reached the Assistant Commissioner in late afternoon. It was brought by the inspector designated as the Interpol contact, who handed it to him without comment.

Sir Henry read swiftly:

> We regret that extensive search of our files has not thus far established identification for the person you seek.
>
> The description furnished to us was general, lacking specific details, which made it impossible to pinpoint a particular individual.
>
> When you are able to develop further details, we suggest they be forwarded to us immediately.
>
> It should be noted, in the interim, that both the Rome and Brussels Police Departments have reports through informants of an individual, answering the general description, who is believed to be prominently engaged in terrorist activities.
>
> No name for this individual has as yet been sup-

plied. We have requested Rome and Brussels to make every effort to develop further information, with special emphasis on obtaining subject's name and/or aliases.

The Assistant Commissioner reacted to the report stoically. "Well, it's no more than we expected. We knew we weren't giving them much to go on."

"Yes, but you always hope," the inspector said. "What do you think of the last bit about terrorism?"

"Haynes raised that possibility," Adams replied thoughtfully. "I hope to God there's no basis to it. It's bad enough to deal with a single loony without taking on a whole organization of them. Backed by money, to boot."

The inspector looked at him sympathetically. "You've had a rough one today, haven't you, sir? I heard you were over at Ten Downing Street this morning."

"Part of the job," Adams answered laconically.

When the inspector left, the Assistant Commissioner tilted back his swivel chair and rubbed his forehead rhythmically. He had to get out of his mind the persistent thought that had been troubling him deeply: Somehow he should have been able to find the assassin—if he had done so Travers would have lived. It did no good to cull over the exhaustive, all-out effort he had directed; it had not succeeded.

After an agonizing quarter of an hour, he roused himself and phoned for a dinner tray. A long night stretched ahead of him.

The sounds of Big Ben were drifting across the city, sonorous deep-toned notes announcing the advent of midnight. Peter Wycoff looked around the unfamiliar computer section of the War Department. It was vast, seemingly endless, much larger than his own impressive section at Scotland Yard. "You've really got the equipment here," he remarked to the army major sitting next to him.

"Just as well, isn't it?" the major said. "That was quite a job you brought to us, wasn't it now?"

"A bitch," Wycoff agreed readily. "But it looks like you've got it well in hand. I'm very grateful to you."

"No need to be. To tell you the truth, I'm enjoying it. Bit of a challenge, you might say." The major eyed Wycoff appraisingly. "Ready to tell me what's on the fire?"

Wycoff laughed and took a sip from a mug of tea. "You just don't trust me, do you, Major? Actually, I've been telling you the truth—I don't know. The Assistant Commissioner simply called me in and told me in detail exactly what he wants. Why he wants it, what he's going to do with the information, is his business. I didn't ask, he didn't tell me."

"But you must have a pretty good idea."

"Possibly. Let's put it this way—suppose I asked you about the design of a hush-hush tank or something. If you knew, would you tell me?"

"I would not."

"I rest my case."

"Very well." The major pulled over a chair and propped up his feet. "I shall have to do my own theorizing. Let's see. I get a call from General Leonard, who I gather has been talking to your Assistant Commissioner. I'm to expect a visit from you, and I'm to extend every cooperation. In due course you arrive, and what do you want?"

"I know, I know," Wycoff replied.

The major ignored him, and went on blithely. "What you want is no small favor, chum. You hand me a list of specifications. You calmly say you want my computers to run through every damned man who is or has been in the services; you want the names of everybody who matches all or most of your specifications. Let's see— you give me these criteria." He began ticking off with his fingers. "Male, British, age under fifty, tall, probably slender, possibly dark hair, an officer or noncom since he led men, a crack shot, possibly a classical scholar in Greek mythology of all things, wounded in the fighting in Ireland, physically handicapped as a result, probably a crippled hand." He glanced over at Wycoff. "Have I forgotten anything?"

"Nothing. Now can we change the subject?"

The major wouldn't be put off. "You even have the bloody cheek to tell me how long the job will take. 'From what I would guess your equipment to be,' you say, 'I should think seventy-two hours would see to it.' " Crossing one foot over the other, he added musingly, "You were pretty much on the mark there at that. How come? Have you been dating one of the girls here? Digging into our secrets?"

Wycoff chuckled, fingering his trim beard. "How did you guess? The beard gets them every time."

"I daresay." The major shrugged. "Well, I suppose I could make an informed guess on what your section's capability might be. Computer buffs are like car collectors, I guess. You get to know what the other fellow has." He broke off as a subordinate brought him a long printout. "Have a look," he said, handing over the sheets. "It would seem we're narrowing down the search rather rapidly now."

Wycoff scanned the lists. "Right." He nodded with satisfaction. "We're smack on schedule."

Chapter 10

THE ASSASSIN STOOD in St. James's Park, staring along Birdcage Walk to the ornate stone facade of Buckingham Palace. There was a slight wind, churning the misty September air, increasing its bone-chilling factor.

Immobile, as absorbed as a field marshal surveying a battlefield, the assassin welcomed the wild thoughts that coursed through his brain. There before him was the bastion of royalty, massive, impregnable, arrogant. Somewhere, in those second-floor rooms to the right of the gates, walked Majesty, aloof and unfeeling.

His fingers slowly clenched as the rage swept over him. We shall see how secure you are, Majesty, he vowed to himself. It has come down to you and to me. You have seen fit to deny my just demand. More, you have caused your police to treat me as if I were a fool. Now we are at the time of reckoning. You have been warned, and you have not listened. Now we shall see who is the fool.

As the night deepened, he finally left his vigil and walked the deserted streets, striding along purposefully, caught up in a euphoric sense of power. There was nothing beyond his capability—nothing. He reveled in recalling that he had warned the police he would kill again, and they had been powerless against him. All their resources, all their vaunted prowess, had availed nothing.

He came at last to his home and set about the task he had been savoring all evening. With a drink at his hand, he began to compose a new letter, debating each word, weighing each exact shade of meaning. He worked steadily, with total concentration, swept up in an exultation that his words were pronouncing a sentence of death. When he had finished, he reread the letter again and again, picturing vividly the fear and anguish its receipt would cause.

There remained the step of putting the letter into its final form. Opening a drawer in a bureau, the assassin pulled on a pair of light cotton gloves and lifted out the back newspapers he had been saving. Referring to the draft of the letter propped up next to him, he hunted through the newspapers to find each word. Whenever a word was located, he cut it out carefully and placed it on the table. When all the words were assembled, he meticulously pasted them on a blank sheet of paper, spelling out his message.

The night was almost over when he had finished doing this and addressing the envelope in the same manner. Suddenly he was tired, with a weariness that seemed to drain energy away, leaving him inert and spent.

He gave himself a moment to recover, then got up and took the letter to a mailbox well away from his neighborhood. Exhausted, he returned slowly and made his way to his bedroom. Still fully clothed, he threw himself across the bed and was instantly asleep.

"I think it's time we had a talk," Jill Blake said, speaking quickly while her courage held.

Haynes was knotting his tie. Hand poised, he turned from the mirror to face her. "I suppose you're right," he agreed quietly.

She led the way into their airy living room and seated herself on the divan. Motioning him to a place next to her, she began resolutely, "Did I ever tell you I got engaged in my senior year at Vassar?"

"No," Haynes answered.

"Well, I did. He was a boy from Dartmouth. A big, handsome guy with a Back Bay family as nice as it was illustrious. All my friends thought I was the luckiest girl in the school."

"What happened?"

"I gave him back his ring." Her blue eyes were fixed unwaveringly on the opposite wall. "The day after graduation. He was pressing me into moving up the marriage date, and right in the middle of all his arguments about why we should—they were pretty good arguments, too—I just took off the ring and handed it to him. Want to know why?"

"Why?"

She turned to him, her face taut. "I asked myself the same question at the time. He was really nice, and he loved me so much, and there I was, pulling off the ring. But I couldn't stop—it didn't make sense, but I couldn't stop until I had handed him the ring. It wasn't until the next day that I knew the reason: I just didn't love him. It was as simple as that."

Haynes spoke gently. "Why are you telling me this, Jill?"

She glanced around the room absently. "My ferns aren't doing so well, are they? Maybe I should try some plant food." She smoothed her skirt with an agitated motion. "You want to know why I'm telling you?"

Haynes took her hand and clasped it in his. "Jill, Jill, you're babbling. What's wrong?"

She shook her head miserably and pulled away. "I'm not doing this very well, am I? And I wanted to. But no matter—it's important to me that you know exactly how I feel."

"Don't talk about it now, Jill. Wait until you calm down."

"No, let me go on. I never told you I was engaged because I didn't want to hurt you. I didn't want you to know that I had ever been that deeply involved with anyone. I wanted everything between us to be new and fresh. Does that make sense?"

"Yes, I suppose it does."

"Well, it sure made sense to me. Because I was so much in love with you, and I thought you were in love with me. Which brings us to your question—why I'm telling you now." Haynes waited quietly. "To tell you the truth," she went on, "I'm not really sure I know. Maybe it's because I'm hurt and I want to hurt you too. If that's the reason, it's mean and petty, and I shouldn't feel very proud of myself, should I? But you've got to understand, Tom. I love you so much." She paused, trying hard to keep the tears back. "I never thought I could feel so damned miserable."

"All right, out with it," Haynes urged softly.

She waited an instant, getting control of herself. "Who is she, Tom?"

"Hope Marston," he replied slowly. "I met her when I first went up to Scotland."

"You've been seeing a lot of her, haven't you? Those times when you said you wouldn't be home—you were with her, weren't you?"

"Yes."

She was sitting rigidly, her hands at her sides. "What is she like, Tom?"

"Jill, there's no reason why you should be torturing yourself like this."

"I'd like to know, Tom. Please."

"All right, if you must. She's quite beautiful; I'm not going to lie to you. Actually, her name is Lady Hope Marston. She's divorced. She lives in the country, not too far from Glasgow."

"Lady Hope Marston," Jill repeated bitterly. "That's a lot more impressive than a secretary in the American embassy, isn't it, Tom?"

"That's not fair, and you know it."

"Do I? All right, so it isn't fair. How is it, by the way, that your lady is in London? Did she follow you here? Did she decide she just couldn't exist without seeing you?'' She stood up nervously. "I can't blame her, I suppose. I know the feeling.''

"This isn't getting us anywhere, Jill.''

"Isn't it?'' She whirled about angrily. "I think it is. It's bringing us right up to the big question: Do you love her?''

Haynes answered reluctantly. "I wish you hadn't asked that, Jill. I knew you would, and I know, too, that you deserve an answer. But the truth is I just am not sure. My thinking is all mixed up. That's all I can tell you.''

"I see. Well, at least you're honest. And what am I supposed to do, just sit around until you make up your mind? Eeny, meeny, miney, mo. Do I choose Hope or Jill? Or better still, how about I love Jill, I love her not, I love Jill, I love her not. When you find the answer you can let me know. How does that strike you?'' She faced him coldly. "Well? Aren't you going to say anything?''

Haynes shook his head. "There isn't much I can say, is there? Except that I'm sorry, dreadfully sorry. You've got every right to feel hurt.''

"You're sorry?'' she exploded. "I've got a right to feel hurt? Do you have any idea of just how hurt I am? I can't sleep, I'm driving myself nuts with all kinds of images of you and her making love; I can never put it out of my mind. Never, not for one damned second! Do you have any idea how much agony there is in living like that? And you say you're sorry?'' Abruptly, she broke off and struggled to compose herself. "All right, Tom,'' she continued dully, "you're right. This was not the time to talk about it. Maybe I should never have brought it up at all. You don't owe me anything. You never made me any promises. When we started living together, neither of us said anything about the future. But can I tell you something?''

"Of course.''

"I hoped, Tom—oh how I hoped. Every week, every day I hoped you would ask me to marry you. I used to make up reasons why you hadn't. Like maybe it was because your work took you away a lot. Or maybe you just needed a little time to adjust to the idea. Pretty stupid of me, wasn't it? I never was able to admit to myself the real reason—you just didn't want to.''

"Jill, please, can we drop it for now? I hate to see you like this.''

"Fine," she agreed miserably. "Only before we do, there's one thing we should settle. Where does this leave us? Do you want me to leave? Or are you planning on walking out? Or what?''

"We'll do nothing," he said firmly. "Neither one of us is in any shape to make any rational decisions right now; we're too emotionally charged up. Let's just try and put everything on hold for a while.''

"I see. And meanwhile, I suppose, you'll be spending every night with her. Don't you think I have any pride?''

"She left for Scotland yesterday afternoon.''

"Very well, then," she answered wearily. "We'll play it your way. We put everything on hold—just the way you want it.''

The Assistant Commissioner stared at the letter on his desk as if it were an asp. He could not take his eyes from it. It lay there, an evil thing, filled with poison.

"How did it come?" Haynes asked. "This morning's post?''

"Exactly. Like the other two letters: London postmark, words clipped from a newspaper. Listen—" Adams's face was drawn, his jaw firmly set, as he began to read.

YOUR MAJESTY—

I OFFERED YOU LIFE IN RETURN FOR £100,000, A GRAIN IN YOUR MOUNTAIN OF TREASURE.

EVEN THOUGH I MUST TO MY LAST MOMENT SUFFER THE ANGUISH OF THE FALTERING HAND, YET I WAS DISPOSED TO BE MERCIFUL, TO GIVE YOU THE OPPORTUNITY TO FULFILL YOUR MORAL DUTY.

BUT IN YOUR GREED AND ARROGANCE, YOU DID NOT. MORE, YOU PLOTTED MY RUIN WITH YOUR ACCURSED POLICE.

I SOLEMNLY SAY TO YOU, YOU HAVE CHOSEN DEATH. WHEN PATROCLUS FELL, MY RAGE WAS UNTAMED, ONLY TO BE SATISFIED WITH BLOOD. IT IS THAT SAME RAGE THAT YOUR PERFIDY CALLS FORTH IN ME NOW.

CHARLES I DIED BECAUSE HE MOCKED HIS SUBJECTS, AND DEEMED THEM BASE. YOU WILL DIE FOR THE SAME REASONS, AND IN THE SAME WAY. THERE IS NO MERCY LEFT IN ME. ALL OF YOUR POWER, ALL OF YOUR POLICE, CANNOT SAVE YOU NOW.

WITHIN TEN DAYS, YOUR DEATH WILL BE AT HAND.

MAKE YOUR PEACE WITH GOD.

ACHILLES

Adams pushed the letter away and slowly swung sideways in his swivel chair. "Did you ever hear any tapes with messages from the Royal family?" he began musingly. "Once in a while you hear them played on radio stations. Christmas greetings, messages to Parliament, that sort of thing."

"Not that I recall," Haynes replied.

"No, as an American, I don't suppose you did. The radio stations usually play them on nostalgia shows. 'Do you remember this year?' 'What were you doing when you heard this?'—that type of program."

"I see."

"It's funny, but I'm thinking of one of those tapes now. The Queen was a little girl, maybe eight or nine, and her mother and father—then the King and Queen— broadcast a Christmas greeting. After they had finished, the King announced that his daughter wanted to add her Christmas greeting. This tiny little voice came over the wire, speaking so earnestly, being so careful to pronounce each word clearly and correctly." The Assistant

Commissioner smiled wryly. "Does it seem to you odd that I'm remembering that now?"

"No, it doesn't."

"There are other things I remember, too. A photograph of her in the newspaper, reviewing the Horse Guards—she's their colonel, you know. She had just come to the throne, right after she had turned twenty-one. She was sitting her horse, sidesaddle of course, primly and with obvious concentration on doing the job right. She's been that kind of queen, you know—do the job right. Do you understand what I mean?"

"I think so."

"No, I don't believe you do. Don't misunderstand me. I mean that you've got to be one of her subjects to know what the Crown means to us. There's a love and a reverence quite unlike any other emotion." He brought his fist down on the desk hard. "That's why this letter tears at my entrails. I feel anger, yes, and frustration. God, what frustration. But above all, fear: deep-down, clammy, ugly fear. And that is the one feeling I cannot permit." He swung his chair forward sharply. "So much for personal reactions. Please forgive me."

"For what? Because you're not a machine?"

Adams tapped the letter. "That phrase he uses—'When Patroclus fell, my rage was untamed.' Does that mean anything to you?"

"No, I'm afraid not."

"It didn't to me either. So I called your Professor Harte over at the museum. He tells me Patroclus was Achilles' best friend; he was killed in the fight for Troy by the Trojan prince Hector. Achilles went mad and hunted him down and killed him. You'll recall that was the scene on the vase found next to Lord Travers's body—Achilles with the upraised spear, Hector at his feet."

Haynes nodded. "I remember. I also remember that the psychiatrist who met with us—Dr. Morton, wasn't it?—said that our killer merges his identity with Achilles. Do you suppose he had a friend killed, someone he now identifies with Patroclus? Maybe in the fighting in Ireland?''

"Possible, I would think.''

"One thing else in the letter particularly interests me. He talks about the Queen dying for the same reasons as Charles I, and in the same way. If I recall correctly, Charles I was deposed by Cromwell.''

"Right. He was pretty high-handed with Parliament—arbitrary and pigheaded would be better words, actually. They rose against him, and eventually it cost him his life.''

"Just exactly how did he die?''

"How? He was beheaded. In the Tower.''

Haynes rubbed his chin reflectively. "Achilles never misses a chance to mention 'the faltering hand,' does he?''

"No, he doesn't.'' The Assistant Commissioner looked at his watch. "Look, Haynes, I asked you to come here because I expect our computer report in about five minutes. Our computer chief phoned me from the War Department to say he'd be here with it about nine.''

"Did he give you any idea of what it shows?''

"Just that he'll have what we asked for. I didn't want to hold him up by getting into details.'' Adams gestured toward the letter. "Now that we have this, I pray more than ever that the report turns up something.''

"It should.''

"We'll know soon. I've been spending the night organizing our follow-through on the list the computer turns up. We've pulled a lot of our people off other assignments; they're ready and waiting. I want every name on the list checked thoroughly, and as fast as humanly possible.''

A buzzer sounded and the Assistant Commissioner picked up his phone. "Very well,'' he said, placing the phone back in its cradle. His tension was apparent as he turned to Haynes. "He's here. Now for the moment of truth.''

Peter Wycoff entered the room briskly. Only the lines of fatigue around his eyes testified to the sleep he had missed during the past seventy-two hours. "Good morning, sir," he said, unsnapping his briefcase and drawing forth some papers. "Just as you ordered." He referred to the top sheet and read aloud quickly. "The names of every British male, age under fifty, who physically is tall, probably slender, possibly dark hair, who served in the armed forces as an officer or noncom, is a crack shot, possibly a classical scholar in Greek mythology, wounded in the Irish fighting, physically handicapped as a result, probably a crippled hand."

"You believe you've dug out all the possible candidates?"

"Yes, sir, I do." Wycoff extended his list. "Only two of the criteria gave us any trouble. Any special skills are noted on a service record, of course. But it's possible a man could be a classical scholar and not have volunteered that information. Also, the exact nature of a wound—a hand wound, for example—is not always detailed. What we did, then, was to include a man if he met all other criteria, even in the absence of information about classical scholarship or a crippled hand."

The Assistant Commissioner was holding the list with great care, as if it were a precious object. "I understand. How many names are there?"

"Fifty-six, sir."

"I see," Adams answered quietly. "Fifty-six. A longer list than I hoped for, but shorter than I dreaded." He studied the list grimly. "May God grant that one of these men be Achilles."

In his university days, Haynes had made the acquaintance of a janitor who cleaned the dormitory where he lived. The janitor fancied himself an amateur philosopher, spending much time dispensing wisdom as he saw it, oftentimes neglecting his duties as a result. To the students, of course, he was a garrulous old fool. Yet one thing he had said had remained in Haynes's thoughts over the years: "People, like horses, run true to form. All you have to do is establish the form."

Time and again, the basic common sense of that belief had brought itself home to Haynes. Two of his friends had divorced their wives because they were cheats, and had promptly married women who did the same thing. Another of his classmates had lost much of his inheritance in a worthless franchise, and then lost the rest of it in two equally foolish investments. Still another had gone to prison for embezzlement, won a parole, and promptly reembezzled.

Now the amateur philosopher's maxim kept intruding itself into Haynes's consciousness. He recognized that the man they sought had run true to form in one vital respect: He had always done exactly as he had said he would do. In his first letter, he had specified that by the time it was received, he would have killed; Lady Lawton had died. In his second letter, he had threatened to kill again if his demands were not met; he had done exactly that. Was there any reason to believe he would not attempt to fulfill precisely the promises in his third letter?

Haynes was remembering that one of those promises had been the Queen would die in the same way as Charles I. That had been by the headsman's ax. Was it too wild, he asked himself, to wonder if the assassin had determined to kill the Queen with an ax? In Achilles' sick mind, would it not be logical? Had he not accused the Queen of Charles's "crime"—mocking his subjects? Then wouldn't it seem justice to punish the same crime with the same instrument of death?

Haynes could not reason away the insistent questions. Instead, they became even more demanding, more aggressive. Suppose the assassin was not only planning to use an ax, his imagination demanded—but the very ax that had been used on Charles? Do you know it doesn't exist still in a corner of some museum? Or in one of the hundreds of collections of antiquities throughout England?

He succeeded in rejecting that thought as too improbable, but another was waiting to take its place. All right, then, it said, granted that the actual ax doesn't exist, could you deny that similar axes do exist in ceremonial England? How about the Beefeaters or the Yeomen of the Guard—wouldn't they have them in their arsenals? Couldn't a determined god, an Achilles, somehow acquire a headsman's ax to take his revenge?

In the end, tired of the struggle, Haynes surrendered to his imagination. He inquired where he might find an expert in the types and probable storage places of ancient weapons and was directed to a Lieutenant Stevens of the Yeomen of the Guard.

He caught up with him in a cluttered office of the Guard's headquarters. Haynes explained the reason for his visit, and was subjected to a long, curious stare.

"You're serious, Mr. Haynes?" the lieutenant asked. "Yes, I suppose you are. You want to know where an ax such as the one that dispatched Charles I might be found. I hope you'll forgive my asking, but are you a writer or a historian? Something like that?"

"A writer," Haynes said evenly. "And an amateur history buff. Right now I'm working on a piece about hand weapons, modern and ancient."

"I see." The lieutenant completed posting entries into a ledger and shoved it aside. "How did you get hold of my name?"

"I asked around for the name of an expert on ancient weaponry."

"Indeed? Who recommended me?"

"Charles Harrison over at New Scotland Yard. He's in their laboratory. I gather they've called on you quite recently for a professional opinion."

The lieutenant thought for an instant. "Harrison. Oh, yes. Chap in his late fifties? Rather dedicated to his work?"

"That's the one."

"I'm flattered. He's a stickler. Well, where shall we begin?"

Haynes smiled apologetically. "If you don't mind a foolish question for openers, does the ax used on Charles I still exist? That very ax?"

The lieutenant stared in surprise, and then laughed heartily. "That would be a bit too much to ask, wouldn't it? No, I'm afraid the best we can do is to show you what one would look like." He allowed himself a dry joke. "The style in headsmen's axes hasn't changed much in three hundred years."

"I daresay. I told you a moment ago I'm a history buff. Do you think it might be possible for me to acquire an ax like that for my collection?"

"Not really," the lieutenant responded. "There are quite a few around, of course, but they're locked up in the vaults of organizations like ours, for example. And they're not for sale, if that's what you mean."

"That's disappointing. Just as a hypothetical question," Haynes added, "how difficult would it be to steal one?"

"It's a good thing you're not serious. You'd have a bit of a time doing it."

"Security is pretty tight, then?"

"Quite." The lieutenant propped his long legs up on the battered desk and settled into a more comfortable position. "Tell you what. If I were you, I'd try one of those costume places that specialize in supplying props for plays. You'd be sure to find what you want there."

"Yes, I'm sure you're right," Haynes agreed, suddenly realizing that he had overlooked the obvious. The lieutenant was right—a costume supply house in any city could provide a headsman's ax. So much for my bright idea, he mocked himself. There simply wasn't any point in trying to learn specifically where the assassin could obtain a weapon that could be freely bought almost anywhere.

"Lieutenant Stevens," he said, putting as good a face on the matter as possible, "thanks very much for your help. I won't need to take up any more of your time."

"No need to worry about that," the lieutenant answered cordially. "This isn't exactly the most demanding job in the world."

"As a matter of fact, I don't have much of an idea what the Yeomen of the Guard do."

"Not much, if the truth be told. It's a part-time assignment, really. We show up to guard the Queen's person at various ceremonies." The lieutenant chuckled. "Oh, and once a year, on the day Parliament opens, we check to make sure no one has hidden any gunpowder there. After all, there might be another Guy Fawkes around."

"How many yeomen are there?"

"About eighty. There's a captain, three other officers, and the rest enlisted."

Haynes decided he had shown enough polite interest and decided to leave. The lieutenant stood up promptly. "I'll walk out with you," he said. "I'm about through here, and besides it's too nice a day to spend indoors. I think I'll go on over to the river and do a bit of sculling. Won't have much more chance before it gets too cold."

"I imagine you're rather good at it," Haynes answered, eyeing the lieutenant's long, lean frame.

The lieutenant grimaced. "Frankly, I'm afraid I'm spending too much time at it these days. It's getting to be a bloody career." He shook hands warmly. "Well, I'll leave you then. Good luck with the article."

The debate was intense, at times verging on the acrid. A senior inspector spoke strongly for one segment of the group. "Assistant Commissioner," he said solemnly, "we do not believe there is any choice. You must pay this man the £100,000 he demands. He has killed twice. Now he threatens that the Queen will die within ten days. No man in this room, including you, sir, has the right to play fast and loose with the Sovereign's life. We must accede to his demands."

Sir Henry Adams sat at the head of the table, his massive shoulders hunched forward, his expression impassive. "You are aware that at this moment we have a massive effort underway, checking through the names we received from computer section?"

The inspector stood his ground. "I am aware of that, sir. I am also aware that there are fifty-six names on that list. It will take time to run them all down. Can you guarantee that will be completed by the end of today? Or tomorrow? Can you even guarantee the killer is on that list?"

"No, I cannot."

"Then I respectfully ask you to bear in mind, sir, that we do not even know how much time we have. The killer did not say he will act at the end of ten days—he said *within* ten days. That could be this very minute, or the next hour, or in three days. We simply do not know. I say we must defuse the threat now. Pay the money."

"Just how do you propose to do that?" the Assistant Commissioner countered. "Granting all you say, have you forgotten the man doesn't trust us? What makes you think he will ever believe us again?"

"Very well," the inspector shot back. "I recognize what you're saying, of course. What I meant was that we should attempt to pay the money. Run a large ad in the personals. Address it to Achilles. Say that this time there will be no tricks. Plead with him—yes, plead. I see nothing wrong with that when the safety of the Crown is at stake."

A gray-haired official reacted angrily. "But I do. If we've gotten to the point where we have to grovel to murderers, then this country has reached bottom. We've never given in to coercion. We never should. What you're proposing is shameful and degrading."

The meeting grew steadily more volatile. After almost an hour, the Assistant Commissioner called for order. "All right, we've heard from everybody, and I believe we've reached a compromise. The one position all of us support is that, through the Prime Minister, we should acquaint Her Majesty with the threat against her person. If she wishes us to pay Achilles' demand, we shall do so." He glanced around the table. "That is agreed, is it not?" There was a general murmur of approval, and Adams went on. "I have no doubt whatsoever what the Queen's answer will be. But at least, since she is the one at hazard, the decision should be hers. We are also agreed that we will ask the Queen, through the Prime

Minister, to avoid any public appearances whatsoever
until we have found and apprehended Achilles. Does
anyone have anything further to add?''

There was an expectant wait but no one spoke. The
Assistant Commissioner pushed his chair back and got
to his feet. "Adjourned," he said crisply.

Chapter 11

INTEROL'S FINAL REPORT was conclusive:

> Please refer to our earlier communication.
>
> As noted therein, the Rome and Brussels Police Departments had received reports through informants of an unidentified individual, believed to be engaged in terrorist activities, who answered the general description of your subject.
>
> We regret that intensive efforts by Rome and Brussels have failed to develop either the individual's name and/or aliases. In addition, both departments caution that informants from whom original information was obtained have in certain instances proved unreliable.
>
> In our judgment, there are no further steps we can take to effect identification of your subject in the absence of additional specific information from you.
>
> We are therefore placing the file in suspended status.

Haynes finished reading the report and tossed it on the table. "That pretty much takes care of the international angle, I should say. If there had been anything to it, it seems to me Interpol would have turned up something."

The inspector handling the Interpol contact agreed. "Well, it was worth a try," he added. "Nothing risked, nothing gained."

"There's still one thing that bothers me," Haynes said.

"What's that?"

"We still don't know what he was doing in Athens, do we?"

One hundred and twelve men had been assigned to work on the list of fifty-six names produced by the computer search. They had been organized into two-man teams, with each team responsible for one name. Their instructions had been simple: Find the man who is your responsibility, interview him thoroughly, and satisfy yourselves beyond any doubt that he is not Achilles. If there is even the slightest uncertainty, bring him to Scotland Yard for further investigation.

The overall minute-by-minute direction of the teams had been delegated to Inspector Thomas Granby. A dour Cornishman, his reputation had been built on methodical, relentless digging to uncover every last detail. His first action was to secure from the War Department the service records, including photographs, of all fifty-six possibilities. Before parceling them out to his teams, he had copies made for his own use. Then he sat down and painstakingly read each record; employing his astonishing capacity for absorbing detail, he speedily acquired an overview of the entire list.

With his teams already at work on their preliminary investigations, Granby ran the fifty-six names through the Criminal Records Division. If any of the candidates had been in trouble outside their army life, he was vitally interested in knowing what kind of trouble, and why.

Not at all to his surprise, given his view of people, he

learned that seven of the fifty-six had been found guilty of violations. All were no longer in the services, and all had committed their offenses since leaving it. One had been involved in a hit-and-run case, two in alimony problems, and three in drunken disputes.

It was the one remaining case that commanded his attention. Captain Robert Anderson had been convicted twice, both times of extortion. Writing letters to obtain money seemed to Granby a training ground for the biggest extortion target of all, and he promptly called the team he had assigned to locate the ex-officer. "This one looks more likely than the others," he commented. "Just where do you stand?"

The sergeant who was the senior member of the team answered smartly. "He's known at none of the addresses listed in his file, sir. His prison release on his second offense was six months ago, and he seems to have gone right off the earth since then. No visits to his friends, no calls to his family. Nothing."

Granby was alarmed. "I don't like that. What are you doing, then?"

"I've sent Jenkins over to the prison, sir. It occurred to me Anderson might have told some of the inmates where he'd be going. Meanwhile, I'm asking around his old neighborhoods to see what we might turn up."

"Keep me posted," Granby snapped. "The sooner we find him, the better I'll feel."

The sergeant spent an unproductive day, showing Anderson's photograph to housewives, store owners, and the neighborhood bobbies. None showed the slightest sign of recognition, although two commented that the fleshy face, largely hidden by a heavy beard, could be almost anyone.

It was late in the afternoon when the sergeant saw Jenkins pulling in to the curb. From his grin, it was obvious that he had good news. "I think I've got something," he announced. "It was a good idea, that, sending me off to talk with his chums in the prison. Wait until you hear what they had to say."

The sergeant listened with mounting astonishment.

"Are you sure?" he demanded when Jenkins had finished. "They weren't putting you on, were they?"

"No, I'm sure of it."

"All right, then, let's go." Hastily the sergeant opened the door of the car and got in. "Take Gower Street—the traffic won't be so bad there."

Jenkins drove expertly, threading through the jumble of cars with a sure instinct. In a remarkably short time, he had managed to get deep into London's East End. Turning into a side street, he slowed down, passing through a district of dilapidated homes, boarded-up stores, and curbs cluttered with refuse. "Ahead there, Sergeant," he said, "that must be it."

A moment later he found a parking space. The sergeant led the way as they approached a rickety structure that had obviously once served as a restaurant. A faded sign proclaiming FISH AND CHIPS hung loosely at one corner, and through the open door part of a counter was still visible.

They joined a small knot of people who were making their way inside. Most were dressed in haphazard odds and ends, and some exuded a sour whiskey odor. The interior of the building was stark. A rough coat of whitewash had been applied to cover some of the dirt; benches had been set out to provide seating space; and an attempt had been made to remove the grime from the windows.

A cross fashioned of metal had been placed on a counter to convert it into an altar, and in back of it stood a muscular, clean-shaven young man. His hand holding a Bible swung idly as he waited for the crowd to be seated. Satisfied, he bowed his head and intoned loudly: "Praise be to God! Praise be to Jesus! Praise be to the Holy Spirit!"

The sergeant instantly recognized the former Captain Robert Anderson, minus his beard, and settled down with interest to listen to the sermon. At the outset he was skeptical, but as the preacher thundered home his warnings, eyes burning with zeal, he became convinced of his sincerity.

With a final, urgent plea for righteousness, the preacher wound up his sermon and walked among his tiny congregation, greeting each member individually. When he came to the sergeant and Jenkins, he extended his hand with a slight smile. "Welcome to my humble church, gentlemen. You're the first law officers I've had here."

"How did you know we're officers?" the sergeant asked. "Does it show that much?"

"It does to those with my background," Anderson replied dryly. "Uniform or not, it makes no difference. I rather think your visit must be official, gentlemen—am I right?"

"You are."

"Very well." Anderson brought them to an area of the building that had been converted into a semblance of an office. He tilted his head gravely as the sergeant asked him to detail his activities since leaving prison.

"Of course," he agreed without rancor. "You know, gentlemen, for perhaps the first time in my life I have nothing to conceal. When I was in prison this last time, the good Jesus saw fit in His wisdom to make me a born-again Christian. I glory in it, and in telling His story."

The sergeant filled most of a notebook before he ended the interview. "All right, Mr. Anderson," he remarked cordially, slipping the notebook into his breast pocket, "we'll check everything you've told us, of course. If it holds up, we'll not be needing to talk with you further."

On the ride back to the Yard late that night, the sergeant chuckled. "Granby won't be pleased," he confided to Jenkins. "He had that poor bugger tagged as a real possibility. But to tell you the truth, I'm glad; it isn't often you see them get themselves on track like that."

All over the United Kingdom, the teams were busy, fanning out through the cities, through the countryside, and even in two instances to the offshore islands. Urged on by a sense of overpowering urgency, they worked steadily, interviewing, checking, sifting through information. They worked almost without respite, skipping meals or bolting a sandwich, going sleepless, fighting off fatigue.

Yet their progress, in view of the urgency, was slow. Few of the teams were lucky enough to find their man as quickly as Captain Anderson had been located. Six of the men on the list had emigrated, and tracing them proved difficult; others had simply dispersed without known addresses into the cities and towns. Only a handful was brought to Scotland Yard for additional questioning, and none proved to be even a remote possibility for Achillles.

The Assistant Commissioner, huddled with Inspector Granby, became progressively more alarmed. After two days of crash effort, only eighteen of the fifty-six had been eliminated. Two days had passed, and it was sickeningly apparent that many more would be needed to complete the job.

It had become a horrifying game of Russian roulette. If indeed the man who was Achilles was on the list, there was a chance that he would be among the first to be found of the remaining thirty-eight as yet unlocated. There was an equal chance that he would be among the last.

The minutes and the hours were drifting away. All that could be done was being done. The initiative, beyond any doubt, now lay only with the assassin.

The petite woman came forward with a welcoming smile. "Good morning, Madame Prime Minister," she said in a tiny, girlish voice.

"Ma'am." The Prime Minister made an abbreviated curtsey. "I believe you have met Sir Henry Adams."

"I have had that pleasure," the Queen answered warmly. "How are you, Sir Henry?"

"Quite fine, ma'am," the Assistant Commissioner

replied. As always, it was difficult for him to realize that this gracious, feminine person bore the weighty title of Queen of the United Kingdom of Great Britain and Northern Ireland.

The Queen led the way to a corner of the audience chamber. Seating herself on a divan covered with richly embroidered tapestry, she motioned her visitors to nearby chairs. "If I were given to guessing," she said, "I would think that this must be a serious matter. The Prime Minister and a high-ranking official of New Scotland Yard forming a delegation—that is most unusual."

"It is a serious matter," the Prime Minister replied. "Suppose you give us a briefing, Sir Henry."

The Assistant Commissioner, speaking in a flat, unemotional tone, explained all that had happened since the receipt of the first letter.

The Queen listened attentively, her face composed. "I see," she said quietly. "Do you have at this point any idea of what his quarrel with the Crown is?"

"We believe it has to do with a wound he received during the fighting in Ireland, ma'am."

"Then his resentment is not too illogical, is it?" the Queen commented. "After all, he was fighting for the Crown."

"In that sense I suppose you are right, ma'am."

The Queen looked from one to the other inquiringly. "Just what is it you wish me to do?"

The Prime Minister undertook to answer. "First, ma'am, we would like to know whether you wish us to pay Achilles' demand. There are many who believe that should be done."

"No! Not one cent is to be paid, with or without my knowledge. Not one cent."

"Very good, ma'am," the Prime Minister said. "Then we must ask you to forgo public appearances of any kind until Achilles is found."

"But that is quite out of the question," the Queen protested. "There are events that have been long planned and cannot be changed easily. Moreover, there is a vital central point: Would you have your Sovereign cower in the face of threats?"

"No, ma'am, I would not. But I would have my Sovereign exercise proper precautions in a dangerous situation."

"Proper precautions," the Queen repeated. "That is a nice-sounding phrase, but just how shall it be defined? Is it proper procedure to change our schedules because a poor sick mind plans us harm? I do not think so. Is it not a far better concept to believe that proper procedure lies in discharging one's duties properly?"

"With respect, ma'am, I do not." The Prime Minister's features tightened. "As the leader of Your Majesty's government, responsible for its well-being in all respects, I must therefore insist that you do as we suggest and temporarily eliminate all public appearances."

Suddenly there was amusement in the Queen's eyes. "You know," she said slowly, "from time to time I have noticed the phrase 'the Iron Leader' used in the London dailies. If I had been under any doubt as to who was meant, I have no such problem now." She turned to Adams. "You have been quite silent during this exchange, Assistant Commissioner."

"Ma'am, the Prime Minister's views are also my own."

"Fiddlesticks," the Queen answered bluntly. "Very well, your consciences can be clear: You have done your utmost to convince me. And I thank you, for I sense that your concern springs as much from affection as it does from concern for the Crown. But you did not really expect me to agree, did you?"

The Prime Minister sighed. "No, ma'am, we did not. But I now ask you if at the very least you will permit us to increase your security. We have discussed that as the next best alternative."

"Just how do you propose to do that?"

"Through the use of more security personnel."

"We would see no objection to that, provided it does not reach a point where it is obvious and therefore indicates fear on our part."

"It will be done as you wish, ma'am," the Prime

Minister agreed. "We appreciate your receiving us."

As the Prime Minister's limousine pulled away from Buckingham Palace, the Assistant Commissioner spoke reflectively. "Did you get the feeling, in there, that we might just as well have been meeting with Queen Victoria? The same determination, even if under a more friendly exterior."

"I know exactly what you mean," the Prime Minister replied. "And they call me the Iron Leader. I could take lessons from that lady."

Hope Marston was worried. She walked back and forth in her spacious library, waiting for her call to London to come through. Occasionally she nervously pushed back her black hair or adjusted her dressing gown. When the phone finally jangled, she was there in three quick steps and snatched up the receiver. "Tom?"

"The very same." His voice, in the imperfect connection, sounded unfamiliar and faint.

"Can you hear me?"

"Just barely. Wait a minute. Let me signal the operator and see if she can clear this up." There was a pause and she could hear him talking to the operator. Suddenly the volume seemed to be tripled and he boomed in her ear. "Better?"

"Too much so," she laughed. "Tom, it's so good to hear your voice. I called yesterday and left a message asking you to ring me back. Didn't you get it?"

"Yes. I got it."

"Oh?" She was suddenly fearful. "Then why didn't you call back? Didn't you want to?"

"What makes you say a thing like that?" he demanded.

"Well, I might as well tell you. When we talked—let's see, last Monday—I asked you to come up here for the weekend and you said you couldn't. Then we talked a couple of times after that, and you seemed preoccupied, almost as if you were a million miles away."

"No, not a million," he said seriously. "Just four

hundred or whatever it is from here to there. Hope, I want to see you so much. It seems to me you're on my mind constantly."

"Then why didn't you come for the weekend?"

"All right," he responded, "I'll tell you exactly why. First of all, I'm working on a project at the moment that I simply cannot leave. But even if that weren't so, I've been doing some deep personal thinking. I want to be absolutely right in my conclusions. It means not only my own happiness, but the happiness of other people too."

"Jill and me."

"If you will."

There was a suggestion of pleading in her answer. "You've got to make the decision, and you should be sure. But you can't blame me for praying."

"Hope," he said softly. "I just told you how I miss you. You're so very, very lovely."

"Thank you, darling, I'll hug that. And please don't make it too long—I love you." She hung up the receiver slowly.

The assassin stood naked, head thrown back, arms stretched high. A table before him had been covered with a sheet to serve as a makeshift altar.

"O Zeus," he intoned, "there stands before you Achilles, the son of Thetis, nymph of the sea. Even as you rule on Mount Olympus, surrounded by the gods, serene in your wisdom and justice, there is in this accursed city a false ruler—a woman of infinite avarice and treachery. She sends men to fight and die for her, and cares not. Patroclus, my beloved friend, fell in her evil service; I have suffered the faltering hand. O Zeus, I swear to you, in the presence of Aphrodite, goddess of love, that I shall strike her down without mercy. Vengeance—in thy name, Zeus, vengeance." He brought his right fist down on the altar with a mighty blow.

The young woman lying on the bed watched with a mixture of fear and fascination. She lay propped against the pillows, her clothes thrown carelessly on the floor next to her. A tendril of smoke curled from the marijuana cigarette she was loosely holding. "Look here, mate," she called now, "why don't you give over that crazy talk and come lie next to me?" She patted the bed invitingly, extending the cigarette.

The assassin did not answer. His shoulders were slumped, his head bowed. She studied him warily, with the skill that comes from experience. This was an odd one, she knew, but there was no denying that she had seventy-five pounds tucked in the pocket of her dress. In the beginning he had seemed normal enough, even pleasant. But the marijuana had set him off: dragging the table about, ripping the sheet off the bed to cover it, and now yelling this wild stuff. She eyed him carefully, continuing her mental inventory, and finally decided that he was harmless.

"Come on, love," she coaxed. "You haven't even begun to get what you've paid for." The assassin turned, and she wiggled her hips provocatively. "Come on, love, I'm getting horny."

His eyes remote, the assassin came to the bed and sat down next to her. Almost absently he caressed her shoulder with light, rhythmic strokes. "Zeus," he said slowly, "I will do your bidding with Aphrodite; soon I will make love to her. The gods and goddesses must be served, as you have ordained. But you know, mighty ruler, that it is not love that is in my heart tonight. It is vengeance."

The young woman ran her hand over his organ and giggled artfully. "My name is Helen, love, I told you that. Call me by my right name—wouldn't that be nicer?" She continued to trace her hand over his organ, professionally assessing his lack of response. "Relax, love," she coaxed. "Would you like to talk a bit first?" He shook his head. She resumed her ministrations and suddenly she felt his organ swelling, rising beneath her hand. It surged to full tumescence. She lay back and gently drew him on top of her. "Now, love," she cooed with practiced ardor, "give it to me good."

The assassin entered her. As his buttocks rose and fell steadily there rose in his throat a deep-toned murmur, growing in intensity. "Mighty ruler," he called sharply, pausing in his thrusts, "I service Aphrodite as you have commanded. Be with me, then, when soon I strike for vengeance. My life will be forfeited—this I know. But grant my vengeance success. For behold, as you have commanded, I service Aphrodite." He resumed his thrusts, savagely, with mounting intensity.

The woman lay beneath him, feeling his inexorable probing, astonished to be experiencing a faint responsive stirring. It had been several years since sex had brought her pleasure; yet now, caught up in his frenzy, the faint stirring became a flood of exquisite sensation. Fingers digging into his heaving urgency, she came to climax in great, shuddering spasms, and simultaneously felt him empty himself into her.

She lay exhausted for several moments, and then gently pushed him off her body. He rolled inertly at her side, already asleep. His forehead was dewed with perspiration, and the tension lines of his face had softened. For a long time she looked at him, debating what she should do. He had paid her the money for the night; that had been their agreement. But now she was afraid—her own matching reaction to his wildness had shaken her confidence.

Thoughtfully she reached a conclusion that seemed to her fair. She dressed hurriedly and withdrew half of the seventy-five pounds from her pocket, placing the notes on the bureau where he could not miss them. She moved to the door and glanced at him one last time. It was best to leave, she told herself. When you stop being impersonal, it's time to go. Softly, she pulled the door closed behind her.

The assassin woke many hours later. Struggling to free himself from his miasma of exhaustion and a pounding headache, he lay on his back, eyes taking in the curtains stirring in the morning breeze, the make-shift altar, and the rumpled bed.

The rumpled bed . . . There had been another bed, so like this in its jumble of crumpled sheets, so long ago. . . .

PART TWO

PART TWO

Chapter 12

THE ASSASSIN HAD been christened George Acton Barrett. His father, John Barrett, was a salesman for a firm selling industrial supplies. At the time his son was born, in 1940, he had been turned down several times by the armed forces. A brief bout with tuberculosis had left him with weakened lungs. Despite this, or more probably because of it, he had become obsessed with reading about the war exploits of healthier men.

His role model was the British officer. To him, all officers, by the very fact that they held a position of great authority, must be courageous, cool, and decisive. Whenever he passed an officer on the street, he would study him avidly, committing to memory every gesture, every facial expression. No matter that most appeared to him arrogant; in his view, that was their due.

He had the good sense not to act during his selling hours as if he were commanding a battalion in Tunisia. But the minute he returned to his home at night, he would bring with him a cold hauteur, ordering rather than asking, unconsciously using his wife and infant son as troops under his all-knowing leadership.

In later years, George Acton Barrett was to recall vividly the contrast between his authoritarian father and his mother. A diminutive woman of blond, almost ethereal loveliness, she had come to London from a Devonshire farm, romantically determined to do her bit in the war effort through factory work. Her modest typing skills, acquired in a crash course, earned her a job in the office of a small metal stampings manufacturer. It was there that she met John Barrett. After a short courtship, punctuated by her persistent refusal on moral grounds to make love, she married him and promptly became pregnant.

Her name was Maude, and in her secret thoughts she felt that gave her a special kinship with Maude Adams, whose meteoric acting career had enthralled her as a child. Through the years, she had longed to be an actress, but knew instinctively she would never have either the courage or the ability to face an audience. That did not prevent her from frequent trips into fantasy, where she held forth in packed, hushed theaters.

To the infant George, his mother's fantasies were much kinder than those of his father. She would cuddle him to her by the hour, reading aloud in a soft, beautiful voice from some play she had bought in a nearby secondhand book store.

He would nod happily, not understanding, not caring. He adored her.

He was almost six before he realized how unhappy his mother was. As the hour for John Barrett's return from his job would draw near, his mother would grow tense, scurrying about their small kitchen, anxiously peering into various pots and pans to check the progress of the evening's supper.

At some point, the door would open suddenly. The thin figure of his father would be there, standing straight and immobile. With a quick step he would advance into the room, saluting his wife with an imperious nod and his son with a disinterested glance.

Immediately, Maude would ladle out the contents of the pans and the meal would usually be consumed in silence. His father would chew each mouthful with meticulous thoroughness, finally swallowing it with a quick gulp. Opposite him his wife would eat sparingly, occasionally leaning over to cut a piece of meat or butter some bread for her son.

On one such occasion, his father finished his meal and retired to the bedroom, giving a sharp command: "I'll expect you in the bedroom soon, Maude." George saw his mother's eyes slowly fill with tears. He stared in amazement, for she had never cried in front of him before. Steadily, inexorably, the tears flowed from her eyes and coursed down her cheeks. Then her hand reached out and covered his, her mouth managing to form a weak, grotesque smile that was meant to be reassuring.

It was then that he sensed his mother's unhappiness, and it was from that moment that he began to hate his father.

There were few children in the neighborhood where the Barretts lived. As a result, George spent almost all his waking hours in his mother's company. They would take walks together, often with a young artist who lived close by.

Jean Ardmore was a strapping girl who painted very bad pictures. An aunt in Surrey had provided for her modestly in her will, and the small income was enough to keep Jean in food and oils and pay for her flat. Somewhat on the horsey side, with dark hair arranged in severe coils and long, prominent features, she seemed formidable and forbidding. Nothing could have been further from the truth. Her disposition was invariably cheerful and outgoing.

It was this friendliness, plus the painting, that attracted Maude Barrett. She found her new friend a welcome antidote to her somber life, and creating oil pictures seemed to her a profession almost as noble as the stage.

The two women were chatting idly on a hot July afternoon when Jean suddenly turned serious. "Perhaps I shouldn't bring this up, but why do you go on wasting your life?"

"What do you mean?" Maude answered defensively.

"You know very well what I mean. Your husband. If ever I've seen a pompous ass, he's it. And the way he treats you and the boy. Why do you put up with it?"

Maude's frustration spilled over and she turned forlornly to her friend. "What choice do I have? If I left him, how could I take care of the boy? I was barely able to support myself before I married."

Jean would not let up. "Do you want to go through life without being loved? You deserve better than that."

"Give over, please," Maude pleaded. "There's nothing I can do."

The day that was to mark the end of George's childhood world began like almost any other. John Barrett set off, as usual, to his place of business. His morning went well. But after a hurried lunch of fish and chips, his stomach erupted into pain and nausea. By mid-afternoon, feeling steadily worse, he reluctantly took the tube for home.

He was surprised to find young George playing alone on their tiny lawn behind the iron fence. "What are you doing out here by yourself?" he demanded impatiently. "Where's your mother?"

George regarded him anxiously. "Inside. She told me it was all right, if I stay inside the fence."

"She did, did she? We'll have a word about that. Come along, then." Barrett turned the doorknob and was astonished to find the door locked.

"You're sure your mother's in here?" he said. At George's nod, he started to knock, but then thought better of it and took out his key. The door swung open. Low sounds could be heard from the bedroom at the end of the hall. Barrett advanced swiftly, his expression one of total bewilderment. With George a dutiful step behind, he pushed the bedroom door inward and suddenly froze. Peeking around him, George saw something he did not understand. His mother and Jean Ardmore lay on the bed naked, their bodies entwined on the rumpled sheets, their lips pressed together passionately.

There was a pause and then a great roar burst from Barrett. "Out, you bloody lesbian, out!" He grabbed his wife and threw her heavily to the floor. "Out, God damn it! Now! Now!" He kicked her brutally. "Out! And don't ever come back!"

George never saw his mother again. If Maude Barrett ever made an attempt to see her son, George never knew about it. As he grew older, he would speculate that his father might have destroyed any letters, or that he had left strict instructions with the part-time housekeepers he hired to prevent a personal visit.

In any event, by the time he started school, George's memory of his mother had almost faded away. He had a dim recollection of a golden-haired woman whose arms had made him feel warm and secure. He also had a deep resentment toward her, feeling that somehow she had abandoned him—a conviction nurtured by his father's infrequent references to her as "that bastard slut."

At school, he learned quickly, not so much through brilliance as through determination. Word of his progress was in due course relayed to Barrett Senior, and led to a decision that was to have a cataclysmic effect on his son's life.

George must go to Sandhurst, his father decided. Obviously he had the brains and the drive to assure entrance. And there, at the Royal Military Academy, he would become an officer, a member of the inner circle Barrett had admired all his life. This chance to live his own dreams vicariously soon became an obsession, and Sandhurst, Sandhurst, Sandhurst became the watchword that George was to hear through the coming years.

By the time he was thirteen, he had grown into a tall, slender boy whose good looks and serious behavior invariably impressed his elders. They also impressed the girls in his class. They were at the age where attracting a first boyfriend becomes an overwhelming need, and many of them decided George was their target. The knowledge of his mother's fall from grace was still very much alive, and he turned the girls away with a coldness that bordered on distaste.

His male classmates, already avid for their first sexual experience, would have classified him as an incorrigible sis except for one thing, his skill in sports. In soccer football, he was an outstanding forward whose speed and quick eye piled up his goal record, and in a rugby scrum his bruising style was much admired.

Outside of school, George found little to occupy himself, until the day he walked into the home of a music teacher. He was to pick up a classmate who would accompany him to soccer practice, but the rotund little man who greeted him shook his head genially.

"I'm afraid your friend isn't here," he said. "His mother rang up a while back to say he wouldn't be making his lesson today. Bit of a sore throat, I gather."

"Thank you, sir," George answered idly. His eye had been caught by the old-fashioned upright piano which held a prominent place in the living room.

The teacher followed his gaze. "I see you're looking at my piano," he commented. "I don't blame you. It's an old-timer, made by a firm in Kent. Do you play?"

"No I don't." As a matter of fact George had never seen a piano outside a showroom window or in a television concert. "How hard is it to play one of those?"

"That depends," the teacher answered. "Would you like to see how we go about it?"

George nodded. There was still half an hour before the soccer practice was to begin, and this seemed as good a way as any to pass the time.

The teacher led him to the piano, and in a general way explained the reading of music, illustrating his remarks by playing brief passages. "Now let's see you try something," he remarked, seating George at the piano and arranging his fingers on the keyboard. "All right, then," he went on, "you're about to play a chord. You remember I explained about chords to you a moment ago? Go ahead—strike the keys.''

George brought his fingers down sharply. The sound that filled the room startled him, but he felt a great pride in having created it. Eagerly he struck the chord again, and then a third time. The music teacher was watching his face with keen interest. ''You like that, eh? Here, let me show you another.''

Three days later George dropped in again and found the teacher between lessons. Encouraged by a warm reception, he asked permission to try the chords again. At home that evening, he found his father in a rare expansive mood and impulsively took a plunge. ''I wonder if you'd let me take piano lessons.''

''Piano lessons?'' his father echoed incredulously. ''What brings this up?''

George quickly explained. Surprisingly, his father listened without interruption and then answered civilly. ''Well, I must say playing the piano would be a bloody odd skill for a future officer. But I don't mind telling you, George, I'm pleased by the work you've been doing at school. I had another note from your master today. All right, then, you're entitled to a bit of fun. You may have your lessons. Provided, of course, they don't cost too much.''

Thereafter, each Thursday afternoon, George would present himself for his lesson. He would avidly drink in the teacher's instructions; and since he had no piano at home, it was arranged that he could practice at odd times during the week.

His progress was astonishing. Within six months his teacher made up his mind that a call on Barrett Senior would be in order. He picked a time when George would not be there. John Barrett received him with condescending coldness and motioned him to a chair. ''So you're the piano teacher George has been telling me about? What is it you want?''

''Your son has a real talent,'' the teacher began soberly. ''How great it actually is I don't feel competent to judge.''

Barrett nodded his head in satisfaction. "George is pretty good at most things."

"I see. What I'd like to suggest, Mr. Barrett, is that we take him to the Royal Conservatory for evaluation. If they're favorably impressed, they can make it possible for him to take advanced studies."

Barrett stood up angrily. "Advanced studies? For what purpose?"

"Why, to qualify him for a career in music. Perhaps even the concert stage."

"I thought that's what you meant," Barrett answered nastily. "You think a career in music might be just the thing for him, do you?" He studied the teacher from head to toe with deliberate insolence. "If he does well, I suppose he can look forward to being as successful as you are. That jacket you're wearing must have cost all of two quid."

The teacher reddened with humiliation. "Look here—" he began.

Barrett's index finger shot forward like a spear. "No, you look here. Let me tell you something, Mr. High and Mighty Piano Player. George will be going to Sandhurst. Sandhurst, mind you, not some bloody conservatory. And I'll tell you something else: I'll not pay to have you filling his head with nonsense. There'll be no more lessons. Not a bloody one."

Fifteen days after his eighteenth birthday George entered the Royal Military College at Camberley, in the gently rolling Sussex hills.

In the summer of 1959, an overwhelming proportion of the incoming Sandhurst class consisted of the brash, confident sons of prominent families. George Acton Barrett, officer cadet, candidate for the Royal Commission List, son of a salesman, was very much in the minority.

At the outset, he gave the matter no thought whatsoever. Tearing into the curriculum with fierce determination, he soon held the class record in virtually every athletic competition; in the classroom, he was similarly dominant. Yet in one respect he was far behind: making friends. Time and again, he began conversations only to hear them trail away. He even tried to share the candy-and-nut packages with which a proud Barrett, Senior, kept him supplied. Polite refusals resulted, and in due time he came to recognize they were not caused by lack of appetite.

Yet George kept hoping. He did acquire one friend, a teacher's son from Coventry. Harold Porter was slight, weighing less than ten stone, and his myopic eyes, when his glasses were removed, gave him the look of a bewildered owl. But there was nothing wrong in the way he saw things.

"Look here, George," he remonstrated, "you've just got to recognize we're background scenery to these bloody snobs, and that's all. They've never seen us at the right Mayfair parties, or at Ascot or wherever, and they probably never will. Just be grateful you're here getting a good education for a good career, and it's all free. Why beat your head silly trying to change something that can't be changed?"

George refused to accept his friend's judgment until the week of the Leadership Rating by Peers. On Monday, he was assigned to a tactical project along with eleven other officer candidates. They were directed by their Officer in Charge to work as a team. Each cadet would make his maximum contribution to the successful completion of the project; at the end of the week, each would be rated by all other group members on his leadership qualities.

George saw in the project an opportunity to make his breakthrough. From the moment the group met, he called upon his every resource; at night, he stayed up far longer than his classmates, poring over textbooks, planning for the next day. His work paid off. Thanks largely to his input, his group made remarkable progress, completing their project with an A rating, much to the dismay of other similar groups.

So he awaited with confidence the results of his

leadership rating by the other group members. Beyond any question, it had to be the highest; and with that public recognition he was sure he would be taken into the fold.

The Officer in Charge summoned the group to his office after the Friday evening meal. "You already know your mark as a group," he began, "and again I congratulate you. I now have the leadership rating of each of you as seen by your peers. As you know, every man, in a secret ballot, rated the eleven other group members on a scale of zero to one hundred. I emphasize the word *secret*—we wanted your true evaluations. And now we have them." He took a list from his pocket. "Very well then. At the very top of the list, with a composite rating of ninety-six, stands Officer Cadet Stuart Kingsley. Congratulations, Kingsley."

A compact cadet with a thin-featured, arrogant face raised a hand in acknowledgment. The Officer in Charge looked again to his list. "In second place, with a composite rating of ninety-one, Officer Cadet William Lawry."

George listened with disbelief and a sick numbness as the reading continued. As if in a haze, he heard the officer winding up his report. "And in last place, with a leadership rating of sixty, we find Officer Cadet George Barrett. Gentlemen, you are dismissed. Good night."

The group members made their way out into the hall, congregating around the cadet they had elected to first place. They were bantering back and forth spiritedly when George, walking heavily, passed nearby. Suddenly, unable to control his rage, he whirled around. "Kingsley," he said bitterly, "you did nothing to earn your rating. Absolutely nothing." He glared balefully at the other cadets in the circle. "As for you, you're nothing but a bunch of obedient, stupid sheep."

There was a brief silence until Kingsley stepped forward. "Well, well," he said coolly, "I see you have your wind up, Barrett. It's time you understood something, once and for all." He pushed a finger forward in sharp emphasis. "You fancy yourself as a leader. And so you are. You're equipped to lead men, but only enlisted men—grocers' sons or miners' sons or whatever. You are not equipped by birth or any other quality to lead gentlemen. That's why you'll never reach field grade, let alone senior officer rank. Never!"

George involuntarily drew back his hand. Then, helplessly recalling the penalty for inciting a fight, he paused, fist still cocked. The cadets in the circle waited expectantly.

His back rigid, George turned and walked away. From then on, he was to hate anyone from a family of wealth or position with a violent, consuming hatred.

If it hadn't been for the constant support of his old friend Harold Porter, George might never have made it through Sandhurst. After his day of humiliation, he did a minimum amount of work, straddling the ragged edge. The bitterness was always there, and the seething anger.

As the weeks passed, he struggled against depression; more than once he was close to quitting. But Porter was always there, hammering away at his persistent theme: Stick it through, take your commission, and then keep your eyes peeled for something better.

George listened just enough to stumble along. Until the day his study section was introduced to ancient history. Suddenly he was engrossed. The Romans and the Greeks, battling for a world they little understood, sent his imagination soaring.

He had found new heroes: Marc Antony, Hannibal, Cato, Ulysses. Of them all, none approached the special worship he reserved for Achilles. Here was the noble figure after which he resolved to pattern his own life. Here was the greatest of warriors, the uncompromising champion interested only in victory. George felt he understood the god's lust for eternal fame, his pride that drove him to conquer, and above all his sensitivity to insult.

"No one stepped on him and got away with it," he

explained to Harold Porter. "Can you imagine how he would have stuck it to those bastards we call our classmates?"

"Give over." Porter shook his head chidingly. "What's done is done—forget it. And stop harping on Achilles, for Christ's sake. You'd think he was your twin brother or something."

No wonder, George thought somberly. We're so alike as to be one.

At long last, there came a cold February when he was duly commissioned a sub-lieutenant in the armies of Her Majesty the Queen. A graying Barrett Senior showed up for the ceremony, pride glowing, ramrod-straight as befit the father of a future field marshal.

George was posted to Gibraltar, and spent thirty-seven dreary months there, in a bleak colony three miles long by three-quarters of a mile wide, where the wild Barbary apes roamed the cliffs above.

He occupied himself with aimless drilling of troops already letter-perfect in close-order marching, in cursing the chronic shortage of palatable water, in reading ancient Greek history, and in football matches that provided an outlet for his anger and frustration. His plan of remaining in the army only until he found something better was completely blocked. There was no place to go, and no way to develop contacts.

The orders transferring him to NATO headquarters near Mons, Belgium, seemed like a release from prison. His duties would be routine: liaison at the lowest level with American military personnel. Glad to be off the Rock, he boarded a military transport and flew north.

The next morning, anticipating his first encounter with the Americans, he took a jeep to a small, concrete building. A smartly uniformed sergeant escorted him into the office of the American lieutenant colonel who would be his superior. "Sub-Lieutenant George Barrett reporting, sir," he said, extending his orders.

Lieutenant Colonel Francotti propped his chin on a

hand and regarded him speculatively. "One thing you'll find about Americans is that we don't mind asking questions when we're curious. You've been down at Gibraltar for three years. How come no promotion?"

"I didn't exactly overexert myself," George said flatly.

"Why not?"

George shrugged. "Does it matter?"

Francotti hunched forward intently. "Let's put it this way. Where I grew up in the States, it's Little Italy. So I wanted out, and with a lot of luck and a lot of hard work, I got where I sit now. Not bad for a first-generation Italian. And I like it. So I don't want anybody or anything lousing up my act. Capish?"

"If 'capish' means do I understand, yes."

"It does. You know why they sent you here?"

"You requisitioned someone with a history background, I understand. About the only thing I got an A-Pass in at Sandhurst was history."

"Right. Now around here we provide historical background. If the wheels develop a hypothetical plan for fighting in an area of Germany, or France, or whatever, we're the boys who come up with the local history. That way, the brass knows how to get maximum cooperation from the local citizenry. You with me?"

"Yes."

"Fine," Francotti said dryly. "Now listen good. My section here runs well, real well. And it's going to continue running well, and you're going to help. Do that, and we get along just fine. Capish?"

"Capish," George answered with amusement.

From the start he liked the easy casualness which was the American hallmark. If there were any distinctions among them, he never noticed what they were; not once did he hear anyone inquire about anyone else's schools or family background. It seemed to him their conversations centered only on women, sports, and food, in that order.

At first, he was unable to enter into the good-natured bantering, which seemed to be second-nature to the

Americans. Gradually, however, he was able to hold his end up passably, although he was never able to relax completely in give-and-take.

Perhaps the biggest difference between his time in Belgium and his Gibraltar tour was in his study of ancient history. In Gibraltar, it had amounted to an obsession, and at times the strange bond he felt with Achilles was so overpowering as to be almost frightening. In Belgium, in the relaxed, informal company of the Americans, whatever need his study provided was far less acute. Weeks would go by without his picking up one of the thick history volumes stacked near his bed.

He did develop a new passion that was remote from history: target shooting. The NATO base, smarting from a series of rifle-match losses to other bases, determined to build a completely renovated team. A call went out to all interested personnel: Successful candidates would rate special privileges—frequent travel to matches throughout Europe, with first-class treatment all the way.

George fancied himself a fair shot, and decided to make the try. A burly master sergeant, chewing gum rhythmically, greeted the candidates on a firing range at 7:00 A.M. "All right, you guys," he began in a raspy voice, "I see some of you are officers. That don't cut no ice with me; the only thing I want to know is whether you shoot good. So now we find out."

In late afternoon, the sergeant called the candidates together and held up a hand. "Okay, that's it. I'll take you, you, you, you, and you." A pointing finger described a semicircle; George was the last man selected.

In the weeks that followed, he immersed himself in shooting. He learned about windage, elevation, the techniques of breath control. In his first match he finished third, and two matches later gained his first win. Encouraged, he intensified his practice efforts, and shortly began a string of victories that even the sergeant found impressive.

Driving back from a match in Paris, the sergeant glanced at him challengingly. "I'll tell you something,

Barrett," he commented. "I thought you had potential, but man, you're turning out to be something else. The all-Europe is coming up in two weeks. Last year I finished fifth, and I hope to do even better this time. I figure what I need is an incentive, so you know what I'm going to do?"

"What?" George asked.

"I'm going to enter you as well as myself. You know that carbine I bring to practice every once in a while?"

"Of course." The sergeant's love for his carbine was well known; rumor had it that he had used it with spectacular results during the Allied invasion of Normandy.

"That gun's been with me quite a while," the sergeant said quietly. "Tell you what. If you score better in the all-Europe than me, it's yours."

George stared at him in amazement. "Why in the world would you do anything like that?"

"I told you. I need an incentive to really pour it on. Ain't no way I'm going to let anyone take that carbine away from me, let alone no student of mine. Understand?"

"I suppose so," George replied unenthusiastically.

The day of the all-Europe was clear and cold. George was relaxed as he took his position, feeling he had nothing to lose. Waiting a moment to build his concentration, he picked up his rifle and sighted with calm deliberation. By three o'clock, much to his astonishment, he found that he had placed third. The sergeant was seventh, two places below his showing of the previous year; immediately after the results were announced he paid his debt.

George looked at the American carbine the sergeant had placed in his hands. It was a short rifle, but he knew its reputation for accuracy at close range. "You sure you want to do this?" he said.

"I never welched on nothing yet," the sergeant answered dully. "It's yours."

The barrel of the gun, polished to a high gloss, reflected the rays of the setting sun. George ran a finger along its length. "I'll take care of it," he said, with a sudden pride in ownership. He could not foresee the use to which he would put his prize in the years ahead.

George was thirty-one when he met Marcia Welles. He had been at NATO for seven years and felt almost a fixture. His captaincy had recently come through, testimony to the steady string of excellent efficiency reports he had earned over the years. His intention of leaving the army was still there, but far in the back of his mind, overridden by his day-to-day routine.

The orders sending him to Washington for a month of detached duty came as a particularly welcome surprise. Even though he would be working out NATO liaison matters with his counterparts in the Pentagon, there would still be ample time to see something of the States.

From the moment he arrived, his hosts planned a full social schedule. His first night he was taken to dinner by two officers, the next saw him whisked off to a play, and on the weekend, despite his protestations, he attended a house party in Virginia. It was there that he saw a young woman sitting alone in a chair on the broad veranda. Something about her seemed familiar, until he realized she could have been part of a Renoir painting. He studied her covertly for several moments and then, much to his astonishment, walked over and introduced himself.

"How long have you been in the States, Captain?" she asked gravely.

"I just arrived Thursday," he answered absently, thinking he had never seen anyone so beautiful. Her black hair was curly and cut short; the delicate heart shape of her face was accentuated by dark eyes and short, arched eyebrows. "You said your name was Miss Welles?"

"That's right. Marcia."

He nodded, wishing desperately he could think of something to say. All his life he had scrupulously avoided any serious contact with women; now he found himself feeling clumsy and inadequate.

As if aware of his problem, she maintained a sympathetic silence. "I'm not very good at this," he blurted finally. "Will you have dinner with me?"

She looked startled, as if that were the last thing she had expected him to say. "I don't know," she replied uncertainly. "I'm afraid—"

"Please."

She seemed confused and reserved. "I don't go out very often."

"Please," he repeated urgently. "Make an exception."

"All right," she agreed with a quick smile. "I'll be very glad to have dinner with you."

The next evening, George picked her up at her Washington apartment. Their dinner went well from the start. Seated across from her in a French restaurant, watching her dark eyes in the candlelight, he found himself talking with a freedom he had never known. She wondered about the reasons he had chosen Sandhurst, and he answered by telling her about his father's obsession with military heroes, even describing in an emotionless tone his mother's defection.

In return, she explained she was an only child. Her mother was dead and her father—a former ambassador to France—had been killed in an accident three years before. She had spent much time in France, where her family had owned a château near Paris. It was still hers, she explained; she just hadn't gotten around to putting it up for sale.

He found to his delight that, at twenty-six, she had never been married. Long before the dessert course, they had agreed to meet the next day.

That was the beginning. They dined out frequently, and on weekends they visited the National Zoo, the theater, the Air and Space Museum, and the bustling shops of Georgetown. They laughed spontaneously and often at the antics of the giant panda, the grimacing of a comedian, or a private joke. It was an enchanted time.

They were exploring each other's likes and dislikes, learning to communicate, liking each other more with each passing day.

At the outset, they settled into the habit of sedately kissing good-night at the end of each date. But inevitably the kisses became more prolonged, and George would drive back to his hotel in the discomfort of sexual desire. Once or twice he tried to get past the kissing stage, but Marcia gently dissuaded him with an understanding but nonetheless unmistakable firmness.

Only one worry clouded his days. His month in Washington was speeding by, and he began to panic. He simple could no longer conceive of a life without her; yet it was irrational to hope she would marry him. One evening, as they were taking coffee in the living room of her apartment, he summoned up his courage. "I've got just five days left, you know," he began tentatively. "Not much, is it?"

"No it isn't," she replied quietly.

He took her hand in his. "I love you, Marcia. This is a crazy thing to ask, but I've got to ask it. Will you marry me?" He was watching her intently, and saw her body tense. "Look," he went on miserably, "I said it was crazy. I'm sorry—I should have known better. A captain's pay isn't exactly what you're used to, is it?"

"It isn't that," she replied quickly. "Please don't think that, George."

"I don't blame you," he said bitterly. "Let's forget it."

"George, it isn't that. Believe me." She placed her hands on his shoulders, her eyes filled with tears. "Listen to me. I love you, I want to marry you, but I just can't. It's such a big, big step."

He touched her cheek gently. "Why not? What are you afraid of?"

"I don't know," she answered hesitantly. "I'm just afraid."

He sensed a confidence building in him, a feeling that now was the time to act boldly. "You said you love me. If that's so, there's nothing to be afraid of. Nothing."

He drew her to him. "I'll tell you what we're going to do. Right up to the time I leave, we're going to concentrate on having a good time. No more heavy discussions. Then after I've gone a week or so, you'll have had time to think it through, and you can write me your decision. How does that sound?"

"Fine, George. I do love you so. It's just that—"

He placed a finger over her lips. "Quiet, Marcia. Remember, no more discussions."

Driving back to the city, he was filled with a great exultation. She loved him; she had told him so twice. Everything was going to be all right—he was sure of it.

His mood of euphoria sustained him only through his farewell to Marcia. Back in Belgium, he was in despair, sure that each incoming post would contain the dread refusal that would tear him down forever. She had promised she would write within two weeks, and the waiting became agony, constant, deep.

When the news did come, it was totally unexpected. A corporal in George's office answered the telephone and held it out to him. "For you, Captain."

"George?" Marcia's eager voice sounded as if it were coming from another planet. "Can you hear me? We have a bad connection."

"I can hear you." The thudding of his heart had begun with her first word.

"George, I hope you don't mind my calling you at work. I simply couldn't wait to tell you."

"Tell me what," he said fearfully, his arms and legs suddenly weak, awaiting the blow.

"I'm going to marry you," she shouted happily. "I love you and I'm going to marry you. No more doubts, not a one. Do you still want to marry me, George?"

"Thank God," he said, tears rolling down his cheeks as he absorbed the incredible news. The startled corporal was eyeing him from the corner of the room.

Two days before Christmas, they were married in a church on the base. They spent their first night in Brussels, at a huge old hotel featuring an enormous dining room, dark oak trim, and excellent food. After a seemingly endless wedding supper, punctuated by sips of champagne, they retired to their room. George was nervous; in the entire British Army, he told himself apprehensively, there probably wasn't another thirty-one-year-old virgin.

His worries were groundless. Their lovemaking was tentative and gentle for a few brief moments. Then the repressed sex drive of years exploded and he kissed her body with a wild, unslakable abandon. She lay still, and suddenly responded with a frantic urgency that matched his own. He entered her, and they worked together, mounting successive platforms of sensation to a shattering climax that left him limp and drained.

In the days of their honeymoon, spent in Paris, they wandered along the Left Bank, pausing occasionally to gaze at a painting, never seeming apart in their opinions. In the evenings, with the frantic haste of their first night behind them, they settled down to exploring each other's body and achieving a deep, soul-stirring satisfaction.

Their existence was idyllic, and continued idyllic after their return to the NATO base. As their first summer together drew near, they considered and rejected many places to spend George's projected leave. In the end, they decided to spend the time at Marcia's château in France. She would have the chance to see its condition, and undertake arrangements for its sale. So on a rainy July morning they loaded their Volkswagen to overflowing and set off in holiday spirits.

George's first glimpse of the château enchanted him completely. The setting sun cast a patina of gold across its stone walls, and brought to its towers a gleaming, fairyland quality.

While the caretaker busied himself with their bags, Marcia led the way into an exquisitely furnished drawing room. Designed in the Directoire style, the pieces blended to produce an inviting, warm atmosphere.

"It's beautiful, isn't it?" she asked. "I'd almost forgotten."

George didn't answer. He was staring at the concert

piano placed before the softly draped windows. Its polished surface gleamed, reflecting the rays of a lamp placed nearby. With reverential attention, he touched the keyboard, taking a sensual pleasure in the feel of the keys. "What a magnificent instrument," he said, almost inaudibly.

"Play something, George," Marcia urged. "I remember you said you studied for a while."

"It's been a long time. I'd be pretty rusty."

"No matter. This isn't Carnegie Hall, is it? Go on."

George sat down on the bench. His hands poised over the keyboard and then came down with authority. The opening notes of Lizst's Hungarian Rhapsody resounded in the room, powerful, commanding.

He played carefully at the outset, concentrating on bringing the score to mind, willing his fingers to recapture their former flexibility. Gradually his confidence built. His hands became a conduit through which the music flowed, soaring in crescendo, compelling in its wild abandon. Sitting erect, eyes closed, George let the music sweep him upward in its power and beauty to the dynamic, stirring climax.

The sound of the final notes drifted away. He sat motionless, still at one with the music. Marcia was silent for a long moment, until at last she spoke in an awed tone. "My God, George, that was brilliant—there's just no other word."

"Spoken like a loyal wife." George swung around on the bench; his face was strained and pale.

"George, what's the matter? Do you feel ill?"

"No, I'm all right." He shook his head dejectedly. "I hate to admit it, but touching a piano after all these years has gotten to me, I'm afraid. I'd forgotten how much I loved it."

She studied him with tender concern. "George, I want to ask you something," she said, getting up and coming to take his hand. "You've never really been happy in the army, have you?"

He started to protest, but finally smiled ruefully. "No. The last few years I had myself pretty well convinced that I was. Way down deep, though, I knew different. I just didn't want to admit it."

She gestured toward the piano. "This is what you really want, isn't it?"

"Yes, I suppose it is." He shrugged his shoulders disconsolately. "But there's no sense in thinking about it. There wasn't any sense when I was a kid—there certainly isn't any now. Besides, how do I know I could ever be good enough?"

"You'd be good enough," she answered earnestly. "I'm sure of it. You know what we're going to do? There must be a top teacher in Brussels. When we get back, you'll play for him, George."

"And?"

"If he says you have enough talent, that it's possible, you're going to try. You'll practice and practice and you'll make it. I've never been more certain of anything in my life."

Thus it was that George became a student of Maestro Fauchon. Three nights a week, he drove the sixty kilometers to Brussels. So he would be able to practice on the other nights, they purchased a piano; after much tugging and hauling, it was installed in their living room. There was one compensation in his grinding schedule. Month by month, slowly at first but then quickly, he sensed that his playing was mounting far beyond the ordinary.

On an icy November night George arrived at the maestro's studio. Grateful for the welcoming warmth, he shucked off his overcoat and arranged himself at the piano. He glanced quickly at the music on the rack and began to play the *Moonlight Sonata*. As the notes of the Third Movement died away, he leaned forward, relaxing, releasing his concentration. There was a light touch on his shoulder. He turned to find his teacher regarding him with great seriousness.

"You are ready," Monsieur Fauchon said. "I have given all I can to you. Now it is time for you to give to your audiences."

When George drove his Volkswagen into the driveway of the cottage, he sprinted through the snow. As Marcia opened the door, he caught her up in a bearhug, ecstatically babbling his news. They talked until late at night, agreeing that he would submit his resignation from the army in the morning. Beyond that there would be infinite plans to make—and time to make them. Sailing on clouds, mellowed with wine, they went to bed and made love with joyous enthusiasm.

At nine the next morning, letter of resignation prepared, he presented himself in Colonel Francotti's office. The colonel, his expression tense, spoke quickly. "Captain, you have orders. I wish they could have been different."

George took the sheet held out to him. He scanned it quickly, reading the terse, relentless paragraphs. One sentence burned into his consciousness, again and again: "Captain George Barrett will report immediately to the Commanding General, Belfast, Northern Ireland, for assignment to an infantry unit."

George entered the seething cauldron of Northern Ireland in the first month of a new year.

His farewell to Marcia had been especially trying. She had managed to smile, talking animatedly of an early return. He agreed, outwardly confident, yet each knew he might be back in a month, a year, or never.

In Belfast, he went directly to army headquarters and made one more try to have his resignation accepted. He was shown into the presence of the general's chief of staff and snapped to attention. "Captain Barrett reporting, sir."

The officer behind the massive desk surveyed him with a cold glance. "I know who you are, Barrett. We were at Sandhurst together. Remember?"

"I remember," George had answered after a long pause. He could not believe his crushing luck. The thin-featured, arrogant colonel was unmistakable.

"It would be hard for you to forget," Colonel Stuart Kingsley said sardonically. "After all, your classmates

—including me, I may say—rated you last in the Leadership Rating by Peers. That's not the sort of thing one sloughs off, is it?'' George fought to keep his anger buried. ''I rather imagine you also recall who was rated first,'' Kingsley went on acidly. ''I was. You started enough of a flap about it at the time.''

''With the Colonel's permission,'' George said carefully, ''may we talk about my reason for seeing you?''

''Of course, of course,'' Kingsley replied with mock expansiveness. ''My corporal tells me you want to leave the army. To become a pianist, I believe.''

''Yes, sir.''

Kingsley's jaw jutted forward belligerently. ''Let me tell you what I think, Barrett. You were mucking around in some damned history unit at NATO, playing at soldier, drawing your money with your arse set neatly in butter. Then the minute the army asks you for a change to do a bit of what you're supposed to be paid for, you scream to get out. Your request is denied. What's more, I'll guarantee you a lively assignment. Dismissed.''

George blundered out of the office, a mist of hate isolating him from his surroundings. An hour later, a jeep dropped him in front of a Catholic school on the edge of the Ballymurphy district. The Forty-third Infantry Battalion was housed in half of the building. Sandbags placed in the middle of the corridors divided the troops from the students on the other side; an almost visible aura of tension filled the air.

An orderly guided him to a cloakroom that was now serving as an office for the commanding officer. For the second time that day, George was astounded. His friend Harold Porter, wearing the pips of a major, myopic eyes making him look more like an owl than ever, rose to greet him. ''Holy Christ,'' he yelled exuberantly. ''George Barrett! What in hell are you doing here?''

''Looking for the CO.'' George grinned. ''I'm his new man. Don't tell me you're it.''

''That's me. The dirtiest job in the whole goddamned army, and I'm stuck with it.''

They talked over a bottle of brandy until well after midnight. "It's shit here, George," Porter said morosely. "We can't set foot on the streets unless on armed patrol. We're cooped up like rats in a maze. Out in the countryside it's even worse; take a walk for a hundred yards and it's odds-on a fucking sniper will drill you through the head. What the hell, let's talk about something else. You'll find out soon enough."

In the weeks that followed, George's life became a nightmare of patrols, putting down riots, roping off streets, and living in near terror. A sniper would fire at a patrolling trooper, touching off a house-to-house search that invariably proved fruitless. His patrol would spot a suspicious-looking car and order its occupants to halt for a bomb search; on two occasions the order resulted in a fusillade of shots from the car that miraculously produced no casualties.

By day he would walk the Ballymurphy streets, his men in single file ten paces apart, rifles unslung and at the ready. He looked at the cottages and knew he was staring at death: Behind any of the storefronts, behind any boarded window, concealed behind any soot-blackened chimney, a sniper might already be squeezing a trigger.

His nerves frayed, and he slept fitfully. More and more, whiskey became at once his opiate and his curse; it would procure him an hour or two of sleep, and an awakening with a sick stomach and a pounding head. Harold Porter, anxious for the well-being of his friend, tried unsuccessfully to get him to cut down his drinking. Time and again, George would promise—and keep on drinking.

Gradually, the line between reality and a dream world of fantasy grew cloudy. More than once, he realized with a dull wondering that he had begun to return to his absorption with mythology. Zeus, Hera, Athena, Achilles—once again they came alive for him, oftentimes more real than the faces of his men.

Only one thing kept him going: Marcia's letters. They arrived daily, cheerful, filled with love, giving him hope. Until a freezing March night. He had been dispatched to a makeshift armory set up in an abandoned warehouse, there to requisition additional riot-control guns. With his business concluded, he was trying to summon up the resolve to go back into the cold; a young major, noting his exhaustion, suggested he might do with some tea.

George accepted gratefully. They made their way to a small, cluttered room containing a stove, a table, and some chairs. The major set out cups and saucers, and then brewed the tea.

"How long have you been out here?" he asked, holding out a steaming cup.

"Not quite three months."

"Where were you before that?"

"Belgium. NATO. How about you?"

They chatted idly, comparing their various tours of duty. At one point George mentioned that he had spent a month in Washington, and the major responded with a delighted grin.

"Really? I spent some time there myself two years ago. What were you doing?"

"Liaison."

"They had me in ordnance, out at Aberdeen. Looking over some new guns the Yanks had. Did you like the States, then?"

"Very much," George said, beginning to feel the warmth of the tea. "As a matter of fact, I met a girl there. Her name was Marcia Welles. You know what happened? I—"

The major threw back his head with a bellow of laughter. "Well, I'll be damned. It is a small world, isn't it?" He patted George on the arm, smiling conspiratorially. "Do I know what happened? Let me guess. You fucked her, just like I fucked her, and half the Yank army fucked her—right?"

George stared at him, uncomprehending. "What? You must be thinking of someone else."

"Oh, come off it," the major said impatiently. "Gallantry is all right, but Christ! You know very well who I mean—good-looking brunette, father used to be ambassador to France." He lifted his eyes expressively. "How that girl loved to fuck. The Yanks told me she was a nympho, and were they ever right!" He reached out his hand in a playful poke. "But you found that out, didn't you?"

George hit him with every ounce of his strength. The major catapulted off his chair and fell into a corner, his mouth twisted in a bloody protest. "You crazy bastard," he mumbled, checking his teeth frantically. "What the hell's the matter with you?"

The door slammed shut as George turned and walked through the armory into the bone-chilling night. He would never remember the trip back to his barracks, but it was after two o'clock when he violently shook Harold Porter awake. "I need an emergency leave now," he said harshly. "Two days. Just two days."

The wintry sun was high, touching the trees with a cold light, when George arrived at the cottage in Belgium. Marcia saw him on the walk and threw open the door, extending her arms wide. "Thank God." Her eyes were radiant, filled with tears. "Thank God."

He pushed past her and turned around. "Close the door." Uncomprehending, shocked by his white face and terrible eyes, she gently shut the door and waited. "An officer in Ireland told me you're a nymphomaniac," he said softly. "Is it true?"

Her shoulders drooped as an agonized expression came into her eyes. "I thought it might be that," she whispered after a long moment. "I guess it was too much to hope you'd never find out."

"Then it's true."

"It was," she answered slowly. "It's not true now." She held his gaze with dignity. "When you met me, George, I was finishing treatment. When you asked me to marry you, I wouldn't give you an answer—remember? I wanted to be sure I was cured." Her hands were clenched as she fought to keep control. "When my psychiatrist told me I was, I couldn't wait to phone. I wanted so much to marry you."

"Why didn't you tell me?"

She smiled sadly. 'I was ashamed, George. You have no idea what a degrading, loathsome sickness it is. I tried to tell you, but I just couldn't. I didn't want to lose you." She held his gaze steadily. "But I have, haven't I? There's one thing I want you to know, though, George. I'll always love you. Always."

He looked at her and the dreadful pain rose in him. It tore at him, assaulting his brain with sorrow and the hopeless knowledge that it would never be in him to forget or forgive. It was finished forever. With one last long gaze, as if to store up a memory that must last a lifetime, he turned and left the house.

Sunday morning came to Ballymurphy. Through the long night George had twisted fitfully, drugged with alcohol, trying to escape his deep melancholia. Toward dawn he rose, scraped away at his beard, and tried to brush the uniform in which he had slept.

He found Harold Porter already in the messroom, eyes haggard with fatigue. "We're in for it," he announced glumly. "Some damned idiotic paratrooper panicked and shot a kid. All night long reports have been coming in. Sniping, land mines, the lot. Fucking mess." He gave George a covert, anxious inspection. "Listen, I've got to go over to regimental HQ. Ride along with me, will you? There's something I want to talk to you about."

Their jeep made slow progress. Every corner was a checkpoint, manned by soldiers who looked gray and drawn in the feeble morning light. When they came at last to a long, uninterrupted stretch, Porter plunged ahead reluctantly. "Look, George, we've been friends for a long time. I'm worried about you. You've got to get to a doctor."

"Why?"

"You know you're not yourself," Porter said gently. "I hate to see you so miserable. A doctor can help you."

George was silent. They rode another block, and Porter braked for a turn. "Well, George," he asked, "what about it?"

Neither of them saw the figure crouched at the top of a wall. As the jeep made the turn, an outstretched arm tossed an object into its path. The grenade exploded with a fearful impact, tearing the jeep apart, hurling its occupants in the air. A second grenade exploded an instant later with a blinding flash.

George struggled up to consciousness through a blanket of pain. The shock of the blast had left him confused; it seemed an eternity before he could focus his eyes. Gradually, he was able to realize what had happened and tried to sit up. His limbs refused to move, and the effort set off violent spasms of torment.

He lay still for an instant, calling weakly for Harold Porter. There was no answer. With a sudden, terrible fear, he forced himself to turn his head, ignoring the pain.

The wreck of the jeep lay several yards away. A twisted, smoking hulk, it was covered with licks of flame, and the stink of burning rubber fouled the air. Next to it sprawled the compact body of his friend.

In death, Harold Porter looked more than ever like a startled owl. His eyes were wide and staring through the smashed lenses of his glasses, and his hair tufted in wild angles. There is something wrong with his head, George told himself dully, and then he realized what it was. A clutch of nails, driven by the explosion of a nail-bomb grenade, had imbedded themselves in his skull. Their steel ends protruded, forming a haphazard, obscene pattern.

George closed his eyes in agony, but when he opened them the grisly sight was still there. He lay in torture of mind and spirit, and drifted slowly into a hellish miasma.

The senior psychiatrist at London's Military Hospital rubbed his chin reflectively. "You've been here four months, Captain," he said slowly. "We're not making all that much progress, are we?"

"I suppose not," George answered without interest.

"There's not much more they need to do for you physically." The psychiatrist flicked through the file in his lap. "You had a bad leg break, but that's mended. Extensive lacerations, healed with no complications. Shrapnel in muscle of right hand, removed surgically, with complete recovery." He sighed heavily. "Everybody seems to have done a good job except us. That damned depression of yours—it doesn't budge, does it?" George listened impassively. "Since they shipped you here from Belfast," the psychiatrist went on, "you've been pretty static. You've got to break out of yourself, get back in the mainstream. Do you understand?"

"Yes."

"The nurses tell me you've checked some books out of the hospital library. All of them, apparently, dealt with the history of classical Greece. Is that a special interest of yours?"

"It has been for some time."

"What you need is a major interest—an in-depth involvement in a project, for example. Have you thought of writing a book?"

"That would take research," George pointed out dryly. "It would be a bit hard to do that, wouldn't it? You've got me restricted to the ward."

"Yes." The doctor acknowledged his comment with a tight smile. "Tell you what. There must be good men in the classics here in the city, say at the University of London. You must know who they are. Why not ring one of them up, tell him you're doing a book, and ask if you can pop in for background discussion. I'll authorize you to make outside visits for four hours at first. Longer, of course, as you improve. Why not give it a try?"

"What do I say?" George asked bitterly. "That I'm a patient in the psychiatric ward? Bit of a scare-off, wouldn't you think?"

"Why even mention that you're in hospital? If you

must, simply say you were banged up a bit in Ireland. That's true enough, isn't it?''

''All right,'' George agreed, not wanting to prolong the session. ''If you think it will help.''

After some thought, he decided to approach Robert Chatwin, well known in the field. He had read somewhere that Chatwin had retired from the Oxford faculty and was now living in London. A look in the telephone directory gave him the number. He rang up, explained the reason for his call, and was rewarded with a warm invitation to come by.

Chatwin's book-filled apartment was near Russell Square. They talked at length, debating the precise meaning of certain mythological passages. Chatwin proved to be an amiable host, as quick with a brandy as he was with conversation, and they established an instant rapport.

In the days that followed, he made frequent visits to see Chatwin, and renewed his acquaintanceship with the Tate Art Gallery, the British Museum, and various of his favorite restaurants. Most important, his nights at last became bearable. There were stretches, growing longer, when he slept without the nightmares of the hell in Ireland or the death of Harold Porter. Even his constant anguish over Marcia, a deep emptiness reaching down into his being, seemed to recede in some slight degree.

For the first time he began to believe that his doctors were right. The one thing he had resolutely pushed to the back of his mind, evoking as it did the life and hopes he had shared with Marcia, was his love for the piano. It intruded more and more into his thoughts, demanding, challenging. There is yet meaning in your life, it insisted without let-up. There might even be happiness, if you do what God intended you to do. There is a choice between happiness and misery—but only you can make it.

One morning he awoke feeling refreshed and at peace, with his depression vanished like an evil black cloud. He walked purposefully to the senior psychiatrist's office and requested an interview.

"Well, Captain," the doctor greeted him with an appraising look, "you're looking chipper this morning. What's happened?"

"I want to play the piano."

The doctor was startled. "The piano? There's one in the patients' lounge, of course—"

"Not that," George said impatiently. "It's out of tune, and it never was very good in the first place. It's not in my service record, but I was once very serious about the piano. I was close to my debut. I want to start practicing again, serious practice."

"I see," the doctor answered thoughtfully. "If it means that much to you, I'll see what can be arranged. Perhaps a practice room at the London Conservatory—is that the sort of thing you have in mind?"

"Precisely."

"Good. I'll get back to you in a day or so."

The moment the arrangements were set, George set off for the conservatory. The day was sunny, matching his mood. He walked briskly, breathing the crisp air deeply, reveling in the knowledge that at last he had a purpose.

There were no delays at the conservatory. He was informed that they were expecting him, and was ushered through a labyrinth of corridors to a practice room. Closing the door behind him, he stood for a moment, glancing at the soundproofed walls, glorying in the great Steinway that took up half the space.

He sat down at the piano bench and struck a note on the keyboard. The sound echoed through the room, vibrating into silence. The quiet and the instrument before him combined to give him the incongruous feeling that he was in a cathedral. He was suddenly sure his spirits would be uplifted, borne by the music he would create.

Tentatively, he began to play, exercising his fingers, attuning himself to the nuances of his instrument. A mood of lighthearted exuberance caught him up, and he swung into a lively Mozart minuet, enjoying its bright, cheerful notes. Then—his enchantment deepening—he changed tempo, softly playing the First Movement of the *Moonlight Sonata*.

He was astonished and reassured to find that his long layoff had taken little from his skill. Two weeks, he told himself exultantly, and he would have it all back. Buoyed by confidence, supremely happy, he challenged Tchaikovsky's Concerto No. 1 in B-flat Minor. His fingers flew threw the intracacies of its score, producing an immense volume and variety of tone. The music thundered in the room, electrifying, magnificent. He reached the formidable octave passages and met them triumphantly, reveling in the power and control of his hands, spread wide to span the keys.

For a second he paused, right hand lifted from the keyboard, ready to bring it down in a climactic octave. Unaccountably the hand trembled slightly. He struck the keyboard at precisely the right instant, but the sound was wrong—almost imperceptibly so, but wrong. Impatiently he repeated the passage, his euphoria dampened. More practice than he first thought necessary would be required to reach his peak.

Again his right hand lifted, poised, and again it trembled. Uncomprehending, he tried a third time—the trembling was there. Far down in the recesses of his being, a panic appeared, a faint alarm at first but growing swiftly to become a torrent of fear. He sat immobile, forcing the panic to retreat, perspiration slowly forming on his forehead.

After several minutes he played the Mozart minuet with which he had started, and played it flawlessly. He repeated the *Moonlight Sonata* movement, with no problem. It was time to try the concerto once more; as before he swept through it brilliantly, approaching the arduous octave passages.

He negotiated the first octave smoothly. At the critical instant his right hand again swept upward, fingers spread wide. The hand trembled.

He stopped playing, looking at his hand in horror. In complete despair, he was remembering the shrapnel that had torn a muscle. No, he screamed at himself silently—

they said the operation was simple, a total success. He stood up and raised his right hand before his face. Slowly, suspended in fear, he spread the fingers to their utmost span.

The trembling began. He kept his fingers spread, holding the tension. The trembling increased, until the hand wavered relentlessly. With a bursting rage he jammed it in his pocket, away from his sight. His head bowed as despair engulfed him, washing over him in waves, endless, agonizing.

The senior psychiatrist was putting away his papers, ready to go to dinner, when George burst into his office.

"What's wrong?" the doctor asked sharply.

"I want to see a neurologist. Now."

"Why?"

George held out his right hand slowly. "It trembles when I play difficult octaves." His voice escalated hysterically. "Did you ever hear of a concert pianist who couldn't play octaves? Did you?"

The doctor came around from behind his desk. "Don't go off the deep end, George. Let's find out for sure. Go on over to the neurology clinic. I'll phone Dr. Risdon to meet you there."

The clinic was deserted, except for the neurologist, plainly out of breath. "They caught up with me just as I was leaving," he explained, "and I climbed the stairs from the lobby. I ought to know better at my age. All right, then, what's the problem?"

George managed to explain with some semblance of calm. "I see," the neurologist said, picking up the phone. "I'll have them bring over your records from Central Files. Meanwhile, we can have an X ray done. Can't do much without that." He eyed George sympathetically. "It might have been just a muscle spasm, you know. Suppose you try your best to relax until we find out."

An hour later the X rays were back and the neurologist had completed his examination. "Sit down," he said, pushing forward a metal chair. He propped himself against an examining table, arms behind him, and regarded his patient soberly.

"It's not the end of the world," he started. "You had a rather severe injury of the interossei palmares. In plain English, they're the intermediate muscles of the hand that permit full spreading of the fingers. That bit of shrapnel you picked up tore them up pretty badly." George stared at him steadily. "No question about it— your surgeon did a fine job," the neurologist continued encouragingly. "You'll have full service of the hand. Even playing the piano shouldn't give you any trouble— unless, of course, you push it too hard."

"Like playing an octave," George said bitterly.

"No, not necessarily. You can play two or even three octaves in a row and probably get away with it. But you've got to realize there's still a weakness in the muscle. The moment you spread your fingers wide, you set up a stress situation. Keep it up and your hand will falter, start to tremble."

George hesitated, and finally willed himself to ask the question that had to be asked. "With treatment, with time, will it improve?"

"I'm afraid not," the neurologist said, avoiding his eyes. "Perhaps if you carefully pick the selections you play you can still have your career. Wouldn't that be possible?"

"No, it would not," George exploded savagely. "Have you ever heard of a concert pianist only able to play an easy repertoire?"

The neurologist shrugged helplessly. "I'm sorry," he said.

Hope was gone, and with it George's short-lived peace. His nightmares returned, seemingly more vicious as a result of his brief respite. In an effort to have him cling to some interest, the senior psychiatrist urged him to continue his visits to Robert Chatwin, suggesting again that he undertake the writing of a book on Grecian history.

George agreed to the visits, as much to help fill his

days as for any other reason. He discovered shortly that
a curious thing was happening; he was having trouble
separating his real world from the world of the ancient
gods.

Once again his fixation with Achilles returned. He
brooded more and more over what he considered the
striking parallel between Achilles' loss of his friend Patroclus and his own loss of Harold Porter. Ruefully he
reminded himself that Achilles had acted swiftly in his
rage, seeking out and striking down Hector, who had
slain his friend in battle. What are you doing to avenge
your friend? he taunted himself. He lies in Ireland, un-
noticed, unsung, remembered but not avenged.

Tormented, relentless, he searched for one answer:
Who was really responsible for Harold's death? Was it
the IRA gunman? No, he decided finally; the gunman
had acted impersonally, responding like a robot to the
pressures placed upon him. Who, then, had created
those pressures? Was it the leaders of the IRA—or were
they also pawns, seeking only freedom?

Existing half in the present, half in the past, no longer
caring, he wracked his mind, seeking the culprit. Who
had dispatched Harold to meet death, who had ruined
his own life by sending him to Ireland? Who was
culpable? Who must be made to atone?

One afternoon he found his answer. A chilling rain
was spattering off the streets of London, soaking
through his coat, as he left Chatwin's apartment. On an
impulse he hailed a cab and gave the address of the
hospital. The cab was creeping in the afternoon rush,
moving a few feet at a time along the Mall, when the
grandeur of Buckingham Palace suddenly came into his
sight.

He stared at the great building, its myriad windows,
its banners snapping on their flagpoles in the strong
breeze. Then—without conscious thought—the long-
sought answer erupted into his mind, overpowering,
aflame. Majesty. There was the culprit!

"In the name of Her Majesty . . ." How many times

had he read that phrase in his life, how many times had he heard it spoken? There was the being who took all and gave nothing . . . a woman, evil in her way as his mother and his wife had been in theirs . . . an unfeeling monarch who let men march to their destruction in her name.

Frantically he signaled the cab driver to stop and paid him off. Disembarking, he walked to the immense gates and stood rigid. Hate seethed through him, and a strange exaltation: The guilty one at last was known.

That night he slept soundly for the first time in months and rose with a purpose. The nature of Majesty's atonement had to be set; there were plans to be made. For days he concentrated on the problem, and slowly began to piece together a plan. He examined each step with infinite care, testing it for soundness, until at last he was satisfied.

He continued to see Robert Chatwin regularly, and dutifully reported this to the senior psychiatrist. But these visits were no longer his purpose. He spent a great deal of time in the libraries of London, doing the research that was necessary to his plan; it went swiftly and well. But there was one vital preliminary step that gave him much trouble; he worked on it doggedly, with a growing conviction that it could never be accomplished. Then—three months later, just as he was about to abandon it in despair to try another approach—he met with success.

The next morning he left the hospital, but did not go to Robert Chatwin's apartment. Instead he stopped in at the bank where his pay had been deposited during his illness. Drawing out two hundred pounds, he bought a newspaper, methodically combing through the advertisements for flats to rent.

Circling several, he set off to check them through. It was mid-afternoon when he found what he wanted, a pleasant flat in a quiet section of Chancery Lane. He paid a month's rent and left to buy a suitcase, some clothes, and food.

An hour later, he returned and set about preparing his evening meal. He glanced around his new home, well satisfied with his day's work. Never again, he said to himself exultantly, would he spend a day in a hospital.

His new life was beginning. Achilles was on the hunt.

PART THREE

PART THREE

Chapter 13

ASSISTANT COMMISSIONER SIR Henry Adams was in his office at New Scotland Yard. The October sun shone weakly through the windows, casting splotches of cold light over the floor. The bleakness of the day matched Adams' spirits. As he had done so frequently in the past week, he glanced at the wall clock.

"Six o'clock," he said grimly to the man seated across from him. "Another day almost gone." He slammed his hand down on the desk. "Christ! A madman tells us he'll kill the Queen within ten days. We've just got three days left. And even that is assuming he won't strike before his outside deadline—it could be any moment." He shook his head in frustration. "We have one hundred and twelve men looking for him. We have a list of fifty-six suspects from our computer check—and the chances are very high one of them is Achilles. But we still haven't found him. Christ!"

Inspector Thomas Granby had been listening dourly. "Sir," he answered defensively, "I have just reported to you that we have eliminated thirty-two of the computer's original list of fifty-six. That leaves twenty-four to go. With luck, we would have found our man in the first thirty-two. We didn't. I assure you we are doing everything possible to get through the remaining suspects as quickly as possible.''

''I know, I know,'' the Assistant Commissioner agreed. ''Forgive me, Inspector. I wouldn't have picked you to head up checking the list through if you hadn't been the best man for it. But there must be something we can do to speed up the job. Are you sure more men wouldn't help?''

''No, sir, it isn't a question of manpower. It's a question of time. Tracing a man from one address to another, talking with his friends when he's left no address —that sort of thing. More men would just clutter things up. There's a point of no return.''

The Assistant Commissioner shoved a folded newspaper across the desk. ''I know that. But did you see the morning paper? There's a picture of Her Majesty opening the Trade Fair at Birmingham.'' He gestured toward the telephone. ''Every time she makes a public appearance, I dread hearing that thing ring. It might be news that this madman has struck. We have simply got to find a way to get him, and get him fast!''

Granby nodded. ''The Queen still refuses to give up public appearances, I take it.''

''She's totally adamant. I was talking to the Prime Minister just before you came in. She keeps trying, but the Queen simply will not give an inch.''

''If the Iron Leader can't budge her, no one will,'' the inspector replied dryly. ''This American—Haynes, isn't it?—the chap who put us up to using the computer to isolate the suspects. Has he anything further to suggest?''

''Just as frustrated as the rest of us,'' Adams said glumly.

''I see. Well, with your permission, sir, I'll get back on it.'' Granby gathered his papers. ''If anything breaks, I'll notify you immediately, of course.''

The Assistant Commissioner sighed dispiritedly after the inspector left. Relentlessly, aginast his will, his eyes strayed to the clock.

• • •

Jill Blake put down her magazine and ran a hand through her blond hair. "I thought I could do it but I can't," she said miserably.

"Do what?" Haynes put down his pad and pencil.

"I agreed we wouldn't talk about your Lady Marston. 'Let's put everything on hold'—I believe that was your expression." Her voice began to tremble. "Well, I can't do it. You said you were mixed up in your thinking about her and me. All right, it's been over a week. How much time do you need?"

"Jill, please."

"Look, Tom," she answered bitterly, "I've been watching you for the last hour. You make a note on your pad and then you sit and stare for five minutes. You're thinking of her, aren't you? Tell me!"

He got up and crossed to the divan. Sitting down next to her, he reached for her hand. "Jill, listen to me. There's something I've been working on—it's of enormous importance. And we've hit a blank wall. I've been jotting down ideas we might try now, but the truth is none of them are any good. Do you understand?"

"I suppose so."

Turning her face toward him, he went on gently. "If I've been staring, it's because I've been wracking my brains, trying to come up with something that might work. I'm not thinking about Hope Marston or anything else. How can I do any objective thinking about my personal life right now? Every waking moment has got to be spent on this problem. It's that vital."

"How much longer will it take?" she asked. "It's hardly fair to make me wait until you've finished, is it?"

"Jill, I simply can't tell you what it's about. But I know this: If I could tell you, you'd agree with all your heart that it deserves everything I can give it and then some."

She was looking at him anxiously. "I've never seen you quite so intense. Whatever it is, it has really gotten to you, hasn't it?"

"Yes," he agreed. "It's been a nightmare. I can tell you this much: We've got to find a man—and soon—who is on the verge of committing a terrible crime. Actually, we know quite a bit about him, including letters he's written. We even know he has what he calls 'the faltering hand.' But he's the proverbial will-o'-the-wisp; we just can't put our hands on him."

" 'The faltering hand,' " Jill repeated. "What an odd phrase. What do you think he means?"

"At first we thought he might be referring to a birth defect or something of that sort. But we're pretty sure now that it's a wound he received in Ireland."

"And that still doesn't help?"

"Not so far." He held her eyes steadily. "Jill, please be patient a while longer. Please."

"All right, Tom." She touched his cheek. "Life would be so much simpler—wouldn't it?—if I didn't love you so much."

The swarthy man with thick black hair took a sip of his coffee. "Do you know why this is my favorite restaurant?" he asked. "Just look at that view."

His companion was unimpressed, refusing to turn his head. "I don't have to—I've seen it a thousand times. So we're up on Mount Lycabettus. So that's Athens harbor down there. So who cares? Let's stick to the business at hand. You say the Englishman was here?"

The swarthy man laughed. "The trouble with you, Barcos, is that you have no soul. If it doesn't have to do with money, you're not interested. Yes, the Englishman was here. Two weeks ago. In that very seat you're sitting in, if memory serves me correctly."

"All right, Paul," Barcos said tersely. "He is prepared to go ahead?"

"He is."

"And the price?"

"As I told you on the phone, the price will be fifty thousand drachmas. The initial payment will be ten thousand drachmas. When the job is done, forty thousand more. Is that satisfactory?"

Barcos deliberated for an instant. "It is satisfactory. There still remains the method of payment."

"We discussed that as well. He wanted some time to think it over, but I have his answer now. He wishes it to be in English pounds."

"I would prefer drachmas," Barcos countered. "It would be easier."

"Perhaps," Paul answered smoothly. "But we can't have everything, can we?"

Barcos stared at him sourly. "There is one thing you have omitted to tell me. Your cut."

"The usual, naturally. No more."

"I'll tell you something." Barcos raised a finger in emphasis. "We Greeks are supposed to be tough in a business deal. And we are. But of all of us, I think you are the worst. There is nothing, absolutely nothing, you won't do to gouge out an extra drachma, one way or the other. You've proved that many times. So don't talk piously to me now about 'the usual, no more.' "

"I'm sorry you feel that way. But nothing will be served if we quarrel, right?"

"I suppose not," Barcos agreed reluctantly. "You are empowered by the Englishman to act for him? In all respects?"

"I am."

"Very well. Tell the Englishman we want to proceed with no further delay."

"I will phone him tonight," Paul answered with a satisfied smile.

Haynes awoke from a fitful sleep. The room was still in semidarkness. Moving quietly to avoid waking Jill, he went into the bathroom and began scraping away at his beard. A quick swipe of the razor left a nick at a corner of his mouth. He grimaced in disgust. It was starting out to be another of those days.

Even his cold shower failed to help. Dressing quickly, his head feeling leaden, he let himself out by a side door and began a brisk walk.

The sidewalks were deserted except for an occasional early commuter, bent against the wind, scurrying toward a bus stop. He covered the better part of a mile, sucking in the sharp air avidly. Over and over again, he was probing for the place where they had gone wrong.

He crossed an intersection and paused to adjust a sloppily tied shoelace. All right, he told himself angrily, let's try it again. First of all, we've got a computer list of fifty-six men and we're sure one of them is Achilles. So far, fine. The problem is that it's taking too long to check them through. We've got three days left at the most—maybe less.

Wearily, he slowed his pace. It doesn't take much intelligence to see the problem, he mocked himself. Now how about the solution? More men won't do it. You've thought that through a score of times. For once, focus on something else, try a different approach.

Unaccountably a phrase came into his mind: "For every result there's a cause." All right, he agreed, our result is that it's taking too long to check through our list. What's the cause? That's easy also—there are just too many names on the list to get the job done quickly.

He turned a corner and suddenly stopped. A thought had come into his mind, compelling, demanding to be heard. For several moments he remained inert, concentrating with tremendous intensity. At last he struck one fist against the other and set off at a run.

Half an hour later he was seated in Sir Henry Adams's office. The Assistant Commissioner regarded him hopefully. "You're abroad pretty early, Tom. It's important, I take it."

"It is," Haynes said quickly. "Let me start by asking you why you called me in on this case in the first place."

Adams was puzzled. "You know why. The assassin used an American carbine in his first murder. And there was an American baseball expression in his first letter—a reference to being out after the third strike."

"Precisely. You thought there was an American angle involved. Now let me ask you this: Did we make any use of that information?"

"Not really. It was established very early on that Achilles was British, not American." The Assistant Commissioner leaned forward. "Just what are you getting at?"

Haynes held up a hand. "Bear with me. I'm rechecking my own thinking as we go along. Now then, we come to the specific facts we fed into the computer to get our fifty-six suspects. You remember what they were."

"Of course."

"Let's go over them again. We asked the computer to give us the names of all members of the British armed forces, past or present, who are British males, under fifty in age, tall, probably slender, possibly dark hair, now or formerly an officer or noncom, a crack shot, possibly a classical scholar in Greek mythology, wounded in the fighting in Ireland, physically handicapped as a result, probably a crippled hand. That was it—right?"

"Yes. You've covered it all."

"All right," Haynes said tersely. "Where is there any mention of America? Did we ask the computer anything about the American carbine or the American baseball expression?"

"As you very well know, there just isn't any way we could do that."

"You're absolutely right. But we forgot one thing. That American carbine and baseball reference didn't just come out of nowhere." Haynes clenched a fist in emphasis. "There is one question we could have asked the computer and didn't. Which of the men, at some time in his career, came into contact with the Americans?"

The Assistant Commissioner came upright in his chair. "By God, you're right! It could have been as a military attaché, or an observer in Vietnam, or any number of other assignments.''

"Or he could have been educated in the States," Haynes pointed out. "Or his parents might have lived there for a while. He might even have been born there and acquired British citizenship later.''

"Exactly," Adams agreed animatedly. "But you've put your finger on it—logically, somewhere, somehow, there had to be a connection. Asking the computer to give us that additional information would undoubtedly have cut our list of fifty-six possibles way down.''

"Hopefully to a number we could check through rapidly.''

"I'm sure of it." The Assistant Commissioner flipped the switch of his intercom and snapped an order. "Get Inspector Granby up here immediately.''

The inspector arrived shortly, notebook in hand. He was barely seated before the Assistant Commissioner launched into a quick summary of his conversation with Haynes. Granby listened carefully; gradually his normally dour expression was replaced with a look of excitement.

"It could be the answer," he said as Adams finished. "Fortunately there's no need to feed the names back through the computer. We've got enough information in the service records of each of these men to pick up what we want by a careful sight review.''

"How long will it take?" Adams demanded.

"Not very long," Granby answered grimly. "No more than an hour. I'll simply parcel out the service records of the twenty-four men we haven't eliminated among some of my best men." He stood up quickly. "I'll be back as soon as they've finished. Meanwhile, gentlemen, it might be in order to do a little praying.''

Across the city from Scotland Yard, George Barrett was in the final stages of his planning. Sprawled in his chair, eyes fixed on the ceiling, he painstakingly reviewed

every step he would take. The point on which he dwelled
most was the manner in which he would strike. There
must be no mistake, no way in which his quarry would
escape.

He was under no illusions as to the risk he would run.
The moment he struck, his life might well be at forfeit.
It was not the thought of dying that worried him. After
all, Achilles had perished in battle, and death in combat was honorable. But the thought of failure—that
brought terror to his heart.

The wrongs had been so monstrous, he was remembering. Revenge must not fail; the monarch must die.
Again he went over his plans, searching for any weakness, considering alternatives. Finally, certain that all
was ready, he got up and went into his kitchen to fix his
breakfast.

Outside the window, the day was overcast, with the
dreary grayness that so often blankets London. He fixed
his sausage absently, still going over his plans. When he
had the meal on the table he poured his tea; on an impulse he reached into a cabinet, took out a bottle of
wine, and poured a glass.

As he ate methodically, he took a sip of the wine and
wondered idly what had prompted him to set it out.
Then he remembered, and with the memory there came
a surge of grief. He saw again the cottage in Belgium,
with the lovely face of Marcia across from him. On just
such dreary weekend mornings, they had often had wine
at breakfast, joking that it was their way of defying the
weather, turning dreariness into gaiety.

He stared at the glass of wine and the images followed
one another, each building his agony: the first time he
had seen her, looking like a girl in a Renoir painting . . .
her black hair, curly and cut short . . . walking along the
Left Bank on their Paris honeymoon . . . her faith that
he would one day make his concert debut.

Torn with anguish, trying to blot out the memories,
he hurled the glass into the sink and ran the water to
wash away every drop of the wine. Still the memories

were there. His face was wet with perspiration as he struggled to beat them back, forcing himself to concentrate again on his plans.

Slowly, in what seemed like an endless time, he won his fight. Exhausted, he at last sat quietly, sliding once more into his world where reality merged with Achilles, proud and merciless in his lust for revenge.

His cheeks were still wet with tears as he gazed unseeing, lost in his semicatatonic dream.

Haynes was later to remember the time until Inspector Granby's return as the longest wait in his life. Occasionally he or Adams would make a comment, not caring whether the other responded or not. After a while they gave up even this effort and fell silent, each preoccupied with his thoughts.

The Assistant Commissioner grew restless, and was pacing back and forth aimlessly when Granby suddenly reappeared. He was clearly jubilant, nodding his head in a positive signal.

"We've got two," he announced, holding up his pad. "The first one is a Major James Whitby, forty-four years old. He studied at Harvard for a year, as an exchange student from Cambridge. That would seem to have given him plenty of time to get Americanized, I should think."

"Why haven't we been able to locate him so far?" Adams asked.

"Well, actually, he's still on active duty, stationed in Scotland. They gave him leave three weeks ago, and he's not due back for a bit. They don't have any present address on him really—he simply told them he'd be knocking about, doing some fishing and so on."

"He was stationed in Scotland?" Haynes put in crisply. "The first murder took place in Scotland."

"Right," Granby confirmed. "That struck me too. So I'd say the major is a definite possibility."

"Who's the other one?" the Assistant Commissioner asked.

"Even more of a possibility. Lieutenant Carl Gordon, forty-seven. Spent some months with the Yanks as an observer in Vietnam. Left the service two years ago, and I imagine they must have been just as glad to see him go. A derring-do artist: Always in hot water, reprimanded for gambling on post, for running arrears at the officers' mess—that sort of thing. Fighter pilot."

"How was a fighter pilot wounded in Ireland?" Haynes asked. "There wasn't any air action there."

"True," Granby replied sardonically. "He was mucking about in an off-limits area, drunk, apparently looking to pick up a girl. A sniper dropped him and then a gang got in their licks. If a patrol hadn't heard the shot and come on the double he'd have bought it for sure."

"And now we don't know where he is," Adams commented.

"Correct. When the medics finally got him patched up, he was mustered out at an airfield in Belfast. He did leave a London address for mailing his terminal check and he did pick it up. After that, no trace."

The intercom suddenly buzzed. The Assistant Commissioner leaned over and depressed the switch. "Yes?"

"Sergeant Boles is here with a message for Inspector Granby, sir."

"Bring it in, please."

"Yes, sir." Adams's secretary entered the office and handed the inspector a slip of paper.

Granby glanced at it and then looked up hesitantly. "As long as we were at it, I asked my people to check the files of the thirty-two men on the list we have already eliminated. Just for the record, you might say; whether any of them spent a hitch with the Yanks would be purely academic."

"Nothing like being thorough, is there?" Adams smiled. "You're just living up to your reputation."

"Yes. Well, in any event, one more name turned up. Want me to bother giving you a rundown?"

"Might as well."

"Right." Granby referred to the paper. "Captain

George Barrett. A long tour of duty as liaison with an American section at NATO. Then Ireland. Blown up in a jeep with his CO; the CO was killed. The chap went mental as a result. Spent some time in Belfast in hospital, and then they sent him along to the military hospital here. He's been there ever since, in the psychiatric ward. We verified that—so we've placed him on our eliminated list.''

"Poor bastard." The Assistant Commissioner placed a hand on Granby's shoulder. "Good job, Inspector. As usual."

With Granby gone, Adams sat on the corner of his desk, rhythmically tapping a pencil. "We've got it down to two prime suspects now," he said, "thanks to that brainstorm of yours. Believe me, if we have to tear this island apart piece by piece, we'll find them, and fast."

Haynes nodded. "That Major Whitby in Scotland— the chap on leave—should be the easiest to find."

"I agree. But the fighter pilot really worries me. He's a drifter, and catching up with them can be like trying to bottle smoke." The Assistant Commissioner stood up and resumed his pacing. "Look, Haynes, would you work with my men in tracking them down? That inventive brain of yours might well come in handy."

"I'd like nothing better."

"Good. I appreciate it. One other thing. Aside from Whitby and the pilot there are still twenty-two other men we haven't eliminated. We'll keep going on them, of course."

"That makes sense. We don't have any absolute guarantees that my theory is correct."

"Let's hope that it is," Adams said fervently. "There's no margin for error left. Come, I'll take you down to the men you'll be working with."

Chapter 14

HOPE MARSTON FROWNED, annoyed at her inability to concentrate. For what seemed to her like the tenth time, she reread a paragraph in the book she was reading; again it failed to register. She snapped the book shut impatiently and gazed idly out the window.

The view was spectacular. The lawn of her home, thickened by the Scottish mists, reached to a grove of ancient trees. Beyond them, the hills rose, gently at first, then more steeply, leading like a green-carpeted stairway to the highlands in the distance.

Normally, she enjoyed spending a moment looking at the trees, but this day was different. It seemed to stretch ahead, filled with hours yet to be filled, empty of purpose.

She turned as her maid came into the room. "Mrs. Rogers is here to see you, ma'am," the maid said. "Shall I show her in?"

"Of course," Hope answered. She greeted her neighbor warmly, saw to it that she was made comfortable, and sent for tea.

"I'm on my way into Glasgow to shop," her friend explained. "I thought you might like to come along."

Hope nodded gratefully. "That's a marvelous idea.

Can we stop by Trowbridge's? I've been meaning to get a new coat.''

They spent the day in the city, touring the stores, pleasant behind their soot-blackened facades. Lunch in the oak-paneled St. Enoch Hotel took up a good part of the afternoon; they swapped news, greeted friends who came into the dining room.

It was almost six before Hope was back in her house. Instantly, the moment her friend left, she found herself back in the restless doldrums. Catching up on her correspondence seemed the best way to use up time. Resolutely, she seated herself at her desk, picked up a pen, and spent several minutes staring at a blank sheet of paper.

Finally she crumpled the paper angrily and hurled it into the wastebasket. There just wasn't any sense in trying to blot out what was wrong with her, she admitted grimly. Haynes was in London and she was here, and it was as simple as that. No, it isn't as simple as that, she contradicted herself fearfully; the girl he is living with is also in London—and he will choose between you.

She thought back over their last phone conversation, reminding herself that he was engrossed in a project he could not leave, savoring the tone of his voice when he said he missed her. A picture of him came into her mind—tall, moving gracefully, his features strong and masculine.

She felt the depth of her longing for him and stirred uneasily. Unaccountably, a phrase came into her head— "Faint heart ne'er won fair lady." She rested her head on a hand, and then straightened up quickly, her spirits soaring. There should be another side to that phrase, she reminded herself—faint heart ne'er won a man, either. She thought for a moment and then rang for her maid, her mind made up.

"I'll need your help," she announced. "I'll be leaving for London in the morning."

•   •   •

Sergeant Wilcox shook his head in disgust. "Do you know how many lakes there are in Scotland?" he demanded, putting down a map.

"Thousands," Haynes answered.

"Right. And Major Whitby could be fishing at any one of them. Or maybe he's fishing in England or Wales. Who knows where a chap on leave will go? Talk about a needle in a haystack."

Haynes nodded, thinking that the Assistant Commissioner had chosen well in the men he had assigned to work with him. In the few hours since they had been together, he had developed a deep respect for Wilcox and Sergeant Miller, busy on a nearby phone. Both had shown themselves to be complete professionals, dedicated, quick, untiring.

"As we agreed," Wilcox continued, "I've alerted the communications people to spread the word through the local constabularies. They'll be checking the rental agents in their areas—if Whitby rented a cottage or a fishing camp, we'll know about it soon enough. We've got the word out on his motorcar license plate, too. Or if he calls his military post or any of his friends there, we've got that covered too. All in all, with a spot of luck, we should turn him up soon."

"Good," Haynes said. He turned inquiringly as Sergeant Miller hung up the phone and scribbled some notes. "Any luck?"

"I'm afraid not." Miller's lined face remained impassive. "You were right when you said Gordon would be the tougher of the two to run down. He's not the typical flyboy, that's for sure; any service pilot I ever knew spent half his time drinking with his buddies."

"And Gordon didn't?"

"No. Not from what I've gathered so far. He drank all right, and plenty. He gambled. He womanized. But never with any one of the eight men in his outfit I've talked to."

"They didn't like him?"

"Like him?" Miller snorted. "Five of the eight used the word 'bastard.' One of the others made it 'slimy bastard.' The two remaining opted for 'shit.' Pretty unanimous, I would say.''

"None of them had any idea where he might be now, I take it."

"Not the foggiest."

"So where does that leave us?"

Miller shrugged. "I still have to run through some of the steps we talked over. If they turn up negative, as I rather expect they will, we'll have to go back to the starting line, won't we? We'll need some new approaches."

Haynes absently hooked a foot behind the rung of his chair. "Let's hope something hits before then. Meanwhile, there's something that bothers me. It's that damned American carbine. If either Major Whitby or Lieutenant Gordon is Achilles, he'll have that rifle. It's been used to kill twice. And we don't really know anything about it, do we? At least the most important things."

"I'm afraid I don't follow you," Sergeant Wilcox said. "We know quite a bit about it, I should say."

"Do we? Oh, we know its muzzle velocity and its range. But we don't know how small a bundle it makes when it's disassembled. Or how quickly it can be put back together. Or whether it can be concealed under an overcoat, for instance." Haynes paused and then went on somberly, challenging them. "Before we take Achilles, don't you agree we should know the answer to those questions? That carbine is evidence. Important evidence. We want to know exactly what we're looking for—how it can be hidden, how not. And we certainly don't want him producing it unexpectedly. One of us might be dead."

"I see what you mean," Wilcox agreed.

"You know what?" Haynes said. "I could do with a break—I think it might sweep the cobwebs from my head, maybe give me a chance to do some fresh thinking. There's an officer over at Yeomen of the Guard headquarters—a weapons expert. As a matter of fact, I called on him recently and he was quite helpful. I think

I'll walk over to his office now and see what he can tell me about carbines.''

"Good.''

Haynes hit a brisk pace, enjoying the fall air. Five minutes later he turned into Guard headquarters and made his way through a number of corridors to Lieutenant Stevens's office. He was in luck: the lieutenant was there, unenthusiastically doing paperwork.

"Come on in,'' he called. "You're the chap who was by a few days back, right? Asking about the ax that did Charles I in.'' He shoved his work aside and draped his long legs on a chair. "How's your article coming?''

Haynes remembered he had said he was a writer. "Oh, fine,'' he answered casually. "I've got another one in the works and thought you might give me some help.''

"Glad to, if I can.''

"Are you familiar with the American carbine?''

The lieutenant pondered for a moment. "You mean the one the Yanks used in World War II?''

"That's it.''

"You're writing about that?''

"Yes—plus a number of other World War II weapons,'' Haynes said smoothly. "You do know the carbine, then.''

"Of course—any authentic gun buff would. It was a strange gun, you know. An overgrown pistol, actually. Effective range of only one hundred yards. Poor stopping power. By the way, it's official name was the M1 carbine, not to be confused with its big brother, the M1 Garand rifle. Now that was a gun.''

"You don't think much of the carbine, I gather.''

"I didn't say that,'' the lieutenant said. "For what it was supposed to do, it wasn't half-bad. It was designed to replace the handgun for troops that wouldn't usually be firing a rifle. Tank men, for instance. Or service troops that wouldn't be on the front line. But some combat noncoms and officers used them, too. The idea was that the carbine had a bit more firepower than the pistol, without the bulky size and weight of a rifle.''

"You say it didn't have much stopping power. What do you mean specifically?"

"Oh, it could kill. Don't make any mistake about that." The lieutenant smiled thinly. "But even though it fired a thirty-caliber bullet, it was propelled by only one hundred ten grains of powder. Compare that with the Garand's hundred fifty grains of powder, producing catastrophic impact power. A world of difference, isn't there?"

"How long was the carbine overall?"

"Better you should ask how short it was. As the Yanks measure, it was only about thirty inches long— roughly seventy-six centimeters. The barrel was eighteen inches—forty centimeters."

"Not very bulky, was it?" Haynes commented. "How long would you say it would take to disassemble or assemble?"

"Thirty seconds at the most. Move the barrel band forward, take the hand guard off, lift out the barrel and receiver, and presto, you're done. Reverse the process and it's back together. Simple."

Haynes unconsciously moved forward on his chair. "If it were taken apart and wrapped in a package," he asked softly, "how big would that package be?"

The lieutenant looked at him with intense interest. "That's a peculiar question to ask. Why would you want to know that?"

"Well, it would be one way of showing how compact the gun was, wouldn't it?" Haynes pointed out.

"Yes, I suppose it would. Let's see." The lieutenant thought for an instant. "Your package would be about twenty-four inches long—sixty centimeters. Say three inches wide—seven and one-half centimeters. Not very big at all."

"One last question. How many carbines are there around today?"

"They're collectors' items, of course. But you'll run across the occasional one in a gun shop. Ammo's easy to come by, even though it's low grain."

"Lieutenant, thanks very much." Haynes extended

his hand. "This is the second time you've helped me. I owe you."

"No problem," the lieutenant said cheerfully. "Listen, I remember seeing a detailed description of the carbine recently in one of the gun magazines. If I run across it, I'll drop it in the post. What's your address?"

"Thirty-four Lacey Square. I'll appreciate it." Haynes left and walked slowly toward the exit, gloomily picturing the small package a wrapped carbine would make.

The fisherman ran a hand through his close-cropped blond hair and squinted at the sun. It had climbed almost halfway to its zenith and seemed to hang there, a cold yellow ball almost obscured by drifting clouds.

Ten o'clock, he judged. There didn't seem to be much point in hanging about, braving the chill that was beginning to invade his limbs. The fish had long since stopped biting; fully an hour had gone by since his last nibble. Reeling in his line, he stowed his gear and set off through the woods, moving briskly to get his blood circulating.

The trail led almost straight upward, away from the lake. Resolutely pushing aside branches, he kept to his pace, emerging at the crest of the hill somewhat breathless but much warmer. Pausing for a moment, he looked down toward his cabin, several hundred yards away at the bottom of a valley. He was startled to see a car pulled up next to his Rover; all but hidden, its front end barely protruded from a clump of trees.

Setting off at a half trot, grateful that it was downhill, he quickly covered the distance to the clearing. As he emerged from the undergrowth, two men in constables' uniforms came quickly to meet him.

"Major Whitby?"

"That's right. What am I supposed to have done, Constable? Robbed the local bank?"

The taller of the two officers regarded him unsmilingly, wondering how many times he had heard the weak joke before. "You'll be good enough to come with us, sir."

Whitby felt a flash of irritation. "Where? And what for?"

The constable examined him implacably. "As to the where, sir, the local police station. As to the why, we've got orders to detain you pending further instructions."

"On what charge, damn it?" Whitby exploded.

"We are not charging you, sir." The constable relented somewhat. "Look, Major, we were told to check our area and see if anyone of your name had rented facilities. You had, and we're here. I promise you this: When we get back to town, I'll ring up immediately and see what's to be done with you next."

"Who are these people you'll be ringing up?" Whitby demanded angrily.

"London CID, sir." The constable eyed him speculatively. "If you've done nothing wrong, you've nothing to worry about, have you now?"

When the call from Scotland came in, Haynes took it and was on his way in thirty seconds. He managed to put together a commercial flight to Carlisle and a fast drive in a rented car to arrive at the police station late in the afternoon.

There he discovered a fuming Major Whitby, his temper escalating with the passage of every hour. "What the hell do you want of me?" he yelled. "I've got a right to know, and by God it had better be good."

"Sit down, Major," Haynes replied calmly. "We've got some talking to do."

Before a quarter of an hour had passed, Haynes knew the man across from him, still glowering belligerently, was not Achilles. No, the major snapped, he had not left the town since he had come here. Yes, he could prove it. Every evening he had driven into town for a quiet whiskey at the local pub. Furthermore, just to carry it a bloody point further, he could point out a couple of fishermen who had hailed him every day.

Haynes was satisfied. "All right," he said, "you're obviously not the man we want. But I'm not going to apologize to you, Major. You're in the military. You should understand necessity—and it was necessary that we find you and eliminate you as a possibility."

Whitby was beginning to thaw. "I see what you mean," he said grudgingly, and then smiled. "I'll make you a bargain. Just tell me what the whole flap is about, and we'll call it no hard feelings."

"That I can't do," Haynes answered.

The major nodded. "Very well. I'll respect that." He got to his feet. "It's a bit early, but I believe I'll look in at the pub. Seems to me I've earned a spot or two."

Haynes arrived back in London feeling drained from lack of sleep. As he opened the office door he almost bumped into Sergeant Miller, who was hurriedly struggling into his overcoat.

"Nothing doing on Major Whitby," Haynes greeted him disconsolately. "Waste of time."

"I know. Wilcox told me you phoned in." The sergeant, impassive face animated for once, spoke rapidly. "We've got something new here though. You remember I talked to some of the flying officers who served with Lieutenant Gordon?"

"Sure. None of them knew where he might be."

"Correct. But one of them rang up not five minutes ago. He had dinner with a friend and was telling him about Gordon; the friend insists he saw him at a gambling club in the West End not two nights ago."

"He knew the name of the place?"

"Aces Up Club. He was positive."

"Let's go." Haynes reversed course, his weariness gone.

The Aces Up Club perched at the end of a narrow street, a two-story building incongruously tucked between two imposing residences. Inside, the entrance hall was opulent, with a deep-piled orange rug, polished mahogany period pieces, and a gleaming grandfather's clock. A heavyset man in a dinner jacket welcomed them with courtly dignity; only a slight narrowing of his eyes suggested he had guessed this was no ordinary visit.

"Carl Gordon?" he repeated in answer to Miller's question. "No need to ask if he's been in recently, sir. As a matter of fact he joined our staff last Friday. He's on his break now—you'll find him in the lounge, down the stairs and first door on the right."

There was only one occupant in the lounge, a good-looking man in his early forties, puffing on a cigar and leaning back in a leather chair.

"CID, Mr. Gordon," Miller explained. "Do you have a few moments?"

Gordon looked him up and down coldly. "Should I have?"

"We think so."

"Well, I don't." Gordon studiously blew a cloud of cigar smoke. "I'm on my break. See me some other time. Let's say on December twenty-fifth."

Haynes stepped forward. "I haven't had the pleasure of shaking hands with you, Mr. Gordon." He reached out and took Gordon's free hand in his, moving it up and down, slowly exerting a crushing pressure.

"Jesus Christ," Gordon cried in agony, yanking his hand away. "What the shit's wrong with you?"

"Nothing that a quiet chat wouldn't cure," Haynes replied evenly. "Let's make this the first question— where were you before you started working here last Friday? In London?"

"Look, I've got my rights, same as anybody else," Gordon complained petulantly.

Haynes studied the soft face, china-blue eyes widened innocently and lips twisted in a grimace. This is my day for difficult interviews, he was thinking. "All we want is a few answers," he said, managing to sound affable. "If they're the right ones we can wind this up in nothing flat. Fair enough?"

"Why not?" Gordon said, trying to muster up his earlier bravado. "You wanted to know where I was before I started working here. All right—in Canada. I flew back here last Wednesday. BOAC."

"Canada? What were you doing there?"

Gordon shrugged, wagging a hand expressively. "A little bit of this, a little bit of that."

"Not good enough," Haynes snapped. "This isn't game-playing time. What the hell were you doing in Canada?"

Gordon eyed him with a return of apprehension. "Same as I'm doing here," he answered sullenly. "Running the poker game."

"What club?"

"The Royal Flush. In Toronto."

"They'll vouch you were there until last week?"

"Of course. Besides, Marie was with me."

"Who's she?"

"We were living together in Canada, and she decided to come along when I came home. She hooked on in this joint, too—deals the twenty-one table upstairs."

Sergeant Miller was curious. "You decided to leave Canada in a hurry, I gather. How come?"

"There was a misunderstanding at the Royal Flush," Gordon replied hesitantly. "The stupid bastards accused me of skimming. I quit—I don't have to take bullshit like that."

"Why should you indeed?" Haynes commented dryly. He turned to Sergeant Miller. "Suppose I keep our friend here company while you look into his story."

While the sergeant was gone, Gordon maintained an angry silence. Haynes was preoccupied; his weariness had returned, deeper than ever. He had believed Gordon's account, and now for the first time despair was crowding in upon him, leaden, not to be denied.

It seemed a century before Sergeant Miller returned and drew him to one side. "He's telling the truth," the sergeant said regretfully. "The Yard got onto Toronto and talked with the people at the Club there. They tell a different version than this bastard does about why he left, but the point is he was there when he says he was. His girl Marie confirms it too. And the Yard checked BOAC; he was on their flight from Toronto last Wednesday."

"Then that settles it," Haynes said bitterly. "He couldn't have been in England when the murders occurred."

"I'm afraid not."

Haynes found it difficult to face Gordon. "Very well," he managed finally. "We accept what you've told us. We'll be on our way."

Gordon's insolence was back. "Just a minute," he blustered loudly, "don't think you can come charging in here and push me around. Now I'm going to tell you a few things, chum."

"Are you now?" Haynes said softly, turning back from the door. "Like what?"

Gordon saw his expression and wavered. "Forget it," he replied grudgingly. "Who gives a fuck?"

Sergeant Miller nudged Haynes as they were making their way through the gaming room toward the lobby. "Take a look over there in the corner. That's Marie."

Haynes saw an exquisite blonde wearing a white sheath at the twenty-one table. She was dealing the cards automatically, and returning his glance with an appreciative, inviting stare.

"I guess it pays to be a bastard," Miller sighed. "If that's a sample."

It was three o'clock when Haynes entered his flat. He undressed quietly, careful not to disturb Jill. She was sleeping restlessly, one arm outflung, her brow wrinkled. Sliding into bed, he felt the welcome comfort of the sheets; his last conscious thought was a sickening realization that he had failed.

At six o'clock he was up and with his breakfast made. The blackness of his mood was still with him, intensified by a call he had made to the Yard. The Assistant Commissioner had commiserated with him on the events of the previous day. "It's even worse than you might think," he had added disconsolately. "You remember there were twenty-two others on the original list we hadn't eliminated. Yesterday we managed to rule out ten more, so we're down to twelve. To tell you the truth, I'm beginning to doubt Achilles ever was on our list. God help us if I'm right—we've got nothing else."

Now, Haynes was suffering the full attack of his

despair. His coffee untouched, he clenched his hand in tension. Who was this Achilles, this man who could kill at will, who could threaten the Throne itself, who taunted and defied with impunity?

There were but two days left of the time the assassin had given them. At any minute, he could strike. Haynes could almost feel his presence in the city, waiting, vengeful.

Hardest of all to withstand was the hopeless knowledge that the end of the string had been reached. There was nothing further to do, no further avenue he could conceive that might bring success. He could not yet accept the fact that Whitby or Gordon had not been their man. He had been so sure that isolating those on the list who had been with the Americans, who had had the opportunity to learn about the American carbine and baseball, would be the all-important last link. But you were wrong, he blamed himself angrily.

The day stretched ahead of him, with no way to fill it. You're wrong, he contradicted himself sardonically— there is one way. There is a third man besides Whitby and Gordon who had served with the Americans. True, he has already been eliminated: Captain George Barrett, wounded in Ireland, verified as being in the psychiatric ward of the military hospital.

But you're looking for something to fill time, he goaded himself. Why don't you go and satisfy yourself that Barrett is not your man? After all, you've always insisted on seeing facts firsthand. Admit it, when you come right down to it, in any investigation you've always trusted only yourself.

In the end, he downed his coffee and munched his toast mechanically. All right, he said to himself, you win. At least it's something to do.

The administrator of the Military Hospital, all business, spoke crisply. "You wanted to see me, Mr. Haynes?"

"Yes. Thanks for taking the time."

"That's what I'm here for," the administrator replied with professional courtesy. He moved the nameplate on his desk half an inch, adjusting it to his liking.

Lieutenant Colonel Harrison Arleigh Manley was a meticulous man. He insisted on using his full name, on his nameplate, on his stationery, every place where it might be even remotely appropriate. It seemed to him this was only logical: Arleigh was part of his name, and therefore should be included.

A similar preoccupation with detail had stood him in good stead throughout his military career. From the beginning, he had known his forte would never be in leading troops; making the best of it, he had concentrated on developing his administrative skills, which were considerable. In due time he had served his apprenticeship with the Quartermaster Corps and then switched to hospital administration, where his ability to grasp detail and to work hard had brought steady progress.

"How may I help you?" he asked now.

Haynes explained his association with the CID. "You have a patient here—a Captain George Barrett," he added. "I'd like to ask you about him."

The administrator was surprised. "There was a CID sergeant here three days ago. What's the problem?"

"We don't know that there is any problem. Tell me this—how is Captain Barrett progressing?"

"As I understand it, some headway has been made. But these traumatic cases are difficult—he has a long row ahead. He was badly wounded in Ireland, you know."

"I know," Haynes replied. "I take it from what you say that the captain has been confined here without interruption."

"I'm not sure I understand."

"He hasn't been granted leave, for example? To visit his family, or perhaps friends?"

The administrator responded with a thinly concealed irritation. "Mr. Haynes, the sergeant asked me the same question. I told him no leave had been granted."

Something had caught Haynes's attention. There was a defensiveness, carefully controlled, but present. He was sure of it. He took an instant to think, and then bored in. "Colonel, has Captain Barrett been out of the hospital for any reason since he came here?"

"I told you no leave had been granted," the administrator answered icily. "If there is nothing further, there are people waiting."

"That's not what I asked you," Haynes said, certain that his feeling had been right. "Has he been out of the hospital for any reason?"

There was one lesson Colonel Manley had learned in his army years: Never leave your neck exposed when it becomes obvious it might be chopped off. "Could I ask something, Mr. Haynes?" he asked worriedly. "Is Captain Barrett suspected of having done anything illegal?"

Haynes was implacable. "Once again, for the third time, has Captain Barrett been out of the hospital?"

The administrator nodded tensely. "Yes." He bent forward and tried to smile ingratiatingly. "Look, Mr. Haynes, the sergeant said his inquiry was routine. The fact that you're here tells me it wasn't. That puts a different light on matters, doesn't it?"

Suddenly Haynes was rigid, concentrating with every fiber. "How many times has Captain Barrett left this hospital? When? For how long at a time?" His questions hammered home with cold, staccato force.

There was an instant when the adminstrator didn't reply. An unmistakable fear came into his face; nervously he rubbed the top of his desk, then clasped his hands. "He isn't here," he said weakly.

Haynes stared at him, holding his excitement in check. "What do you mean?" he demanded. "Where is he?"

"I'm afraid I don't know." The administrator reddened visibly. "He'd been permitted to go into the city for a few hours at a time. Twenty-two days ago he didn't return on time."

''And you've heard nothing from him since?''

The administrator's voice was almost inaudible. ''No.''

Haynes was incredulous. ''Then why in hell did you tell the CID he was here?''

''Please, Mr. Haynes.'' The administrator was pleading now. ''You must understand, psychiatry is not an exact science. We do give patients permission to go into the city or home as a means of helping them to return to reality. Occasionally, a patient does return late. But the senior psychiatrist doesn't want that advertised, so to speak. It might look—''

''Inefficient? Incompetent?'' Haynes interrupted coldly.

''No, sir, it's not that,'' the administrator floundered. ''Besides, the patients do return, you know.''

''Always?''

''Well, I must admit there was one incident where a patient did commit suicide. But we're dealing with sick minds—there are no certainties.''

Haynes was seething. ''You took it upon yourself to conceal from the CID that Barrett was gone. Surely you realize how serious that is.''

The administrator, close to panic, stared at him helplessly. ''The senior psychiatrist didn't want late returns mentioned,'' he implored. ''That is his policy, not mine. Besides, when the CID was here, I was still hoping Barrett would be back. Believe me, I've mentioned the matter to the doctor several times since.''

''Where did Barrett go when he went into the city?'' Haynes asked sharply.

''I wouldn't know that. I'm sure the senior psychiatrist will.''

''Then get him here. Now.''

''Of course.'' The administrator jumped to his feet and headed for the door. ''Better if I get him myself. If he's not in his office, I usually know where to find him.''

And you'll have a chance to brief him, Haynes

thought cynically. He waited with impatience until the administrator returned with a stocky man wearing a white physician's coat. "I'm Dr. Coleman," the stocky man said with assurance. "Colonel Manley tells me we've got a bit of a problem."

"No, we haven't got a problem," Haynes corrected him icily. "You've got a problem."

The doctor was startled, but recovered instantly. "A hostile attitude won't help, Mr. Haynes—it is Mr. Haynes, isn't it?"

"Sit down, Doctor. And listen hard." Haynes looked at him steadily. "I have one advantage over you. I know why the CID is interested in Captain Barrett, and you don't. Nor am I about to tell you. But it is a grave matter—extraordinarily grave. Believe me, it will be to your advantage to stop treating me like one of your patients and do everything in your power to help me. Do I make myself clear?"

The doctor measured him thoughtfully. "I understand," he said. "What do you want to know?"

"You gave Captain Barrett permission to go into London from time to time. You must know where he went. Was it his family, for instance?"

"No. His father died some years back, and he is estranged from his wife. There just isn't any family." The doctor half closed his eyes, concentrating. "He would visit a retired history professor—let's see, his name was Chatwin, Robert Chatwin. As part of his therapy, I was encouraging Captain Barrett to write a book. He was interested in history—especially Greek history."

"Believe me, I know," Haynes answered. "What is Professor Chatwin's address?"

"Offhand I can't recall. But there's a record in my office, of course."

"Before we get it, take a look at this." Haynes reached into the file he had brought with him and drew out a photograph. "Is this a good likeness of Captain Barrett?"

The doctor studied the photograph intently. "No, it isn't. This must have been taken a good many years ago."

"Yes. It's an ID photo from his service record. Taken at his first post—Gibraltar. We don't have anything more recent."

"Pity. In the first place, he's wearing a beard here. He's clean-shaven now; his hair is different too. And he's so much older, of course." The doctor shook his head. "But it's more than that, actually. There are some things in his face now that aren't here; he's taken bad bumps over the years, you know." He handed the photograph back. "No, I would never recognize him from this. Never."

Haynes accompanied the doctor to his office and got Professor Chatwin's address. He then asked for a room where he might telephone privately. Waiting for his call to the Assistant Commissioner to go through, he took note of his lack of elation. Instead, there was a grim awareness that the danger was still there—the assassin still stalking his prey.

Sir Adams came on the line. "Yes?"

"I know who Achilles is," Haynes said quietly.

Robert Chatwin was a lively man in his early seventies whose only visible handicap was a stiffness in his legs. Hobbling to a Chippendale table placed against a wall, he picked up a decanter and began to pour a drink, gazing at his visitor with a lifted eyebrow. "Let me know when it's your size."

"Stop right there," Haynes replied. "That will be fine."

Chatwin frowned. "Hardly enough to wet your throat." He poured a second drink twice the size of the first, passed Haynes his glass, and settled down in an overstuffed chair. "Now that we've seen to the amenities," he said, sitting back comfortably, "we can have our talk."

Haynes had sensed from the outset that the professor

would do things at his own pace, refusing to be hurried. "Very well, Professor," he said, taking a polite sip of his drink. "You said you know Captain Barrett?"

"You quote me accurately." Chatwin smiled. "Which is more than I can say for most of the articles written about me in my teaching days. What do you want to know about him?"

"When did you see him last?"

"Now that's a curious thing. He was in the habit of stopping by maybe a couple of times a week. Very enjoyable too, I must say. The chap knows his subject."

"When was he last here?" Haynes prompted gently.

"Must be two or three weeks, I should judge." The professor eyed him curiously over the rim of his glass. "I must say I never knew the CID is interested in history. You did say you represent the CID?"

"I did. Actually, our reason for wanting to talk with him has nothing to do with history."

"Oh." Chatwin shrugged, as if to register his perplexity at the ways of officialdom.

"Have you heard from him by phone?"

"No."

Haynes persisted hopefully. "Did he ever mention anything that might help us to find him now? Any friends with whom he might be staying? Any hotel he particularly liked? That sort of thing."

"No, no," Chatwin responded. "I had no idea where he lived; I could care less."

"He never mentioned the hospital?"

"Hospital?" Chatwin echoed in bewilderment. "Why should he talk about the hospital? He was discharged, of course, or else he couldn't have been coming to see me."

Haynes masked his disappointment with their talk behind a smile. "You've been most kind, Professor. I'm going to leave my number. If you should hear from Captain Barrett, please see if you can find out where he's staying. Then get in touch with me promptly. Will you do that?"

"I will."

"No need to mention my visit to him." Haynes got ready to leave. "You won't forget to let me know? It's very important."

The professor looked offended. "No, I won't forget. I'm not quite senile, Mr. Haynes." There was a quick glint of amusement in his eyes. "I can quote Plato for half an hour without notes. Can you do that, Mr. Haynes?"

"No, sir, I cannot."

"I didn't think so," the old man answered smugly, taking a long pull at his drink.

Paul snapped his fingers imperiously. The waiter scurried over, took the check and his money, and headed for the cashier. Waiting for his change, Paul relaxed, surveying the panorama of Athens spread far beneath him. Heaven can contain no view more beautiful, he was thinking: the sweep of Mount Lycabettus down to the neatly arranged streets bordering the bay beyond, the sky a vibrant blue.

Leaving a modest tip, he reluctantly left the restaurant and took the cablecar down to street level. Hailing a taxi, he returned to his office and settled down behind his desk. It was time to try the Englishman again.

This time, to his relief, the phone was picked up after three rings. "Barrett?" the Greek asked anxiously.

"Yes."

"Paul here."

"I know." The voice sounded listless.

"I've been trying to get you. I saw Barcos; we're set to go ahead."

"The deal is off," George said. "It is no longer possible."

"Off?" the Greek yelled in anguish. "What do you mean, off?"

"Things have changed. There is nothing I can do."

"You listen to me," the Greek exploded. "You write me three weeks ago. You tell me you want to buy a house in Athens—fast. I bust my balls. I find exactly the kind of place you want at the right price. You even come here two weeks ago and tell me to wrap the deal up. And now you calmly tell me the deal is off! Bullshit!''

"I'm sorry."

"You're sorry! What am I supposed to tell that bastard Barcos? I hate the son of a bitch, but he owns the house you wanted, so I put up with his crap to make the deal. What kind of a fool do you take me for?''

"Look," George said, "I'll send you a check for the commission you would have earned. I know you put in a lot of effort."

There was a pause while the Greek assimilated this. "That's very generous of you," he answered with relief. "Are you sure you won't be able to go ahead with the deal? You were so eager."

"It is no use," George answered dispiritedly. "I believed I would be coming into a great deal of money; it was my dream to spend the rest of my life in Greece. Those things will not happen."

The Greek tried for a suitable sympathetic note. "Perhaps you are mistaken. It may yet work out." He switched to a positive tone. "You won't forget to send the check? Oh, and if at some point later on you're in the market again, you'll keep me in mind, won't you?"

"I doubt if I shall ever see Greece again," George said.

It seemed to Jill that her misery came in waves. During the day, when she was busy at her job, she tried hard to hold her thoughts at bay. But even then, she would suddenly be overwhelmed with the agonizing knowledge that her life had been turned upside down.

The nights were worse. With Haynes away many nights, she formed a mental picture of him together with Lady Marston; yet she knew this was not so. Unmistakably, his total concentration was on the project that seemed to absorb his every waking moment.

She could see in him a deep weariness, and a frustration that steadily grew greater. But he would not let up:

She heard him rising quietly before daylight and returning home long after midnight.

Once or twice, in an effort to forget her own worries, she speculated on his search. A man must be found, she remembered him saying, before a terrible crime was committed—a man who described himself as having a faltering hand. Much was known about him, apparently, yet he had still managed to remain free. "The faltering hand"—the phrase seemed to her strange and compelling, challenging her imagination.

But suddenly the wave of her own misery would sweep over her again, driving away everything else. She would sit motionless, a storm of jealousy and fear rising to a frenzy within her, building an overwhelming anxiety that tortured her mercilessly.

From the moment she had first seen Tom, she kept thinking, he had been her life. It was not possible to conceive of a time when he would not be with her—but that time could be very near at hand. Time and again, she would be attacked by an image of him making love with Hope Marston, happy with the choice he had made, beginning a new life. Finally, her hands shaking, a sick lump in her throat, she would force herself to do some household chore; the misery would recede to a constant pain before it returned in fury to wash over her again.

She did not fault him. She knew him so well, and so sensed the turmoil that must be in him too. From the outset, his sense of fairness and decency had always been such a part of him. But she would not want him to remain because of that—love could not be controlled, and without his happiness there could be none for her.

There came a night when she decided not to remain with him any longer. To do so would not be fair to either of them. His choice should be made freely, uninfluenced by her presence, without any further discussion between them. He must make his choice through love—not through sympathy.

The next day—her mind made up—she acted quickly. A few discreet inquiries uncovered a flat that might suit her needs. She planned to look in on it after work, and if it proved satisfactory, to pack her things and move that night. She did not consider telling him in advance. Her resolution must not be tested, or it would weaken. A note left for him, giving her reasons, would have to suffice. Her heart heavy, she knew one request it must make: that he not see her until his choice was made, and only then if he had chosen her.

"It's for you," Sergeant Wilcox said, holding out the phone.

Haynes recognized the cultured accent of Professor Chatwin even through the slurring imparted by several drinks. Instantly he was alert, unconsciously sitting straight up.

"What is it, Professor?" he asked urgently.

"I told you I wouldn't forget," Chatwin announced cheerfully. "You wanted me to call. Here I am."

"You've seen Barrett?" Haynes waited tautly.

"No, no, I haven't seen him," Chatwin answered with infuriating slowness. "But he did ring me up. Not ten minutes ago."

"You found out where he lives?"

"Regretfully, no." A slight pause followed, and an unmistakable sound of swallowing. "Bell makes a great whiskey—you know that? No, I don't know where he lives. I asked him twice, and if I do say so I believe I did it circumspectly." Chatwin chuckled. "Maybe you should find a place for me at the CID."

"But he didn't tell you," Haynes said quickly.

"Didn't even acknowledge the question. Just kept on talking."

"He's coming to see you?"

"No."

"Then why did he call?"

"Now that's a curious thing," the professor replied. "He started out by thanking me for all the help I had given him—our discussions and so on. It almost sounded as if he might be going away."

"Is he?"

"I don't think so." Chatwin took a long moment to answer. "This may sound a bit like the pot calling the kettle black, but the chap seemed to be a mite in his cups. At times I'd swear he was babbling—he didn't make all that much sense."

"How do you mean?"

"It's hard to say exactly. Oh, after he got through thanking me, he started talking about Greek mythology. That's when he sounded confused." Chatwin hesitated. "Perhaps confused isn't the right word. Actually, he talked at times as if he believes he is Achilles. But of course I must have misunderstood him. He'd have to be bonkers to think that, wouldn't he?"

"Yes. What else did he say?"

Chatwin responded with firm conviction. "Now that's the oddest thing of all. Just before he rang off, he told me he'd be in the papers tomorrow evening. He was absolutely sure of it. Tomorrow evening."

"Why?" Haynes almost shouted.

"Of course I asked that. He answered by saying something about a procession. Wait—give me a minute to think."

There was a maddening pause until Chatwin resumed triumphantly. "I have it now. It was something like 'They'll have their procession tomorrow noon, but they don't know I'll be in it, do they?' It sounded as if he was amused or boasting."

"That was the end of the conversation?"

"Except for one thing. I said I didn't understand and he answered with a quotation:

> Think not, my foes, that sacrifice
> Of bulls, or other rich device—
> Shall curb my vengeance-hungry blade!
> An ample blood-price must be paid,
> For those who with Patroclus died.

"Do you recognize those words, Mr. Haynes?"

"No," Haynes replied abstractedly, thinking hard.

"They were spoken by Achilles. The night before he revenged the death of his friend Patroclus."

Haynes didn't reply. His heart was pounding. With dread certainty, he had suddenly realized where and when the assassin would strike.

Chapter 15

NIGHT HAD COME to London, and the city was changing into its evening costume. Piccadilly Circus was ablaze with neon signs—their multicolored flashings reflected from the tops of endlessly circling cars and buses. From the statue of Eros in the center of the Circus Haymarket Street stretched to the southeast. Along its length, restaurants, snack bars, and theaters were beginning to welcome the night's customers, disgorging from taxis and the underground.

In Mayfair, the smart townhouses and apartments were gala with arriving dinner and cocktail guests; in Soho the city's poor had already finished their simple meals. Along Oxford Street, the great department stores were closed, their artfully lit windows displaying furs, jewelry, and furniture.

The Thames flowed through the city, its waters dark in the moonlight, bending sharply at Southwick to pass under the Westminster Bridge. Looming on its bank, the Houses of Parliament made an imposing bulk; its windows were dark except for the occasional light of a late-working member.

This night, among the millions who thronged the London streets and peopled the houses, there were some who were wrapped in their own thoughts and others who met in conference. . . .

Hope Marston was unpacking her bag in the quiet elegance of the Hotel Connaught. She hung her dresses in the wardrobe carefully, examining each with a critical eye, trying to decide which one would be most suitable for tonight.

It must be very special, that was certain. All the way down from Scotland, she had been planning how she would greet Haynes, what she would say to him later. All right, she had said to herself, you're clever. How do you tell a man that you are now embarked on an all-out campaign to marry him? You don't, her feminine logic had counseled. Instead, you should remain in London, see him constantly, love him, until he raises the question.

Now, sure of her course, she picked a dress that had the right combination of simplicity and allure. She laid it carefully on the bed and sat down at the dressing table. With deliberate strokes, she brushed her hair, approving its black gleam. Appraisingly, she surveyed the reflection in her mirror: dark, challenging eyes, lustrous skin, a faultless figure. You have a great deal to work with, she congratulated herself happily.

She debated whether to draw her bath or wait for Haynes to call. An hour earlier, when she had checked in, she had phoned his office. Mr. Haynes was out, she had been informed, but they were expecting to hear from him. Would she like to leave word?

Glancing at her watch, she decided he would be calling at any moment; but she would hear the ring if she left the bathroom door open. Slipping out of her robe, she filled the tub and stepped into the scented water. Its soft warmth gradually produced a state of euphoria, and she lay back, completely relaxed, deliciously daydreaming of the night to come.

In her semisomnolent state she had no sense of the passage of time. But as the water slowly cooled, she roused herself and reached for a towel. In the living room of the suite she again checked the time and was startled to see it was almost half-past eight.

What could be keeping him? Swiftly she dialed the number of his office, hoping someone was still there to give him her message. With relief, she heard the ring answered immediately.

"Yes?" The feminine voice was brisk, efficient.

"This is Hope Marston. Have you heard from Mr. Haynes?"

"We did, Lady Marston. We gave him your message."

Hope frowned. "How long ago did Mr. Haynes call, please?"

"Not five minutes after you rang us up before."

She hesitated. "By any chance, did he say when he would be calling me?"

"No, I'm sorry, Lady Marston. He left no return word."

She hung up slowly. Disbelieving, she was realizing that more than an hour had passed since he had gotten her message. Half-annoyed, half-worried, she absently began to dress.

"Good night, Lieutenant."

"Good night," the officer replied mechanically. He watched the departing back of his orderly, and then relaxed in his chair, returning to his pondering.

In his small office at Yeomen of the Guard headquarters, he was concentrating on his conversation with Haynes, trying to remember the American's specific questions. They had all related to the American carbine, of course: its size, its firepower, how small a package the dismantled rifle would make. Some of them had struck him as odd at the time, not the kind of material a writer would need for an article. Yet Haynes had stated that as his purpose.

His thoughts went further back to the first time Haynes had come to him. The questions then had been about the ax that beheaded Charles I, and later about medieval axes—how easily they could be obtained, and where. Those too had been strange questions.

He shifted his position and continued to meditate. When he had inquired how Haynes had obtained his name as a weapons expert, the answer had been from the CID. How would a writer be connected to the CID? he wondered. The more he deliberated, the more he was certain: Haynes must be associated in some manner with the CID. The thought had occurred to him earlier, but now there could be no doubt.

With the certainty, he reached in his drawer for the slip of paper on which he had noted Haynes's address. He had offered to send him an article detailing the merits of the carbine, but now the matter was more urgent. He had something further to tell him—something important. With Haynes in the CID, it was vital that he see him at once. He studied the address. Thirty-Four Lacey Square. Not that far away at all.

Getting up quickly, he picked up his overcoat, turned out the light, and left.

The National Affairs Editor of the London *Times* was wishing he hadn't eaten Dover sole for dinner. For some reason he had never isolated, it never failed to bring a slight queasiness; tonight—with his incoming basket piled high with unedited copy—the feeling was more acute.

He rubbed his ample stomach lightly and regarded his assistant with a testy glare. "A fine help you are," he groused, gesturing toward the stack of copy. "Couldn't you have gotten through more of this stuff?"

The assistant sighed, accurately diagnosing the source of the complaint. "Your stomach's acting up again, I see," he answered patiently. "You seem to have forgotten you had me researching the Manchester by-election."

"I know, I know." The editor waved a hand imperiously. "The load's heavy enough now, but tomorrow will be even worse. That damned opening of Parliament ceremony—it's hard to believe it's that time again.''

"How many times will this make you've covered it?"

"Let's see. My first time was in 1960. Jesus, I'm getting old—right?" The editor shook his head wearily. "Every year, the same damned procession. The same bloody pomp and circumstance. The same bloody speech, when you come right down to it. Why the hell don't they just start the sessions without all the folderol? Besides, I'm put to the trouble of writing a story every time. The same damned story, I might add.''

"Maybe the procession tomorrow will be different." The assistant grinned. "Who knows?"

"I'll bet," the editor answered sourly. "I'll just bet."

New Scotland Yard was a command post, flashing orders, receiving reports, in the all-out citywide search. Hundreds of bobbies, elite men all, scrutinized the faces of passersby, mentally comparing them to the photograph in their pocket. Teams of detectives were contacting every rental agency in the city, checking every hotel, every rooming house. Newspaper reporters, and radio and television newsmen, had been summoned to the CID.

All of the searchers had been told the identity of the man they sought: George Acton Barrett. None had been told why he was wanted, except that the reason was of the most urgent national priority.

At the center of the vast effort, Assistant Commissioner Sir Henry Adams was closeted with his top aides. Despite the ordeal he had borne for so long, he issued directions with crisp authority; the most critical moments had arrived, and with them a new inflow of energy.

He listened to an inspector and shook his head adamantly. "No, I don't care how insistent the reporters are. Why we want Barrett must remain our business for the moment—and only ours."

The inspector nodded. "I've told them and told them

that, sir. But you know how they push. Two of them are saying they won't even run Barrett's photo tomorrow morning. They're demanding more information.''

"They'll get nothing," Adams snapped. "And tell them, unless they cooperate, I'll deal with them personally when this is over."

Another aide claimed his attention. "That possible identification reported by a patrolman in the East End turned out to be a negative, sir."

"Very well." Adams turned to Haynes with a grimace. "I'd feel a lot better if we had a decent photo to work with. That service shot of Barrett is useless—too damned old."

"True," Haynes agreed. "I don't think we'll ever nail him that way. But he's got to eat and sleep and live just like the rest of us. Somebody is bound to remember him—a restaurant where he goes, maybe, or a hotel clerk, or a store."

"If only he had some relatives somewhere," the Assistant Commissioner said. "But there's no one. We've even been on to NATO—Barrett was stationed there for a number of years, you'll recall."

"No luck?"

"Absolutely nothing. We talked with a Colonel Francotti there who apparently was quite close to Barrett. He hasn't heard a word from him in months; neither has anyone else at NATO, as far as he knows."

"How about the estranged wife?"

"We tried that as well. She seems to have vanished completely—we haven't been able to get anything on where she might be."

"The men he served with in Ireland?"

"Nothing there either. He wasn't in Belfast that long, you know. And the only friend he seemed to have was his CO—the chap who was blown up in the jeep with him."

"Major Harold Porter," Haynes said. "He's got to have been the one Barrett calls Patroclus."

"I suppose you're right." Adams dug out his pipe. "You know what makes this whole thing so frustrating?

First of all, of course, the threat to the Crown is so horrifying. But beyond that, we learn more and more about him, yet everything seems to hit a blank wall. It's almost as if he were made out of smoke."

They were interrupted by Inspector Granby, carrying a sheaf of papers. He nodded to Haynes and then addressed himself to the Assistant Commissioner. "I've completed the check you wanted, sir."

"And?"

"He's not on any of the lists, sir."

"Not surprising." Adams looked over at Haynes. "You didn't expect he would be."

"No, but I was hoping," Haynes answered. "Professor Chatwin was so insistent that Barrett said to him 'They'll have their procession tomorrow noon, but they don't know I'll be in it.' " He glanced at Granby inquiringly. "You're sure you've got there the names of everyone who'll be in that procession?"

Granby held up the papers. "Come noontime tomorrow, these organizations—and only these—will participate in the ceremonies opening Parliament. And every member of those organizations is listed here, even the officials of the House itself. Barrett's name does not appear anywhere."

"Thank you, Inspector." The Assistant Commissioner thoughtfully rubbed his jaw. "If he's not in the procession in any official capacity—and we didn't think he would be—he's got to be planning some way of getting into it. That puts it right up to our security, doesn't it?"

"Yes," Haynes responded. "It's got to."

Adams beckoned an aide. "Set up a conference for half an hour from now. I'll want the Chief of Metropolitan Patrolmen, the Chief of Detectives, and the head of Buckingham security. Plus any of their security experts they want to bring along. Do you understand?"

"Yes, sir." The aide inclined his head in assent and headed briskly toward the door.

The Chief of Detectives, summoned from his dinner at a West End restaurant, was the last to arrive. The

Assistant Commissioner immediately convened the group. "Gentlemen," he began crisply, "some of you do not know anything of what I am about to tell you. Up to now, we had hoped to keep the matter completely confidential for many reasons, not the least of which was our worry about how the press would handle it. Let me explain." He quickly took them through the events of the past days. "As you can see," he ended solemnly, "our security tomorrow must be impenetrable. Your comments, please? Chief Scott?"

The Chief of Patrolmen was a slender man whose steel-framed glasses gave him a deceptive pedantic look. "You want my comments, Sir Henry?" he replied incisively. "I have one—don't permit the Queen to appear. Under any circumstances."

"I couldn't agree more. But she is a very courageous and determined lady. She won't hear of it."

"I can picture every foot of the route of that procession," the chief insisted urgently. "There are any number of places where a sniper could conceal himself. If this man is half the shot you say he is, he couldn't miss."

"Her Majesty will not change her mind. I am sure of it," the Assistant Commissioner responded. "We had best occupy our time by considering how we can make our security airtight."

"You know as well as I do there is no such thing," the chief said acidly. "But I can see what you're up against. All right. How about tripling our normal assignment of patrolmen?"

"How far apart will that station your men?"

The chief did a mental calculation. "About fifty feet, I should judge. We'd have an even heavier concentration at Parliament itself."

"Good." Adams noticed the head of detectives was trying to gain his attention. "You have something to say, Mike?"

"Yes. In line with what Chief Scott has said, I'll increase the number of my people too. Suppose we put a detective on the roof of every building along the route. With binoculars, they'll be able to command a pretty wide sector.''

"That should help. What about the interiors of the buildings?''

"I'll have them checked out forty-five minutes before the procession. After that, we should forbid entry. It would be drastic, and we'll get a lot of flak, but I think we should do it.''

"Go ahead," Adams said. "Now what about communications? Bill—your recommendations?''

A communications expert answered without hesitation. "Every patrolman should have a walkie-talkie, of course. The same for Mike's detectives. That won't pose any problem—they'll be outside. But for the people inside the Houses of Parliament, we'll use different equipment; I wouldn't want to take the chance on a garbled transmission.''

"Where do you want your communications center?'' Adams asked.

"I've been thinking about that. It seems to me the best bet will be to set it up in a van. Let me work out the details with Chief Scott and Mike.''

"Excellent." Adams addressed the group as a whole. "One of the things that bothers me most is that the Queen will be traveling along the route in the golden ceremonial coach. Those horses move along pretty well, of course, but it's still a slow process. All we'd need is a snarl in the front of the procession, forcing the coach to halt. How can we make certain that doesn't happen?''

The conference continued intensively until about ten o'clock. The Assistant Commissioner summed up and then looked around the table. "Does anyone have anything further to say?'' He paused a moment. "Very well, that's it. May God be with us.''

He shook hands with each man as he departed, and then slowly walked back to his chair. "How do you think it went?'' he asked wearily.

Haynes answered sympathetically. "You've done

everything possible that could be done."

"Except one," Adams said bitterly. "The one thing that matters: find Barrett."

In her bedroom suite, the Queen sat at her desk, reviewing the speech she would make to declare Parliament open. More than once, she read a passage several times, debating the exact emphasis she would place upon it. The room was chilly, the only heat coming from a fireplace in one corner, for she preferred to work that way.

Satisfied at last, she walked to the window and gazed out over the darkness of St. James's Park to the myriad lights of the West End. As on so many occasions in the past, she was musing on the continuity of the throne. Tomorrow she would summon Parliament to their great task, as her father before her, as her ancestors for scores of years.

There was a soft ring from her telephone. Surprised, she picked up the receiver and listened carefully. "She wishes to see me now?" she asked in her precise way.

"Yes, ma'am," her secretary responded. "The Prime Minister is most emphatic. At once. Sir Henry Adams is with her."

"Very well, then. Send them up immediately." The Queen walked into her sitting room, and a moment later there was a discreet knock on the door. "Enter," she called, and then smiled warmly. "Good evening, Madame Prime Minister. And to you also, Sir Henry."

"I'm sorry to bother you this late, ma'am," the Prime Minister said. "But we've come to you with an urgent appeal. You simply must not appear in the procession tomorrow."

The Queen indicated a divan covered in a burgundy velvet. "Please sit down. Both of you look so distraught —what has happened? I presume, since you're here, Sir Henry, it has to do with this man who calls himself Achilles."

"It does indeed, ma'am. We now know who he is. We

also know when he plans to do you harm. Tomorrow, during the ceremonies opening Parliament. As the Prime Minister has stated, it is out of the question for you to appear.''

The Queen regarded him gravely. ''Why do you use a euphemistic phrase like 'do you harm,' Sir Henry? Wouldn't it be more accurate to say 'kill'?''

''It would indeed, ma'am, but where you're concerned I cannot bring myself to speak the word.''

''This man who intends to kill me—what is he like?'' The Queen bent forward attentively. ''When we talked before, you mentioned he had been wounded in Ireland. Do you now know how seriously?''

''Yes, ma'am. Quite seriously. His physical injuries have healed, but his mind was affected. As a matter of fact, he was confined to the psychiatric ward of the military hospital here.''

''From which he escaped,'' the Prime Minister put in disgustedly. ''Ma'am, this man is extremely dangerous. I must insist you send someone in your place tomorrow.''

The Queen gently held up a hand. ''I would like to hear more about him. What is his name, Sir Henry?''

''Barrett, ma'am. George Acton Barrett.''

''He has a family?''

''No, ma'am.'' The Assistant Commissioner gave a quick summary.

The Queen listened intently. ''He is estranged from his wife,'' she said thoughtfully, when he had finished. ''I wonder how much pain that caused him. And the loss of his friend on top of that. Poor man—he has suffered so much.''

The Prime Minister had been waiting impatiently. ''Ma'am, may we now consider who will be delegated to read your speech?''

The Queen looked at her reflectively. ''You know, Madame Prime Minister, just before you arrived I was thinking of my father and grandfather. In the same circumstances, do you think either one would have done as you ask?''

"That is a hypothetical question," the Prime Minister evaded.

"But please indulge me and answer it," the Queen smiled.

"If you insist, ma'am. No, I do not believe they would."

"Then you will understand why I must refuse you."

The Prime Minister shook her head ruefully. "Ma'am, jurisprudence lost a great barrister when you were born royal."

The petite woman answered seriously. "Madame Prime Minister, we are deeply appreciative of your concern. But you know the motto of the English throne: '*Dieu et Mon Droit.*' God and my right. With a right, there is always a responsibility. We have never evaded our responsibility. We do not intend to begin now."

"With respect, ma'am, I point out that you have a responsibility to your people."

"That is true," the Queen replied quietly. "And we have always considered that responsibility to be the upholding of those institutions and traditions that are the warp and woof of our history. Would you not agree the opening of Parliament each year is the most important and visible symbol of our freedom, so dearly earned, and so gallantly defended so many times in the past. To shirk our duty here, above all else, would be to betray our people and our trust. Our word is final—we cannot accept your recommendation."

The Prime Minister stood silent for a long instant and then replied gravely. "Then there is only one thing left for me to say, ma'am."

"What is that, Madame Prime Minister?"

"I am proud to be one of your subjects, ma'am. Very proud indeed."

Chapter 16

JILL BLAKE WAS packing her clothes. She would succeed for a few moments in holding back her tears, then a dress or a blouse would remind her of a time when she had worn it for him. It seemed to her she was tearing her life apart, rushing to a hopeless future. But her determination never wavered. He had to be alone to think things through.

Now, as she began to strap up her bags, the dreaded moment was close. She had taken a new apartment, and it was almost time to call a cab. At least she could be grateful for one thing: He was not here—she would be spared the agony of saying good-bye.

Finishing with her bags, she sat down at a desk in the living room and began to compose a note. It went quickly; she had gone over in her mind a score of times what she wanted to say. She was reaching for an envelope when the door knocker sounded. Puzzled, hurriedly wiping her eyes, she crossed to the door and opened it.

A tall man was standing there, smiling politely. In the light from the lamppost next to the walk, it was clear he was well groomed, dressed impeccably. "Good evening," he said cheerfully. "I'm Andrew Stevens. Please forgive me for disturbing you at this hour. But I wonder if I might speak to Mr. Haynes. It won't take long.''

"I'm afraid he's not here," Jill answered. "Actually, I don't believe he'll be home at all tonight."

"Pity. Let me explain. Mr. Haynes called on me twice at Yeomen of the Guard headquarters—I'm a lieutenant on their staff. He asked me to stop by if I came up with anything more."

"I see."

"It so happens I do have something. It's rather vital I see your husband tonight. Can you tell me where I might be able to catch up with him, Mrs. Haynes?"

Jill didn't bother to correct him. "Come in," she said, opening the door wide. "I can give you his office number but I doubt he'll be there. Perhaps you'd care to leave a message?"

"That's very kind of you." He entered and glanced around appreciatively. "This is a very cozy room, especially on a chilly night like this."

"Thank you." She tried to cover her own preoccupation by making conversation. "You said you're with the Yeomen of the Guard. That must be interesting."

"No, as a matter òf fact, it isn't really. It's just a part-time thing, you know. And at times rather boring."

She nodded absently and indicated the telephone on a corner table. "If you'd like to try Tom at his office, you'll find the number on a pad there."

"Thank you." He stood up and suddenly stopped, looking into an adjoining room. "I see you have a piano, Mrs. Haynes. I didn't happen to notice it when I came in."

"Yes. We've been using that room as a combination den and catch-all. The piano takes up most of the space, I'm afraid."

"Do you play?" he asked pleasantly.

"No. I wish I did; it's always been one of my ambitions. It was here when we came—we took the flat furnished."

Abstracted, not listening, he walked to the piano.

Reaching forward, he touched the keys lightly, listening critically. "It's in good tune. Perhaps you won't mind if I play something—it's been quite a while."

"Well, I don't know," she answered uncertainly. "It is rather late. The neighbors might not appreciate it, don't you think?"

"Actually, they're some distance away, aren't they?" he said with gentle insistence. "Just for a moment or two. Please!"

She managed a smile, trying to make the best of it. "Very well."

He sat down on the piano bench, staring at the keys, seemingly caught up in his thoughts. Then—quickly— he raised his hands and struck the opening chords of Tchaikovsky's Concerto No. 1. The music poured into the room, powerful, magnificent.

She listened in awe as he played with flawless skill, calling forth from his instrument a soul-stirring majesty. His head was erect, aquiline features sharply outlined, a look of somber dedication on his face.

The music was building to a climax, relentless, compelling—when suddenly he stopped. He held up his right hand, staring at it in revulsion, his expression contorted. The hand was trembling—faintly at first, then more and more, until all control was lost.

An agonized cry burst from his lips. "Behold, Zeus, the obscene burden you have given me. The faltering hand!"

Jill felt the fear sweep up from her vitals. Paralyzing. Chilling. She gazed at him in horror, her breath suspended.

He roused himself and turned to face her, his eyes frenzied. "I see your husband has told you about me, Mrs. Haynes," he said tonelessly. "Then I was right in fearing him."

"I don't know what you mean," she protested weakly.

"Unfortunately, you do. The questions he asked could only have come from someone who knows or believes I might be Achilles." He took a step toward her. "Yes, Mrs. Haynes, I am the one who signs his letters Achilles. I am George Barrett. I am the one whom the gods have cursed with the faltering hand."

She repeated feebly, "I don't know what you mean."

"Don't you? If you could see your face, Mrs. Haynes, you would realize there is no point in denials. You have heard all too well of the faltering hand." He took another step toward her.

"Please!" she whispered. "Please!"

"I came here to kill your husband, Mrs. Haynes," he said quietly. "It is my bad fortune he is not here. Nonetheless he will not stop me tomorrow. Not him, not anyone—and not you." He stepped close to her and clasped her hands.

She gazed up into his face and found there a deep sadness. His voice was grave. "I, Achilles, must exact vengeance on a treacherous ruler. You are innocent, Mrs. Haynes. Yet the last evil she will cause must be your death."

Jill opened her mouth to scream. But his hands were at her throat, imprisoning its air, pressing hard. Her body thrashed as she fought to breathe. Then, in her torture, there came a black mist. It rose swiftly, inexorably, until she slid from consciousness.

The assassin relaxed his hands, listening intently to the sound of an automobile in the street. Satisfied that it was passing by, he gazed at her for a long moment. His eyes slowly filled with tears; he remembered another gentle woman and a gentle time, gone forever.

Slowly he walked to the door. Without a backward glance, he opened it and stepped out into the night. His sadness deepened. So much tragedy has brought you to this time, he said to himself. So much deception. But it had been the will of the gods—his course had been clear. He thought back to his last weeks in the hospital . . .

It had been a time of dedication. Vengeance had filled his mind to the exclusion of all else. Unremittingly, he had considered and rejected plan after plan, until at last he found the one he knew at once was right.

It required that a relative of the Queen must die to lend credence to his first letter. If his demands were not met, then a second must perish. So be it.

It never occurred to him that the Monarch would not bow to his demand. He thought long and intensely, debating what he would do with the vast sum he would realize. Finally, he had made his decision—he would purchase a villa in Greece. It was only fitting: Achilles should take his place among the gods, in the land of greatness.

The Monarch would surrender to his will; he was sure of it. But his military training was ingrained, impossible to ignore. You must consider all eventualities, it said to him. It is unthinkable, yes—but suppose the Monarch does not yield? Are you then prepared to fulfill your threat and claim her life? Even if your own might be forfeit?

There was no hesitation. Vengeance, at any cost, must be obtained. If need be, he would exact the ultimate price, and run the ultimate risk.

With the plan set, it was time to begin putting it in motion. He frequented the reference room of the library, researching the Queen's relatives, selecting his first target and, if necessary, his second. A sense of power surged through him; life and death rested on his choice.

With the final selection of his targets, he delved deeply into their life-styles. It was surprising how much information could be gleaned from a shelf of periodicals: The nation obviously hungered for detail after detail concerning their betters. News of their country homes, their smart flats in town, their motorcars, clubs, sports, hobbies—all was there for anyone determined to dig. He was able to chart, with astonishing ease, the specific steps he would take.

A heady sense of infallibility enveloped him. It was this that led him to conceive an idea which appealed to him irresistibly. How richly ironic it would be, he mused, if he could place himself in a position close to the Queen. He would be able to observe her during her time of ordeal, savoring her sorrow at the death of a relative, her anxiety at the threat to her person. The idea was so daring, so godlike in its boldness, that it possessed him completely; he knew he would not rest until he had made it reality.

But how could it be done? Obtaining a position on the palace staff would be impossible; furthermore, it would take his full time, destroying the mobility his plan demanded.

Then what? One overcast morning, absorbed in his problem, he paused near Buckingham Palace. A detachment of Yeomen of the Guard was drawn up in line, ready to assist in a ceremony. It struck him instantly: Wherever the Queen might discharge her official duties, there you would likely find the Yeomen.

Three days later, a strategy firmly in mind, he presented himself at Yeomen headquarters. He requested an interview with Captain Pierce, the Commanding Officer, and was soon shown into an austere office.

"Yes?" Pierce asked brusquely.

George adopted an imperious tone. "My name is Stevens, Andrew Stevens," he lied smoothly. "I've decided I should like to join the Yeomen."

Pierce surveyed him coldly. "So you've decided, have you? Has it occurred to you we might have an input into that?"

"Naturally," George replied, pretending to be unabashed. "But that doesn't change the fact that I would like to join, does it?"

"Why?" the captain demanded hostilely.

"Why would I like to join?" George shrugged. "Does one always have to have a firm reason for one's actions? Family tradition, I suppose. My grandfather was in the Yeomen." Research is a wonderful thing, he was thinking sardonically.

For the first time Pierce unbent slightly. "Who was that?"

"The earl of Ashford."

"Indeed?" The thawing was very noticeable now.

"You're the present earl's son, are you?"

"Second son." George managed a half-rueful smile. "I won't inherit the perks, regrettably."

"You have military experience?"

"If you can call four months at Sandhurst military experience, yes."

The captain studied him curiously. "What happened there?"

"Are you by any chance Sandhurst?" George replied.

"Yes, I am."

"Then you know." George smiled a man-to-man smile. "Let's say I wasn't cut out for hitting the books. Not with all the good-looking women there are in the world."

Pierce laughed. "We're not exactly Sandhurst here, but we do have our rules and regulations. You might not find them to your liking."

"I've calmed down a bit," George said lightly. "By the way, I've just thought of something." He reached in his coat pocket and brought out an envelope, taking a letter from it; carefully he placed the envelope so Pierce could not miss seeing the address. "Let's see, it's here somewhere," he went on, pretending to scan the letter. As he had expected, Pierce's eyes were fixed on the envelope address—"The Honorable Andrew Stevens, Connaught Hotel."

"Here it is," George announced. "A friend of mine dropped a letter by my hotel—he mentions meeting a general on a shooting trip. I thought he'd written Pierce, but it's something else, actually."

"Too bad," the captain said jokingly. "I could do with a relative among the brass, couldn't I?"

George smiled politely, congratulating himself. He was sure the envelope address had done its job. One more way to establish an identity—good family, good address. No need, naturally, he was thinking with amusement, to mention he had scrawled the letter and envelope himself.

Pierce was speaking now in a semiapologetic way. "We've got a full complement now, so I won't be able to have you with us immediately. But we do have a lieutenant who's thinking of resigning in the next few months or so. Why don't you keep in touch?''

"Of course," George answered, hiding his disappointment. "I hardly expected to join today—right? I'm leaving tonight on a bit of a trip—suppose I pop in when I get back? We might have a drink together.''

"Good idea," Pierce said enthusiastically, clearly pleased to see more of an earl's son.

During the next weeks, George called on the captain twice, cementing their acquaintanceship. He was quite comfortable in his assumed identity as Andrew Stevens, knowing full well from his research that the actual Andrew Stevens was in Australia, beginning a two-year stint as a Unilever executive.

It was reassuring, too, to know that he had also rented his flat in the name of Andrew Stevens; the hospital would find no trace of the missing George Barrett.

All in all, his plan was progressing perfectly. There remained the one hitch—Captain Pierce was reporting that his lieutenant still hadn't made up his mind to resign. George waited impatiently, but reluctantly decided he should wait no longer. He would have to forego the added pleasure of observing the Queen's reaction to her coming ordeal at first hand; he would proceed as originally planned.

On a frosty morning, he dropped by Yeomen headquarters to make one final check. This time, unexpectedly, he found Captain Pierce beaming cheerfully. "Glad you came by, Stevens," he announced. "You'd never guess what's happened."

"The lieutenant is resigning after all?" George asked quickly.

"No—he's decided to stay on. But Lieutenant Hanfield—he's another chap we have—is leaving. The bloody fool's going off to marry some woman in the wilds of Wales. He's even going to live there, if you can imagine anyone that daft."

George covered his elation with a nod. "Absolutely daft," he agreed.

Within a week he assumed his new duties; as expected, they took very little time. There was no longer any reason to delay. He would travel to Scotland, to the rendezvous he had planned with his first victim. The time for action was finally at hand.

George came to realize he had been walking the streets aimlessly. It does no good to remember, he lectured himself wearily, especially to remember the gentle girl you have just strangled.

He stood for an instant, staring up at the star-filled sky. Tomorrow will be the culmination, he was thinking, the day of vengeance. It might well be, too, his last day on earth. The thought brought him no fear. Death, in so many ways, would be welcome.

Chapter 17

THE COACHMAN WAS up and about his business in the royal stables before dawn. With painstaking care, he went over every inch of the Royal Coach, testing the axles and wheels with judicious tugs and pushes, examining the polish on the giltwork and side lamps with a critical eye.

It was a ritual he had performed for many years, on each day when the Queen was to ride in the Royal Coach. Of all the solemn ceremonial occasions, he considered the annual opening of Parliament the most important—so his inspection this morning was even more meticulous than usual.

Satisfied at long last, he filled his pipe and enjoyed his first smoke of the day.

Not far away, in the Hyde Park Barracks, the two squadrons of the Household Cavalry stationed there were beginning their morning. Each trooper dressed in the magnificent uniform: scarlet tunic, tight white trousers, gleaming black boots, knee-high with flaring tops, and a plumed steel helmet. There was an air of expectancy; the great procession would soon begin to form.

The Foot Guards, in their barracks, were also making ready for the day. Against the chilling late-October weather, they wore long greatcoats over their scarlet tunics and blue trousers; their towering bearskin hats, hallmark of the brigade, would offer additional protection.

There was bustle, too, in an orderly room at St. James's Palace, headquarters of the Yeomen of the Guard. A group of early-morning arrivals was busy brewing their morning tea, looking incongruous in their uniforms, unchanged since Tudor days—scarlet doublets, black velvet hats, and white ruffs.

All the pomp and glitter, all the paraphernalia were now in full preparation. Centuries-old tradition was demanding that it be served once again, to the most minute detail.

Thousands of the people of London, who would later line the route to and from Parliament, witnessing the splendid spectacle, were making ready too. Many were reading their morning newspapers over their breakfast or, in the case of especially early risers, in their offices.

Their interest was focused on a three-column photograph occupying a prominent position on the front page. Above it a black headline announced—"THE CID WANTS THIS MAN." A block of copy set in large type below the photograph identified the wanted man as George Acton Barrett, and explained the CID wished to question him on "a matter vital to the national security." Anyone having knowledge of his whereabouts, or having seen him, was urged to call at once a telephone number prominently displayed.

Every newspaper printed the story with the same amount of space, the same large type, and the same wording. For all its grumblings about the lack of additional information, Fleet Street had closed its ranks in support of the government.

* * *

There was one Yeoman of the Guard who had yet to make his appearance at Guard headquarters. George had made an effort to get some sleep. But as he expected, it was useless; at four o'clock he gave up completely and got up and dressed. With ceremonial deliberation, he bathed and dressed, then sat himself down at his kitchen table.

Picking up the glass cutter and the pane of glass he had purchased two days before, he set about cutting two small squares of glass. Pleased with the performance of the cutter, he threw the squares of glass and what remained of the pane into a wastebasket.

Placing the cutter carefully aside, he added to it a roll of electrician's tape. A glance at his watch showed him the morning newspapers would have arrived by now at the corner kiosk. They promised a way to spend the hour before he must leave, so he stepped out into the chilly air, walking quickly.

He came to the kiosk and reached out for a paper. Suddenly he stopped, his heart pumping strongly: Staring back at him was his own likeness, beneath the ominous message—"THE CID WANTS THIS MAN." Hurriedly, keeping his emotion rigidly in check, he paid for the paper and returned to his flat.

With the paper spread out, he read the article three times. Then, buoyed by a tremendous relief, he sat back and felt himself begin to relax.

This is no threat to your plan, he told himself reassuringly. In the first place, the picture is so old no one could possibly recognize you. In the second place, they are looking for George Barrett. This flat is not listed in the name of George Barrett; nor does that name appear anywhere in the lists of those who will be in the procession today. In the third place, and most important of all—they are not looking for a Yeoman lieutenant named Andrew Stevens. You were right, he said to himself, in thinking that Haynes was working with the CID. But you were wrong in believing he had identified Lieutenant Stevens as Achilles.

A tremendous exultation rose within him. He would take his place in the procession, secure in the knowledge that Lieutenant Stevens was not sought. Once again there would be no interference, once again he would triumph. Once again he would work his will—Achilles invincible.

Rising quickly, he placed the glass cutter and the electrician's tape in his pocket. It was time to go; the hour of vengeance was nearing fast.

The procession would travel from Buckingham Palace along the length of the Mall, turn right along the eastern edge of St. James's Park, and thence proceed to the Houses of Parliament.

"We've got a problem practically every foot of the way," Sir Henry Adams said grimly. "Even with all the precautions we're taking."

Haynes nodded in agreement. They were seated in the CID communications van, parked behind a clump of trees near Parliament Square. The radios hummed continuously as reports continued to come in from various positions along the route.

A sergeant wearing earphones turned from his station. "They've completed the deployment of the bobbies, sir. Every fifty feet."

The Assistant Commissioner looked up from a map he was studying. "How about the men on the rooftops? Any word there?"

"Just coming in now, sir." The sergeant adjusted his earphones and listened intently. "Inspector Granby reports they'll be all set in another few minutes, sir."

Adams looked at his watch. "Forty-five minutes to go until the procession starts. Right now our people are starting to check the interiors of the buildings along the way. To tell you the truth, Haynes, I'm hoping very much they'll turn Barrett up."

"You think that's where he'll be?"

"It seems to me a strong possibility," the Assistant

Commissioner answered. "Look, he's not in the procession itself—we checked that. He can't stand out in the open and get a shot off. He can't go to the rooftops—we've got that covered. All that's left for him is to pick a spot in the interior of some building. Some place with a good overview of the procession. If I'm right, we'll get him."

"We'll know soon enough," Haynes said soberly.

They waited anxiously. The first report came in: Negative for a block of commercial buildings on the Mall. Other reports began to arrive, at first slowly, then with increasing speed. Negative, negative, negative—the word seemed to echo in the van with an almost physical presence.

With each report, Adams's concern grew greater, until finally he spoke heavily. "There can't be many more buildings left. It's beginning to look bad. Very bad."

Haynes kept his silence, acutely aware of his own mounting despair.

The radio hummed again; the reports slowed to a trickle and then stopped.

The sergeant looked at the Assistant Commissioner half-apologetically. "That's the lot of them, sir. All negative."

Adams bowed his head, wearily passing a hand across his forehead. "God be with us now," he said fervently.

The Queen was dressed in a flowing white gown, calmly awaiting the summons to her coach. Through the windows of her sitting room, she noticed the day was clear, with a bleak quality to the light that promised a nip in the air. Her thoughts were centered on the coming ceremony; as always, she was resolved to acquit herself well. The knowledge that somewhere along the way an assassin might be waiting was frightening. But she was deliberately pushing it aside, concentrating on the duty at hand.

A maid approached her deferentially. "It is ten o'clock, ma'am."

"Thank you." The Queen rose and walked to a table. The Imperial State Crown—the most valuable piece of jewelry in the world—rested on blue velvet, its gems blazing.

She surveyed it thoughtfully, again feeling the sense of closeness to her ancestors the crown inevitably brought. Its history spoke to her, in so many powerful ways.

This, she reflected, is the headdress made for the coronation of my great-grandmother, Victoria, almost one hundred and fifty years ago. And there are the four Stars of Africa, and a second Star, all cut from the Cullinan diamond—the largest ever discovered—presented to my great-uncle Edward VII by the government of South Africa.

With an emotion close to reverence, her gaze went from the crown's edging of ermine to the Black Prince's ruby, worn by Henry V at the Battle of Agincourt. Twenty generations of British sovereigns have worn a State Crown with this ruby, she meditated. Near them the four drop pearls, the earrings of Elizabeth I, gleamed with a rosy luster; St. Edward's sapphire, worn in the ring of Edward the Confessor, shone from a diamond-covered cross.

Once a year, on this day, it is my privilege to wear this crown, she said to herself. It is my link to the past, my pledge to the future.

She reached out and lifted the crown from its bed, feeling its two-and-a-half-pound weight. Smiling, she recalled how she used to wear it for several hours around the palace, trying to get accustomed to its weight before the opening of Parliament. With the passage of the years, the practice was no longer necessary.

The Queen raised the crown and placed it firmly on her head. From the action she took new courage, and new strength.

A glance in the mirror assured her the crown fit snugly. Its internal fitting, like that of a Guard officer's bearskin hat, had been adjusted to take the weight evenly on her head. Taking up her long white gloves, she drew them on carefully and left the room.

Her husband joined her in the lift that carried them to the ground floor. Passing through the Queen's entrance, they stepped into the courtyard. Immediately, there were sharp commands and the ranks of Foot Guards snapped to rigid attention. A military band struck into the first strains of "God Save the Queen." The horses of the Cavalry, breaths rising in the frosty air, reacted with nervous movements.

A footman, standing erect, held the door of the Royal Coach. The Queen and her Consort entered, the door closed, and four footmen took their places on the raised step at the rear of the coach.

There were further commands all along the line, and the sound of horses' hooves and the tramp of guardsmen's feet. At a signal from an official, the coachman of the Royal Coach, wearing a tricornered hat, touched his whip to the backs of his team of grays. The team took a strain and the coach edged forward. The great procession was underway.

In the vanguard, the Yeomen of the Guard swung along smartly, heading through the filigreed gates of the palace toward the broad reach of the Mall. One of their lieutenants marched with special purpose, thinking exultantly that his prey—in her Royal Coach—was following him to her death.

Haynes was at the entrance to the Houses of Parliament, talking quietly with the Assistant Commissioner.

The four Westminster chimes, high in the tower of Big Ben, sounded with their phrase from Handel's *Messiah*. "Quarter past the hour," Adams said mechanically, as if speaking to himself. "They'll be coming along the Mall now."

They waited on edge, dreading to hear from the sergeant—standing close with a walkie-talkie—that a shot had been fired. It seemed to Haynes that the world was in suspension, standing still, braced for news of the ultimate outcome.

The walkie-talkie suddenly came to life. "Mobile One, this is Center," a quiet voice said. "Is Mr. Haynes with the Assistant Commissioner?"

The sergeant pushed the button of his walkie-talkie. "Affirmative," he said, answering the query from the communications van.

"Mobile One, we have just had a call from the Metropolitan Police. There is a Jill Blake in Middlesex Hospital—the hospital is asking he come at once."

Haynes felt the fear course through his body. With a quick reaction he took the walkie-talkie from the sergeant and spoke sharply. "This is Haynes. What's wrong with her?"

"No further information, sir," the quiet voice replied. "But the message was urgent."

The Assistant Commissioner had already summoned a bobby with a wave of his arm. "Drive Mr. Haynes to Middlesex Hospital," he instructed crisply. "Fast."

Haynes gratefully followed the bobby to a police car. The officer rammed the car into gear and swung away from Parliament Square. Choosing streets off the procession route, he snapped on the siren. Its wails rose and fell in insistent waves, clearing the traffic before them.

The car hurtled along at a high speed, turned corners with a squeal of tires, and emerged into Mortimer Street. The bobby, clearly a good man in an emergency, floored the accelerator until the hospital buildings appeared before them. Braking hard, he turned into the curved driveway.

Haynes was out of the car before it had stopped, and sprinting for the lobby. Two minutes later, taking the stairs with great strides, he emerged on the third floor and swiftly scanned the room numbers, looking for room 314.

He found it at the end of the corridor. A young man in a doctor's long coat, just leaving, stopped him from entering and took him aside.

"I'm Dr. Larkin. You're Mr. Haynes, I presume."

Haynes nodded. "How is she?" he demanded anxiously.

"She'll be all right. We've got her pretty heavily sedated; her throat hurts, and of course the trauma was very extreme."

"What happened?"

The doctor stared at him in amazement. "You don't know? Oh, I see—they just told you to get over here fast, I suppose. Well, she was strangled. As a matter of fact, she was unconscious when they brought her in. I thought for a while she might have brain damage."

"Strangled?" Haynes echoed in horror, trying to comprehend. "What happened?"

"You'll have to ask Metropolitan Police about that. But I gather, when they brought her in, they didn't know much. Apparently a neighbor of Miss Blake's stops by in the mornings. They ride the bus together—I think that's what the police said."

"Yes. That would be Mrs. Boynton."

"I see. She found the door a bit ajar so she called out. When she didn't get an answer she went in. Good thing for Miss Blake she did—it was touch and go."

"But she's going to be all right?"

The doctor regarded him sympathetically. "Yes. No question; please don't worry. Look, you'll find her groggy. But it's going to do her a world of good to see you—she kept calling for you. So we phoned the police—she seemed to think they'd know where you were."

"I'll go in now. Is there any limit on how long I should stay?"

"Not really. You'll be able to judge."

Haynes thanked him and opened the door. The blinds were drawn; in the dim light she seemed so small and fragile in the hospital bed. Her eyes were closed, and there was a large bandage on her neck.

He gazed at her and the tears filled his eyes. He gave his thanks to God that she lived, and knew in that instant that he had always loved her with his entire heart. Bitterly, he reproached himself for ever doubting it. God grant me, he prayed, the chance to prove my love through every day of the years ahead.

Sensing his presence, her eyes opened. She saw in his expression the answer she had longed for—and a great happiness came to her. Her hand reached out and he took it gently, bending to kiss her forehead.

"Jill, Jill," he whispered. "Forgive me."

She stroked his hair lightly. "It will be fine now, Tom," she said, her voice weak and forced. "Thank God. Tom, listen—"

"Don't talk, Jill."

She shook her head, disagreeing. "Tom, the man came to kill you. He was the man you talked about, the man with the faltering hand."

Haynes was incredulous. "Jill, you must be mistaken."

"No, no," she insisted weakly. "He played our piano and his hand started to shake. Then he began yelling that he had the faltering hand—he was crazy, raving."

"Did he tell you his name?" Haynes asked urgently.

"Yes. When he came he said he was Lieutenant Stevens of the Yeomen. Later he said he was the man who signs his letters Achilles—George Barrett."

Haynes was suddenly rigid. Then, a second later, he stood up hurriedly. "Jill, I've got to leave you for a while."

"I understand." She looked at him anxiously. "But be careful, Tom."

He kissed her tenderly and left. Racing down the stairs, rage poured through him; there was a personal score he had to settle.

He was relieved to find the police car still in the driveway. The bobby, seeing him coming, started the motor.

Chapter 18

THE PROCESSION WAS approaching Parliament Square. On both sides of the road, the spectators stood three deep, watching with mounting anticipation until the moment when the Royal Coach drew abreast, Then— awed in the presence of Majesty—they stared fixedly until the coach had passed well beyond.

The hooves of the cavalry horses sounded a steady rhythm on the paved streets, with the jingling of their riders' accouterments providing a counterpoint. Like so many statues, the bobbies interspersed at regular intervals along the route watched intently; high above, the detectives on the rooftops braced against the chilling wind.

Up at the front of the procession, the Yeomen of the Guard had already reached the Houses of Parliament and dispersed quickly to inspect the vaults. Ever since 1605, when Guy Fawkes had tried to blow up Parliament, it had been their symbolic duty to make sure that this time the vaults held no gunpowder.

The officer who was known to his comrades as Lieutenant Stevens led a detachment of men down to the dank underground passages. Carefully beginning his plan, he turned to his sergeant and affected a worried air. "I don't know what's hit me," he said. "I barely made it through the march; some kind of a virus, I should think. I may have to ask you to take over here."

"No problem, sir," the sergeant answered smartly. "Glad to. This search business is all bloody nonsense, anyway."

Now, at street level, the State Coach had reached the Royal Entrance. The footmen swiftly dismounted from their perch; the cavalry held their mounts in check, the plumes of their helmets stirring in the breeze.

The door to the coach was held open and the Queen, followed by her Consort, stepped to the ground. Head erect, walking slowly, she made her way into the stately building.

Her officers of state were waiting, and escorted her to the House of Lords. There more than nine hundred peers, wearing the rich robes of their rank, stood in deference. The Queen mounted to her throne, placed on a dais carpeted in a vivid red and gold pattern; her Consort seated himself to her left.

Turning to the Lord Great Chamberlain, she spoke in her light, clear voice. "My Lord Chamberlain, please tell the members of the House of Commons that we command them to attend us immediately."

With a bow, the Lord Chamberlain, as tradition dictated, passed the Queen's order to the Usher of the Black Rod. Proceeding to the door of the House of Commons, the Usher struck the door three times with his rod. Upon admission, he strode to the middle of the House, made three bows to the chair, and repeated the royal command. The Speaker of the House, followed by the more than six hundred members present, at once repaired to the Chamber of Lords.

When the muted noises of their arrival had died away, and all had found a place, the Lord Chamberlain approached the throne. Kneeling upon one knee, he extended a printed copy of the Sovereign's speech, already drafted and approved by her ministers.

The Queen accepted the copy. Bidding the assembly

to be seated, she paused for a moment, gathering her resolve. Then—carefully stressing certain phrases as she had practiced—she read aloud at a steady pace.

George notified his sergeant, with a great show of reluctance, that he was feeling even worse. "Perhaps the air might brace me up," he said forlornly. "Carry on here, will you? If I'm feeling better, I'll join you a bit later."

Once out of sight of his men he swiftly scaled the steps to street level. Leaving the building, he walked purposefully to the House of Commons parking lot. Just off it, he saw ahead of him the entrance to the Tower of Big Ben.

As always, a police constable was on duty, making certain that no one entered without a pass. George approached him confidently. "Good morning, Peter."

The constable looked at him with amazement. "Lieutenant Stevens! I thought you and your men would be checking the vaults about now."

"So they are," George answered. "But I have this damned virus, and it's gotten to my stomach. I had to get some air." He shook his head woefully. "It's not doing much good, I'm afraid. I'm right on the verge of being very sick."

"Too bad," the constable said sympathetically. "That's a bloody miserable feeling."

"It is," George agreed unhappily. "Listen, Peter, if I'm sick out here in public it's going to be pretty embarrassing, isn't it? Bad enough without being in a Yeoman's uniform, right? How about letting me step into the Tower? If I have an accident, I promise you I'll see it's taken care of later."

The constable hesitated. He liked the lieutenant, and had gotten to know him during his visits to the Tower over the past fortnight. "I don't know," he said doubtfully. "We're not permitting anyone in today, what with the Queen here. It would be pretty irregular."

"I know that," George said. "But what's the harm,

Peter?'' He suddenly held a hand to his mouth, as if fighting off nausea. ''Please! I need the favor.''

''Very well then,'' the constable said, his decision made. He glanced around to make sure no one was watching. ''In with you. And good luck.''

George entered the Tower and mounted the spiral staircase. There were almost three hundred steps to the clock room, he knew. Climbing swiftly, he congratulated himself on his foresight; in his frequent visits to the Tower, he had worked hard to gain the constable's approval. It had paid off. Not only for yourself, he told himself grimly, but for the constable as well: If he had been refused admittance, it would have been necessary to use the knife strapped to his shin. A third of the way up, he came to a prison cell—once used by Parliament's Sergeant-at-Arms to lock up quarrelsome members. He bent swiftly and groped in the cell, just to the right of the open door. His fingers closed around the package he had placed there two days before. Drawing it out, he tore off the wrapping. Working hurriedly in the semigloom by touch, he assembled his carbine and loaded it with a clip of cartridges.

Almost running now, he climbed the rest of the way to the clock room. He crossed to the south face and gazed through the glass of the dial. One hundred and eighty feet below, well within range, the Royal Entrance to Parliament lay before him.

He placed his carbine on the floor and drew his glass cutter and the roll of electrician's tape from a belt under his uniform. Squatting, he tore off a piece of tape and stuck one end of it to the glass of the dial. He picked up the glass cutter; working with infinite care he cut away a square of glass around a foot in diameter. As it came loose the tape kept it from falling to the street below. He pulled it in and placed it to one side.

Cold air rushed through the opening. Lying prone, he pulled his carbine to him. There was nothing to do now but wait. His watch read ten minutes to noon; the Queen would soon conclude her speech and leave Parliament.

He reviewed in his mind his escape plan. With the shot there would be instant, total confusion—wild milling about, panic, guesses as to the place from which the bullet had come. There would be time to leave the Tower and slip into the frenzied crowd. His thoughts drifted exultantly: It was a plan befitting the bold Achilles, a plan of vengeance and guile.

With ironic delight, he suddenly remembered that carved in the stonework under the clock dial was a Latin inscription. *"Domine salvam fac reginam nostram"*—O Lord, save our Queen. The Lord had better be about it fast, he thought with amusement.

Picking up his carbine, he trained it on the spot where Majesty would soon appear.

The car tore through the streets, siren wailing. The bobby gripped the wheel tightly as he threadneedled through the traffic.

Haynes was hunched over the radio microphone, trying to get through to the Assistant Commissioner. It seemed an eternity before he succeeded in raising the communications van, and there was a further delay before he heard Adams's voice.

"Where are you, Haynes?" the Assistant Commissioner said.

"On the way back. Listen! Achilles is Andrew Stevens, a Yeoman lieutenant. He's there now. Repeat: Barrett is using the name Lieutenant Stevens."

"Understood," Adams answered tersely. "Over and out."

Haynes blessed the Assistant Commissioner's instant reaction; there was no time for questions. He forced himself to wait a full five minutes as the car raced ahead, then called the van again. "Any news?"

A sergeant answered, trying to mask the excitement in his voice. "They've located Lieutenant Stevens's Yeomen detachment—he wasn't with them. The Assistant Commissioner is leading the search for him now. I'll get back to you when they get him."

Haynes hung up the microphone, his body tense. Achilles could be anywhere, inside the building or not. Nervously tapping the seat, willing the car to even greater speed, he waited for the radio to announce the assassin had been taken.

The car was speeding now along Whitehall. The Houses of Parliament loomed before them, with the Tower of Big Ben rising gracefully into the sky.

Haynes glanced at its soaring height. Suddenly another tower came into his mind: the bell tower of the University of Texas, from which a sniper had dealt death. He thought, too, of a book depository in Dallas, with a marksman firing from his high perch.

"Pull in at the Tower," he shouted to the bobby. Achilles is still free, he told himself urgently. What more logical vantage point could he have picked than this tower?

The car jolted to a halt and he was out of the door and running.

Inside the Houses of Parliament the Queen finished her speech with a firm peroration. The assembled Lords and House Members rose in tribute. The Queen moved among her ministers, accepting their congratulations, and moved gracefully toward the door.

It was three minutes to noon. In the clock room of the Tower, far above the street, Achilles waited, sensing the time was almost at hand.

Sprinting wildly, credentials in his hand, Haynes came to the constable at the Tower entrance. "Is anybody up there?" he demanded sharply.

"Just a Yeoman lieutenant, sir. He was feeling poorly and—"

Haynes furiously pushed the constable aside. "The man who would kill the Queen is up there. Get help—fast—and follow me up!" He scaled the steps three at a time, pushing himself unmercifully, gulping for air.

The Queen emerged from the Royal Entrance and moved toward her coach. The assassin moved his carbine slightly, bringing her into his sights, and began to curl his finger around the trigger.

At that instant Haynes burst into the clock room and hurtled forward in a headlong dive. He struck the assassin from the side, knocking him half onto his back. The carbine clattered to the floor and spun against the wall.

George reacted immediately, fighting back with frenzy. Punching, gouging, they thrashed on the floor, two powerful men seeking a killing grip.

Suddenly other sounds were added to the noises of their struggle. There was a turning of gears, movement of release rods, and twitching of bell cables. The Westminster chimes pealed musically. Then—with a thunderous boom that shook the chamber—Big Ben spoke. "Bong"—a stately pause—"Bong." The bell continued to toll, marking the hour of twelve.

The struggle continued. Haynes felt as if his lungs were seared, and his straining muscles an unbearable torture. He saw the assassin's grasp forcing inexorably toward a knife strapped to his leg. With a supreme effort, he fought to reach the knife first.

Then, with a thud of boots, the room was filled with uniformed men. George was spreadeagled on the floor, held immobile by four bobbies.

Haynes was assisted to his feet. His legs shaking, he looked down at the staring eyes, wild, filled with agony.

George's mind seethed with a dreadful knowledge. He was not to gain his vengeance—nor was he to die in battle as a god should. Instead, there was to be humiliation—forever.

Gazing into the hopeless vacuum of the years ahead, Achilles slipped from reality into his private world.

The great bell, thirteen and a half tons of gunmetal, sounded a final majestic boom.

Epilogue

FOUR MONTHS AFTER the opening of Parliament, the publicity devoted to George Acton Barrett at last dwindled to nothing.

It had been a torrent at first. Reams of copy poured from Fleet Street. There were stories about George, many inaccurate, that chronicled his boyhood, his Sandhurst years, his army career; there were demands— *"How Could An Assassin Infiltrate The Queen's Guards?"* *"Why Was A Mental Patient Allowed To Roam The City?"*; there were exposés—*"Reveal How Madman Outwitted The CID"*; there were charges, explanations, conjectures.

Gradually, the copy streaming from high-speed presses slowed. Three weeks after the initial stories a cabinet official sued for divorce, charging adultery; his wife promptly counter-sued, charging homosexuality. A new target had appeared, a new way to sell papers, and "The Army Assassin," as the press had called him, was moved to the back pages.

The articles grew shorter, their frequency decreased, and finally it was over: Except for those who remembered . . .

• • •

It was not over for Hope Marston. Her thoughts returned constantly to her final meeting with Haynes. He had been so kind during lunch; but the kindness could not erase the meaning of his words. He wished her well, but there could be nothing for them—ever.

Now there was another man in her life. There always has been, there always will be, she knew wearily. This one was a surgeon, handsome, confident, pleased with his career and his new mistress, debating whether he should ask her to marry. If he only realized, she said to herself, it makes no difference. Whether it is he, or next month's lover, or next year's—it makes no difference. There will always be, way down deep, the memory of what love was like. There will always be the leaden sense of loss.

It was not over for Sir Henry Adams, Assistant Commissioner of the CID. Time and again, he remembered how near a thing it had been. He took his own role under scrutiny, reviewing in detail each step he had taken, considering alternatives he might have chosen.

His personal standard of excellence had always been extraordinarily high, and it seemed to him he had fallen far short. There was only one honorable action to be taken: resignation.

His decision reached, he submitted his letter. Much to his surprise, it was promptly rejected and he found himself summoned to the Prime Minister's office.

The Iron Leader was most explicit. "Henry," she said, removing her glasses and gazing at him steadily, "I have taken you for many things over the years. Cantankerous, opinionated, stubborn. But never for a fool. Until now." She continued with quiet forcefulness. "If you will remove that hairshirt you're wearing, you'll remember that as long as there is mental aberration, there will be assassins who will target the great. No one can predict their plots, no one can prevent them. All that can be done is to do everything in our power to prevent their success, and to pray.

"Henry, you did both of those things. You are not God. Remember that. But you are an intelligent, able, dedicated servant of the Crown. That is a breed hard to come by. We cannot afford to lose you. Let us hear no more nonsense about resignation."

He returned to his duties suddenly free of his burden of guilt. After all, he reminded himself, one does not argue with the Iron Leader. Particularly when she's such a hell of a woman.

It was not over for Jill Blake, or for Thomas Edison Haynes. Her hospital stay was short, but the trauma lingered. In the beginning, it was severe; she would find her heart pounding, and the terror would return. But with the passing of time, her symptoms were disappearing, and she was confident they would soon leave her forever.

The biggest help to her recovery was, of course, her husband. Their marriage was a simple affair, attended only by a few friends including Sir Henry Adams and her superior at the embassy. But what it lacked in grandeur it more than made up in joy.

For her the years ahead were filled with prospects of happiness: the family they would have, the places they would visit, the happiness they would share. She did not consider these thoughts daydreaming; for her the greatest dream had already come true.

As for Haynes, his life with Jill was all that he would wish. At times, he was perversely grateful to the assassin, who caused him to look into his heart, to recognize the depth of love it held.

It was not over for George, of course. Nor would it be for months, for years, or perhaps forever. During the court proceedings that led to his commitment for criminal insanity, he sat motionless, gazing at the bewigged judge without interest, deep in his semicatatonic world.

As was to be expected, every precaution had been taken to prevent his escape. He was no longer in the military hospital, having been medically discharged from the army and transferred to a civilian facility. In that crowded institution he was assigned to a single room. It was heavily barred, and a guard, stationed nearby, made it his business to glance in frequently. Even at night a light was left burning in his room; the periodic checks continued. Where George was concerned, maximum security took on its full meaning.

Once each day, George was taken through a succession of corridors to a quiet office overlooking a stretch of lawn. He sat in a leather chair, looking out at the trees, while a psychiatrist gently asked him questions.

At the outset, he did not answer, and apparently did not even hear the questions. But the psychiatrist was young, and remembered painfully the mental illness of his mother. So he persisted, determined to bring George back to reality, for only then could any progress be made.

He did careful research on the drugs he would administer, and then closely monitored their effects. With this regimen, and with continued compassion, there came a morning when George turned from the window and stared at his doctor, obviously seeing him for the first time. The beginnings of a communication had been established.

The doctor nourished it with infinite patience. Slowly, at times imperceptibly, it grew, until it became a firm bridge. Then, at long last, George's therapy could begin.

As if a restraining wall had been breached, he began to talk. A great mass of words tumbled forth, confused, often senseless—but always revealing excruciating hurt and rage. The doctor listened, probing gently, suggesting, leading the way back to reality.

More and more, George spoke the name of one person, with an immense, anguished longing. The doctor took note of this fact in reading his report to a recent staff conference:

"The patient George Acton Barrett continues a slow improvement.

Periods of lucidity are observed with greater frequency. The patient's identification with Achilles seems to be abating, although it still remains a factor.

No unequivocal prognosis can be made as yet. For the first time, however, the possibility of a complete recovery cannot be ruled out.

It should be noted that the patient refers with increased frequency and yearning to his estranged wife. Her presence would, it is strongly felt, contribute to his further progress.

Unfortunately, a review of the file indicates no information as to her current address."

The doctor did not know that his report found its way to the CID. Steps were immediately undertaken to locate Mrs. Barrett. So far they were without result, but the CID is persistent and, in this instance, specially motivated.

That motivation derived from the identity of the person who forwarded the doctor's report, with a written notation reading, "Please find her. He has suffered so much."

It was not necessary for Sir Henry Adams to look at the signature, for he had seen the writing many times.

He was aware—since it was his business to know much—that the writer had been receiving all reports relating to the progress of George Acton Barrett, at her request.

He also believed, with absolute confidence, that if the patient ever recovered, she would use her considerable influence to minimize his legal punishment.

The Assistant Commissioner would have it no other way. He had always believed that a great Queen must have great compassion.

Bestselling Books for Today's Reader